PRAISE FOR WARWICK COLLINS

On *The Marriage of Souls*:

'Every now and then, a writer emerges who just gets better and better. These are the really exciting ones to encounter. Their novels carry the promise of so much more to come. Warwick Collins is one such writer. He is the author of several novels and each has been an extraordinary improvement on the last. *The Rationalist* marked Collins out as a writer who would be able to challenge the supremacy of Hilary Mantel, Rose Tremain and Ferdinand Mount. *The Marriage of Souls* confirms that he has arrived.'

Observer

On *Gents*:

'Collins' style is marked by a European sensibility. *Gents* is spare, quirky, funny and profound... A classic moral fable about understanding and respect'

The Times

'Brave and lyrically subversive, this novel is original in every aspect'

Guardian

'Collins' prose is beautifully clear'

Observer

'An uplifting tale which beautifully illustrates how even in the lowest circumstances humanity can stand tall'

London Magazine

'*Gents* is deceptively powerful and realistic… Collins writes without adornment or rhetoric, a polished, shining prose that is neither prurient nor antiseptic, but gazes honestly at human foibles and the essential ironies of modern life. A startling, wonderful book.'

Times Educational Supplement

'Warwick Collins has crafted an amusing, understated and very gently subversive story'

Times Literary Supplement

'Bristling with invention…'

Publishers Weekly

On *The Rationalist*:

'At every moment the quality of the writing surprises and delights'

Guardian

'An erotic, beautifully crafted novel… I was spellbound from start to finish.'

Daily Mail

'Collins subjects the figure of the eighteenth-century Man of Reason to a cool and ironic investigation'

Times Literary Supplement

'A vivid and beautifully written account of the past'

Time Out

'The are echoes of *Les Liaisons Dangereuses* and *The French Lieutenant's Woman*, but Collins manages to avoid all the clichés.'

Midweek

ABOUT THE AUTHOR

WARWICK COLLINS has written ten novels, including *The Sonnets* and *Gents*, and is a bestselling author in France and Germany. His non-fiction work, *A Silent Gene Theory of Evolution*, published by University of Buckingham Press, is considered by leading scientists to be a genuine challenge to Darwin's theory that natural selection drives evolution.

First published in 2009 by Old Street Publishing Ltd
28-32 Bowling Green Lane, London EC1R 0BJ
www.oldstreetpublishing.co.uk

ISBN 978-1-905847-91-4

10 9 8 7 6 5 4 3 2 1

A CIP catalogue record for this title is available from the British Library.

Printed and bound in Great Britain by Clays.

F-WOMAN

WARWICK COLLINS

Everything in Los Angeles, including the people, is designed to impress. You can see it in the cult of physical appearance, in the deep and perfect tans, in the constantly changing health fads, in the bodybuilders on Santa Monica beach. Los Angeles is gothic through and through. You could say that this gothicism is a kind of falsity. But I'd prefer to say it another way. The city's falsity is genuine.
Helen A. Brinkman

People think Hollywood is evil, but they're wrong. Hollywood is false. You have to understand the distinction. The great religions invented the soul, that is to say, the deepest essence, the heart of a man. Hollywood invented the image. The image is the opposite of the soul. It's the not-man.
E. Remington Nesbit

1

In the offices of the Los Angeles *Angel Times*, you could track through the newsroom, underneath the hanging long-lights, past the green-painted aluminium tables at which the reporters were sitting, and not a single soul amongst them seemed to have any life when set apart from the computer terminal on which he or she was working. They were all feeding the machine, the great *Moloch* of news, and it absorbed their entire concentration. It drained the life out of them. Afterwards they went home, and sought to replenish themselves somehow, and then returned in the late morning or early afternoon (for the rhythm of the newsman is different from other mortals), to be drained again by the machine. If there was a single predominant fear in the minds of the editor and the reporters it wasn't darkness; it was whiteness, the eternal whiteness of blank pages, pages that were waiting to be filled by the dark foliage of newsprint.

On that day as on others, reporters were working at laptops on their desks. Most of the desks had flat screens mounted above them, and the screens exhibited the most obvious signs of life. For this was the visual age, and it added another dimension to their occupation. In confining themselves to the written word, they practised an older art, about which there was a certain pride. But it didn't remove the other central anxiety of the newspaperman — that television and the internet were making the news, and that they were just filling in the background, adding a textual detail here, an editorial opinion there.

But these were subtexts to the main theme. That was the point. If you moved through the newsroom, you might hear odd snatches of conversation amongst the reporters, or the cryptic exchange of a piece of information, but it was the visual screens that appeared to be setting down the narrative. Even if it was a disjointed one, it seemed to be the heart of the room.

It wasn't easy to discern at first, this narrative. *"Traffic density is at an all-time high in Pacific Palisades,"* or *"Smog warnings have been issued for the incoming routes at Encino."* It was there, hiding underneath the welter of unremarkable information, but once you found it you knew it was authentic.

On that day in late summer one screen was switched onto a television Channel 23, which could be heard increasingly over the other random noise of the newsroom. It began as a conversation between a local interviewer and a senior police psychiatrist, Dr James Holocenter, on the subject of vigilantes.

Dr Holocenter sat, long-boned and vertical, in a plain wooden chair in his study in the police sub-section in City Hall. The interviewer, a young woman called Jill Everhart, said, *"What do you think of vigilantes, Dr Holocenter? Is it justified to operate outside the law if justice is served?"*

At first the eminent criminal psychiatrist seemed emollient, as though humouring a precocious student: *"Well, it depends what you mean by vigilante. I guess each individual example should be considered on its own merits. An ordinary citizen making a citizen's arrest is some kind of vigilante. Even someone who reports seeing a burglar in the neighbouring house is actively supporting the process of law — is adding, so to speak, his citizen's weight."*

"That seems sensible," Miss Everhart said. *"But let's take another example, perhaps the most notorious current case — the woman who calls herself, if you will forgive me, Fuckwoman."*

There was an electronic bleep across the word "fuck", so that the sound emerged as "F-woman". But that was the strangeness of television news — a few moments' delay before transmission meant that a word could be picked up in an instant and an electronic filter put across it. In some ways the bleep was more obscene than the joyful old English word it attempted to block out. Somehow that bleep brought an extra attention to the word: it gave it additional volume or timbre, it mined its taboos, it generated an added richness or lustre. It was significant, too, that at this point in the conversation Dr Holocenter, the senior police psychiatrist at the Los Angeles Police Department, seemed to become a touch defensive, as though the word had pulled his nerves a little tighter. He pivoted his head toward the interviewer, as if that same offending syllable had caught his attention in the way a dog whistle might attract a stray and perhaps guiltily errant canine.

"What particular point are you making?" he asked.

"The case of someone who over the last few years or so has caught several long-term serial rapists — rapists who, until she intercepted them, seem to have eluded the police. Isn't this an example of someone who's doing the community a good service by acting outside the law?"

The story of the day began to unfold, falteringly at first, but with increasing sureness as the interview developed, as positions were adopted and the story grew, little by little, defining itself with increasing clarity. While the interview proceeded, a small group of reporters standing in a corner at the Vendomat coffee machine ceased discussing the Dodgers and, sipping their coffee thoughtfully, directed their attention to the nearest monitor.

By now Dr Holocenter had subtly adjusted himself in his chair from a position of avuncular detachment to one of greater alertness and perhaps a touch of confrontation. His knees had swung towards Miss Everhart as if he were realigning the axis of his body in her direction. He looked towards her more directly now, as though in the orientation of his elbows and shoulder-blades he was asserting both the concentration of his discipline and the authority of his expertise.

He said, *"The problem is that the particular individual you mention administers her own rough justice by going out into society and, so to speak, humiliating the rapist."*

Jill Everhart paused, appeared to consider, then said, *"In attempting to catch and humiliate the rapist, isn't she doing to him exactly what he does to his women victims? In making him see what it is like being a victim, isn't she engaged in something not unlike psychological therapy?"*

4

"Psychological therapy is one way of putting it." A smile moved across Dr Holocenter's lugubrious features, like a brief patch of sunlight in a corner of a graveyard. *"In this case I would prefer, however, to keep to the judicial aspect."*

"Isn't that exactly what we are discussing?" Miss Everhart persisted. *"Direct, applied justice?"*

"That may be so," Dr Holocenter said. *"But, as in other things, two wrongs don't make a right."*

At this point, Miss Everhart paused to gather herself too. Maybe she was constructing in her mind the right combination of innocence and sarcasm — two elements notoriously difficult to mix — for her next sentence. Whatever her thoughts or calculations on the matter of tone, of emphasis or delivery, what she said next was clearly registered. *"But the evidence suggests that rapists don't rape any more after F-woman has got to them."*

There was a nice silence there, just long enough to allow the audience to know that Dr Holocenter had been forced to think a little, that his reply wasn't pat and prepared, that he was actually in the process of being compelled to work along new ground.

"Frankly," Dr Holocenter said, *"the evidence is still unclear. Maybe something else made those particular rapists stop offending. There are known cases of spontaneous remission."*

Miss Everhart sensed a certain evasiveness in the reply. It was the sign of a man under pressure, of a man perhaps on the run. Her former stance of an interviewer setting up an innocent fact to be debated was set aside. A stronger trace of sarcasm entered the next question. Her voice seemed to lower a little, to become both more mellow and more authoritative. She liked that phrase "the evidence suggests". It sounded objective, so she tried it again.

"Nevertheless, the evidence suggests that spontaneous remission only seems to take place after F-woman has intervened."

Another satisfying pause. Then the police psychiatrist was speaking again in his carefully enunciated East Coast accent. *"That in itself seems to be an observation which requires further proof."*

They appeared to have reached an impasse. Dr Holocenter tried to shift the grounds of his counterattack. He uncrossed his legs, leaned forward with a show of sincerity, folded his hands, let his cuffs rest on his knees. *"Speaking on my own area of specific expertise — that of criminal psychiatry — and setting aside the psychological state of the rapists in question, I believe F-woman herself is something of a psychotic case."*

It was a critical point in the interview. Miss Everhart was being offered an interesting morsel to draw her away from her main line of questioning. It was up to her to consider whether the morsel was sufficiently inviting in itself to justify shifting the axis of the interview. The reporters who had gathered at the TV monitors were absolutely silent, watching to see whether Jill Everhart would take the bait.

"Isn't her own state of mind somewhat academic if she's preventing significant numbers of women from being raped? In this case, doesn't the end justify the means?"

There was something like a collective sigh of relief that she had not taken what was offered, that she had stuck to the central point.

"Well, it isn't quite as simple as that," Dr Holocenter said. "In doing what she does, in the way that she does, F-woman is violating the due process of the law."

Miss Everhart seemed to hover, to compose herself, and then to drive forward. "A lot of people believe the trouble with the police is that because they can't catch these serial rapists, someone like F-woman is simply doing a job that's become vacant."

Perhaps this was getting a little too close. Dr Holocenter had become almost preternaturally still, as though he had instructed his body not to move, not to fidget or exhibit signs of tension. You could sense the heat generated by the television lights. In the newsroom, several more reporters had left their workstations and were gathering at the screen.

Dr Holocenter chose to ignore that question. "In the end, Jill, the serial rapist will make a slip and give himself away. Then we'll catch him. The same applies to F-woman. The fact is, she's breaking the law, and we'll catch her too."

"Well, you haven't caught her yet."

"We will," Dr Holocenter said.

"How can you be so confident?"

"I believe that, like most psychotics, she has a personality flaw, and that's what will give her away."

"Are you prepared to disclose what that flaw might be?"

"Yes, I am. She feeds on publicity. When she captures a suspected rapist, she leaves little notes behind, giving away her identity, like a kind of signature."

"What do you read into that?" Miss Everhart asked.

"It's as if she's seeking approval."

"What kind of approval?"

"All the attendant media coverage that follows these acts seems to serve the same psychological purpose — she seeks some form of approval from the public, or at least from certain members of the public."

"You think that will give her away? Her hunger for approval?"

"That's what will provide us with the final clue," Dr Holocenter said.

Miss Everhart knew she had mined a little gold by then, that in order to counter the problem of answering her question, Dr Holocenter had diverted attention away and onto another subject — the subject of the vigilante's own hypothetical weaknesses. And in order to divert her, he'd offered something of genuine interest in return — the police's psychological profile of F-woman. Jill Everhart was prepared to accept that as some kind of *quid pro quo*.

"Dr Holocenter, senior police psychiatrist, thank you for joining us."

It was something of a milestone: the first time the authorities had discussed the vigilante directly; the first time they had even admitted their hopes to capture her; the first time they had identified what they considered to be her vulnerability. The small group that had congregated round the screen began to break up and return to their desks. Paradoxically, as the newsroom began to function once again, a sense of unreality returned. The glow of the overhead strip-lights bathed the desks in soft light, like a hospital ward. In that artificial luminescence the journalists and researchers, gathered over their screens, seemed to become as pale as ghosts.

2

The newspaper headlines the next day were largely concerned with that single interview. In the *Herald*, on the second page, there was a large article headed:

INTERVIEWER TAUNTS LAPD OVER F-WOMAN

Another, in the *Tablet*, read:

POLICE PSYCHIATRIST CALLS F-WOMAN PSYCHOTIC

Of the two accounts, the story in the *Herald* covered the interview in greater detail. It also provided further background to the several rape cases in which the vigilante had been previously involved:

In an interview with LAPD senior psychiatric adviser Dr James Holocenter, the subject of the notorious figure commonly called "F-woman" was raised by the programme presenter Jill Everhart. The interview was supposedly on the general subject of vigilantes, but during the discussion Miss Everhart proceeded to press home the more controversial subject of F-woman herself, and in the course of the interview managed to undermine the LAPD's customary reserve on the matter.

Until now, LAPD has not commented in any significant detail on the vigilante's activities, preferring to confine its views only to factual briefings on her various assaults on certain rapists in the greater Los Angeles area. Its official view remains that F-woman's activities are merely another aspect of lawlessness, a further example of criminal behaviour with which it is proposing to deal in due course. During the interview, Miss Everhart's efforts managed to generate a more detailed response from Dr Holocenter, which was both defensive and revealing.

Dr Holocenter, one of LAPD's most experienced spokesmen, admitted the fact that LAPD has not managed to catch at least two serious rapists, subsequently intercepted by F-woman, has left them vulnerable to public criticism. Ron Acheson, the so-called "clothesline rapist", had carried out seven serious rapes, mainly in the Van Nuys and Reseda areas of Los Angeles. Targeting one- and two-bedroom apartments much favoured by younger women, before launching his violent attacks he "stalked" his victims and stole their underwear from clotheslines, though he was assiduous in never leaving behind identifiable evidence. Acheson remained at large for several years until the police discovered him tied up in clothesline in a back garden in nearby Sherman Oaks, with a set of women's panties stuffed into his mouth. Found incoherent and babbling, after several days recovering in prison he claimed he had been assaulted and trussed up by the vigilante known as F-woman.

The second rapist was the so-called "Mouseman", Larry Delamous, a former TV soap opera screenwriter who pretended to be a famous film producer and invited out starlets and would-be actresses with promises of roles, before allegedly drugging and raping them. The full extent of his depredations is still unknown because many of the women involved could not be certain whether they had been raped while under the drug's influence. Without concrete evidence, and fearing their claims would be compromised by the fact that they agreed to a date and consented to return to Delamous's flat, they were ashamed to report their suspicions to the authorities at the time. Delamous also relied upon the likelihood of the intrusive legal process leaving his victims nervous of making allegations of date-rape.

Unlike the "clothesline rapist", Delamous's identity was well-known, but like Acheson he seemed invulnerable to prosecution because of the lack of evidence. Whenever suspicion was thrown upon his activities, he was shrewd enough to lie low for months or even years. Police believe he may have shifted his activities to other cities or states. Delamous was therefore as surprised as anyone when, on his way to a date in Tarzana, an old Ford drew up beside him, a woman stepped out, punched him in the stomach, and bundled him into the car. Delamous claims he was then injected in the left buttock with a quick-acting drug — thought to be the same drug he had used on his own victims — and driven in a sedated and depleted state to an unspecified address. After an anonymous telephone call, police found Delamous tied up in a low-rent apartment off Sepulveda Boulevard, beside him a note which read:

Gerbils are nice
For those who like vice,
But Mouses can be
A pain in the ass.

Delamous escaped prosecution because of a lack of any evidence which would stand up in a court of law. But it is also believed he has not offended again. It seems that the experience of being hunted down and caught by a woman, then rendered immobile by drugs and kept against his will for several days humiliated and traumatised him. According to unofficial accounts, he has become a Jehovah's Witness, and now works as a part-time social worker from an address in Anaheim.

Predictably perhaps, F-woman's buccaneering qualities, with even a touch of literary legerdemain, *have endeared her to the radical feminists in the city. She has also found fans amongst the substantial gay population in West Hollywood and Silver Lake. One of her most outspoken admirers is Crispin Grace, editor of the radical magazine* Queens with Spleen, *who recently commented in one of his characteristically charged editorials: "F-woman's reverse gender rapes are symbolic attacks on the whole notion of conventional sexual stereotypes. Her activities amount to a form of cryptic performance art and radical social critique rolled into one."*

For the time being at least, the offender known as F-woman continues to operate outside the law, and the police force remains largely impotent in apprehending her.

The notion of the vigilante as performance artist caught Cynthia Lelague's eye as she read the rival newspaper accounts that morning in the main newsroom of the *Angel Times*. The consistent use of the letter F- instead of the word "Fuck" emphasised the peculiar notoriety of the central figure. Like the televised word, the printed word exerted its own arcane censorship over the name of the feminist vigilante. Referring to her by the honorific of "F-woman", that hissing fricative "F-" seemed to perform the same function as the single bleep on the television channel — it both obscured and burnished the word's meaning. It seemed to Cynthia, as she closed the newspaper, that the abbreviation merely expressed society's moral platitudes concerning the nature of sexual behaviour.

Something of that ritualised, hypocritical decorousness over the earthier facets of sexual activity engaged her as she made her way over to the editor-in-chief's office to talk about the Cipasso case.

3

Her editor, Gore H. Emhard, was something of a legend himself. He had been editor of the *Angel Times* for a good twenty-eight years, since his mid-thirties. He was ideologically deeply conservative in his views, a committed Republican and an active member of the National Rifle Association. Cynthia knocked on the frosted glass door, listened for his gruff "Come in," and entered his sanctum.

Emhard was tapping at a keyboard, putting in some final adjustments on an editorial. He was in his shirtsleeves, and the window was open. She knew he disliked the air-conditioning system, that he always seemed to retain something of the habits of an outdoor man.

She paused while he tapped in his corrections. Without looking up, he said, "What gives?"

"That Cipasso case," Cynthia said. "Want me to find out a bit more about it?"

Emhard stopped tapping and reached for a cigarette that smouldered in an old elephant toe ashtray. He sucked in smoke like a patient drawing in oxygen, wheezing into his lungs. There was nothing he liked more than to annoy her with his habits. He made a special show of stubbing the cigarette out on the elephant's toe.

After a while, he said, "You up to that, Cynthia?"

"What do you mean?"

"Cipasso should be executed," Emhard said. He turned slightly and cocked one eyebrow up at her. "You heard what he did to that family?"

"What exactly?"

"That exactly," Emhard nodded to himself. "He violated them all."

He looked at her standing there, in her shapeless dress, her eyes unblinking behind round glasses. What was it about her? he asked himself. Some kind of social crusader, he thought, a female one, trying to prove something. If there was one thing he hated, it was people of vaguely benign disposition. They never did anything newsworthy, and their attitudes got in the way of the facts.

There were other things that disquieted him about Cynthia Lelague. Her father had been a hippie in his youth, and then (like certain other student radicals of his era) had merged effortlessly into the commercial culture, forming his own business selling greeting cards and making good. Her mother, Professor Fernanda Lelague, was a sociologist of strongly feminist persuasion, a leading light at UCLA. That meant Cynthia was at least a second-generation feminist. Even more than a single feminist, he disliked the thought of a matriarchy of feminist intellectuals.

Cynthia said, "Are you telling me I shouldn't investigate?"

She had a kind of stubbornness, he thought. God knows where it came from. Some kind of unpleasant ferment of muesli, soft environmentalist ethics, stirred in with fashionably progressive views. What went on in the minds of radical young women these days? She eschewed make-up, and clothes that showed off the body. He could live with that. But why did she always have to be so earnest?

"What exactly is it about these rape cases that interests you, Cynthia?" Emhard asked.

She watched him for a while, standing in the doorway, not moving, as though it were a question whose answer was so obvious that it didn't need a reply. Eventually she said, "Rape's a political act. It's got nothing to do with sex. It's using sex to dominate and humiliate."

"Political, huh?" Emhard said. "You think these scumbags think politically?"

"They don't have to. It's something they picked up from society, from other people."

"Society?" Emhard said, with as much irony as he could muster. "That's your line, is it? Don't blame the individual, blame society."

"You know the way men talk about women when they're on their own. We're all carrying our history inside us — including a few thousand years of men's exploitation of women."

"Is that so?"

"You asked me for my views."

"OK," Emhard said. "But if that guy gets hold of you, and your mammy comes looking for my blood, I'm gonna tell her — 'Cynthia wouldn't listen to my advice.'"

"Maybe I don't need your advice on something like this."

It was the way she said it, so calm and reasonable, that stopped Emhard for a moment. It was like some final judgement, an implacable statement of fact.

Unexpectedly, he found himself playing for time. What was it exactly that he heard in her voice? What sort of underlying assertiveness was that? So Cipasso only raped them, he thought to himself. He only left Mrs Marcia Cabrera and her two grown-up daughters, both visiting, living in utter terror in case he came back. It didn't matter that Mrs Cabrera lived on the south side of Venice Boulevard, in a relatively plush area near the ocean; even a good security system and an active local police patrol hadn't kept out Cipasso. And even now, a week later, Mrs Cabrera and her two daughters were so scared they refused to leave their respective houses while Cipasso was at large. OK, so he raped them, thought Emhard savagely, let's all say it's society's fault. Then it occurred to him that to this kind of feminist maybe all men were rapists. To her, Cipasso only differed in that he did it overtly.

"How you going to investigate this, Cynthia?" Emhard said. "Gonna walk the streets in a tight dress and lure him in?"

"That's unfair, Gore."

She looked at him behind her glasses, and he saw a flash of something, a spark of resistance, or perhaps defiance. For a moment he thought she was going to do something extreme, like shout or cry. He hated to see feminists weep. Their tears were not biodegradable. They were acid; they could burn your hand. Who was it who described women's tears as "water power"? Adler, he seemed to remember, the contemporary of Freud, the least known of the trio Freud, Jung, and Adler.

"Are you ordering me not to investigate?" Cynthia said.

Listen to this, Emhard thought. Who's asking the questions here?

He said, "What exactly is it that interests you about this particular case?"

"You know me, Gore. It's not the specifics so much. It's the wider issue. Anything with an overtone of sexual politics."

She even smiled at him, an apologetic or perhaps ironic smile. It seemed to him she was trying to lighten up a little, maybe soften things after her statement that she didn't need his advice. Or, just as likely, she'd had enough of his interrogation, and was getting ready to leave.

She was still standing in the doorway, and it occurred to him that if she didn't wear those long smock things, if she took off her glasses and maybe smiled a little more, she was a handsome woman. She was tall, maybe too tall for his taste, but there was also something oddly and insidiously graceful about her. Once he had come across her in the newsroom unexpectedly late at night. He had been walking back to his office with a cup of coffee from the Vendomat machine and he almost bumped into her. She had been working on some article at her workstation and was getting up and preparing to go home. She must have inadvertently knocked her car keys off the desk and onto the floor, because suddenly, without any apparent effort, she bent down to pick them up with a supple, graceful motion, like a ballet dancer. She didn't have to bend her knees at all. In the course of that movement she had turned towards him, aware that he had stopped and was watching her.

"Sexual politics?" he said now. He nodded, as if he understood. She had surprised him in the past with her special diligence on issues like this one, where some kind of political principle was involved. But he had other things to worry about than the Cipasso issue. The unfinished editorial was still occupying his mind.

"Go find out what you can about him, Cynthia," he said. "Do your worst."

She nodded and turned away.

For a few moments Emhard felt unsettled and vaguely restless. Underneath the pile of articles was a cup of cold coffee. He found the glaze of the handle cold on his fingers and pulled it out from beneath a heap of printouts.

"You owe me, Cynthia," he called out after her.

She heard him, turned, and came back.

"Before you go," Emhard said, smiling in a way that he knew would annoy her — "would you kindly get me another cup of black coffee?"

She nodded, a little reluctantly, and reached forward to retrieve one of the empty cups lurking at the edges of the desk. On principle she refused to take away or wash the others.

Emhard said, "Do me one more favour, will you?"

"What's that?" Cynthia asked.

Emhard said, "Make it the worst you can get."

4

Cynthia phoned Detective Ed Stevens. She didn't have his mobile number so she had to use the official system. It took four attempts to get connected up to him. He seemed to be moving around the building just ahead of the calls that were following him. She had an image of a telephone ringing in one room just as he was closing the door. Finally they caught up with him at Filing.

"Cynthia Lelague, *Angel Times*," she said.

"What can I do for you?"

"Could you give me an update on the Cipasso case?"

"What's happened to Fernando?" Stevens asked.

Fernando Cinares was another reporter. It was Fernando who usually covered criminal cases like this one.

"He's away," Cynthia said. "Anyway, Fernando works mostly on murders, not rapes."

"Oh?" Stevens asked.

"Murders are macho," Cynthia said.

She could almost hear Stevens thinking, have I met you somewhere? Stevens was fishing, trying to form an impression of her. He had floated Fernando's name across her like a fly to get her reaction. Now he told her about the follow-up on Cipasso, a little selectively maybe, knowing that with new reporters on a case you had to establish a *modus vivendi*, a code of official or non-official information, or each piece of evidence could be spread all over the town. There were some things his section wanted to keep to themselves. They had taken samples of sweat and semen. Cipasso's blood belonged to a rare group. Still no fingerprint except a half-thumb on a belt-buckle they were working on, the print partially disguised by scar-tissue. They were building up a case on him. But why should he tell a reporter about the details — a pushy female reporter? A picture of her was coming into his mind. She didn't create any special kind of impact, to be honest: someone he'd noticed at the edge of police briefings; earnest and solid; someone who wore vague, smock-like things.

"How'd you get my name?" Stevens asked.

"Fernando left a note saying you had helped him. Maybe you could help me."

"Maybe," Stevens said.

"Can I come over and talk?"

Stevens looked out over the filing room. He prevaricated. "Right now?"

She stepped in with her whole foot. "Now would be good."

He still wanted to draw a little blood. "So what's the division in your place? Fernando does homicides, you do rapes?"

"Something like that."

"You cut it like that, it suits you both?"

She didn't reply.

This chick didn't flirt, he decided. He was suddenly bored with teasing. "I'll be here," he said, and put down the phone.

Cynthia paused only long enough to go into the women's room to splash a little water on her face and gather herself. Emhard usually managed to get her steamed up and annoyed. He treated her with the familiarity he treated his other leading reporters, but it seemed to her there was also something a little paternal in his attitude towards her.

The women's room was a dingy place, with hardly enough room to move. When the offices were originally built, maybe forty years before, they didn't imagine female reporters would be anything other than an anomaly in a male-oriented business. In her eyes, it was another sign of the old order. If you visited the men's room (she had taken a look in there one evening when there was no one about) you were faced with beautiful tiled floors, polished urinals where the brass gleamed, rows of white porcelain washbasins.

Leaving the women's room, she set off briskly along the green-painted corridor, down an aluminium stairway to street level and out of the revolving doors at the back of the building that led to the car park. There, in the fresh air, she seemed to change. Her stride was purposeful. Her shape, which in the confines of the office seemed like solidity, moved on her frame surprisingly comfortably.

On the sidewalk she swung freely, eating up the pavement. Four blocks, three crossings. The police headquarters was set back twenty feet and had a portico and half-columns. Inside the entrance foyer a policewoman sat behind the armoured glass of the receptionist's cubicle. A telephone rang in the depths of the building. "Harry?" someone kept asking from one of the inner offices. "Harry?"

"I've come to see Ed Stevens. Cynthia Lelague." She withdrew her press identification and held it out.

The policewoman glanced at her card and reached for the telephone. "Detective Stevens?" She insisted on formalities. "Turn left at Homicide. Door marked Filing. The number is F3."

Cynthia nodded.

Away from the newspaper offices, she breathed more freely, as if the outside world were her habitat. She glided over the scrubbed tile floors, found F3 with ease, arranged a smile on her lips, and breasted through the swing doors without a knock.

Three men moved nervously and quickly backwards from a *tête-à-tête* about something. One of them was putting some photographs back in his pocket.

"Stevens?" she said to the group.

They were starting to smile. They thought it might have been the chief and now that it wasn't, they could handle this oversize chick. Two of them were chewing gum.

One said, "You got company, Ed." Then two of them moved off, pushing past her on either side.

"Cynthia Lelague?"

Ed Stevens was one of the gum-chewers, standing with hands on hips, assessing her. He was big, athletic, a little overweight. Now he held out his hand like a commiseration prize. She ignored it.

"The Cipasso case?" she asked.

He moved his gum from one side of his mouth, then to the other. He thought a while about things, then moved it back again.

Cynthia said, "You get A1 for shifting gum, brother. Can you speak as well?"

Something inside Stevens snapped. His jaw stopped for a half a second, then his mouth started to motor rapidly. After a while it stopped again. He thought something. He turned his back on her and walked to the other side of the room. He would freeze her out. Make her come to him.

He walked away with a big man's walk, moving like a gunslinger. But when he reached the other end of the long room, something unexpected happened. He didn't hear anything at first. He didn't detect the slightest movement of her heels across the floor or her breath or the rustle of clothes or anything — and detectives are aware of the space behind them; it is part of their body's intimate domain. She seemed to glide in his wake, to move like something that floated or swam, because when he halted she was right there behind him, and her hand was on his ass. Firm, as if her hand had arrested his butt. She was whispering to him, "So help me, Stevens, you're starting to annoy me."

He felt smoke coming out of the top of his head. He wasn't carrying a gun today but he had a fantasy he would have liked to turn round and just casually blow her away, motor the trigger and watch her slump, then motor it a few more times while she went downwards and out of sight.

Jesus. Standing there in his own room, with this dumpy chick's hand right on his crack.

But he thought about other things. If he did anything remotely violent to her, even so much as pushed her away from him, he could find himself up on an assault charge. And what would the department say about that? Ed Stevens was defending himself against indecent assault in his own office? By some chick? Who'd believe that? He'd be laughed out of the county. When he cooled down a little he knew that the basic facts were: one, he had an iron hand on his rear end; and two, he was dealing with someone who had a good working knowledge of the law.

"Great little ass you have, officer," she said.

All of a sudden his rage turned into something higher, something he could cope with. He started to laugh, just stood there shaking with laughter and tears filling his eyes.

After a while he said, "What kind of wrestling grip do you call that, Miss Lelague? I heard of a double nelson before."

"A double standard, Detective Stevens?"

"That's a new one to me."

"Only feminists can use it."

He had to smile at that one. The chick had half of a sense of humour, at least. He found himself winding down a little more.

"What would happen if I used a double standard on you, I wonder?"

"You'd end up in San Quentin."

She was sharp enough, he could see that. He paused a few seconds.

"You sure do carry journalism to a fine point, Miss Lelague."

"Let's talk about points, shall we, Detective Stevens? Like Cipasso. That's to the point."

She moved her hand off his ass, but not without a friendly pat; to be accurate, two friendly pats. He turned round slowly and looked at her, gazed down from six foot three with the definite, hovering intention to intimidate. But she didn't back off at all, and the eyes he saw staring back at him were remarkable. They were cold and calm and at the same time seemed to concentrate on him.

"Cipasso," she said.

"You want Cipasso?" Stevens asked.

"That's right."

He looked at her a little while longer, taking his time. "OK," he said. "I'll give you Cipasso."

What followed was co-operation at its best. There was a measure of understanding and movement between partners. Big metal cabinets were approached. Keys were called and signed for. Files were opened. Out came documents.

"Do me a favour, will you?" Cynthia said. "I don't just want to see a copy of his birth certificate or his prison record numbers. Give me the dope. I want psychological background."

He considered her for a while, then began to open more files, combing for headings. Criminal Record. Social Background. Psychological Treatment. A special section called "Physiochemistry". Fingerprint analysis, blood type, semen count, and various other headings. Ed Stevens began to sense, not for the first time that morning, the powerful compulsion of a predator on the trail.

Cynthia Lelague seemed to drink it in. And what a background it was. Orphaned aged two. Brought up by his mother's younger sister, herself a convicted prostitute and felon, Cipasso had emerged from the criminal classes. The psychological report said, "Signs of abuse as child. Stepfather suspected." She had an impression of someone raised through a tide of human degradation, someone so surrounded by it that it was all he breathed, all he ate or drank.

"Seems like a nice guy," said Stevens, chewing gum as he peered over her shoulder.

And the victims. That was where she paused. They were always well-off women, women of a certain middle-class standing. She looked at the photos; the victims were in their forties and fifties, housewives and matrons. Each had the curious glow of health on them, of the good life. That was her first lead. What was going on here? Cipasso had exercised charm and somehow he'd got into their houses. He nearly always raped them in their bedrooms. Did he hate the kind of normality he liked to invade? Was it because it was something he never had?

And then Cipasso himself. Pablo. A whippy little street-fighter, all bones and muscle. Not mean-looking, but a peculiar power and intent in his eyes as he stared out at the camera in the mugshot.

Stevens was speaking. She was concentrating so hard on Cipasso and his victims that it was difficult to wrench her attention away.

Stevens said, "The guy could have been a hoodlum. But he's not easily enough controlled. Things are changing. The gangs are moving into white-collar crime. They don't take on board guys who habitually rape women — I mean, not least women who remind them of their own wives and mothers."

"If you know so much about him, how come you haven't caught up with him?" Cynthia asked.

"Some people change. They learn their trade, if you know what I mean. Trial and error. He doesn't make the same mistake twice. This guy's not intelligent, but he has instinct. He learned how to disappear, dissolve. It's as if he lives in a belfry somewhere, only comes out at night." Stevens stopped, then added, "Like, he's dedicated."

"Dedicated?" Cynthia Lelague moved that idea around a bit, looking at it from various angles. "Obsessive, I'd say."

Ed Stevens shifted the gum around his mouth. "You got more than enough for one article now, Miss Lelague. What else exactly are you looking for?"

Cynthia was moving fast down a row of figures on the nature of each crime. She was so involved she didn't seem to hear him. She looked up.

"You're right, Detective Stevens. This person is just a type that interests me."

"Interests you?" Stevens moved around the thought. It was a careful repetition more than a question, but his curiosity hung in the air. He paused, moving his gum back and forth a little more. What sort of interest would that be, he asked himself?

"Rape's your scene?" Ed Stevens had an uncomfortable feeling he might be pressing his luck, and he had memories of that firm hand on his rear again.

"In a manner of speaking. It's a meeting point for a whole lot of social ills, a kind of arena for processes that interest me."

"That so?"

Now she was looking again at the photographs of Cipasso,

as though committing them to memory. Left profile, right profile, front.

"You some kind of political nut?" Stevens asked.

She seemed to consider his question. "I wouldn't say that. I'd say I look at these things from a social perspective."

"Social?" That translated into nut in his language. Stevens was getting restless. She could sense the movement of his distrust building up beside her, like a cloud that was hovering.

"Not a nut, huh?"

She seemed to pause, raising her attention from the documents and photographs in front of her. She closed the file and faced him, and once again he was looking into those peculiarly direct eyes.

He was inclined to withhold his judgement, for the time being at least.

"There's something else," Stevens said, "something you should maybe see."

"What's that?"

Stevens went to a heavy cabinet with rows of drawers, each with an individual key. He worked through a chain of keys, found the one he was looking for, opened the drawer.

"Don't touch it," Stevens said. "They already examined it to try to get DNA samples, but they couldn't find anything that connected it with Cipasso."

She looked down into the drawer. In a sterile transparent bag there was a wig, long and red-haired; not a man's wig but a woman's, carefully combed.

"What's this?" she asked.

"They found it outside the house of one of the victims. There is a theory Cipasso was disturbed by someone when he was on his way out of the house, and he dropped it."

"He was wearing it at the time?"

"No one knows. We're not even sure it was anything to do with him."

She realised he had offered her something unusual, a piece of potential evidence that they themselves didn't know how to interpret. It was a peculiar gesture of trust on his part. Almost against her instincts, she started to feel something not unlike affection towards Officer Stevens.

"Thanks," she said. "I appreciate that."

He said nothing, just nodded and closed the drawer, locking it carefully.

After that they moved apart again, as calmly as two animals that have scented each other in the dark and are prepared to surrender a little working room.

5

That wasn't the only strange object she witnessed that week.

A couple of evenings later Gore Emhard called out her name from the inner office. When Cynthia appeared at the door, Emhard was crouched over his desk, tapping into his laptop.

"You filing anything on Cipasso?" Emhard asked, without looking up.

"An interim report, nothing special."

Emhard was quiet for a few moments, just tapping away.

Cynthia said, "I'll keep tabs on the case."

Emhard might have faintly nodded. He didn't seem greatly interested. She was about to go when he said, "Notice anything different?"

"What about?"

"The environment, maybe."

"National or local?"

"Local."

She glanced over the piled, untidy disk, with its old coffee cups.

"Not that I can see."

"New pencil-holder?"

She looked more carefully. On his desk was a cylinder covered in some sort of skin, a brown and grey tuft of fur.

"You don't recognise it?"

"Can't say I do."

Emhard nodded. He seemed oddly amused. After a few moments he said, "Bison's pizzle."

"A what?"

"Found it in a curio shop on Melrose Avenue. Wooden cylinder for holding pencils covered in the skin of a bison's penis. Five dollars eighty. I'd call it a snip, if the remark wasn't in dubious taste."

"Jesus Christ, Gore."

Emhard was pleased. "Please continue. Don't stint yourself. You're a reporter, Cynthia. Let's have some honesty and directness around here."

"That has to be one of the most tasteless, politically incorrect, and ecologically offensive objects I have ever seen."

"Yep," Emhard said, "that's what I figured."

They seemed to have reached agreement of a kind. They paused for a moment, like people who have concluded a satisfactory deal.

"Have we said what we needed to say?" Cynthia asked.

"I believe so."

She turned and walked past several desks in the main

newsroom to her own desk. Emhard had succeeded in outraging her again — and at the minimal cost of five dollars eighty. And it seemed he'd got a workable pencil-holder into the bargain. She'd have to wait before she could plan her revenge. Meantime, she'd sublimate her energies into another campaign.

She pulled out a map of the area. Cipasso's offences were marked with crosses in soft pencil. The latest one was on Lafayette Street. They formed quite a tight circle, mostly in Venice. Venice was a mixed neighbourhood, hippies and bohemians and yuppies and a few older, expensive properties. Why would anyone commit crimes in such a tight area? Unless they were compulsive, of course.

Maybe a man with Cipasso's complexes had experienced various rejections and insults in that locality? Maybe he thought of the neighbourhood as the scene of a personal humiliation. A psychopath's skin could be very thin. Perhaps just being in Venice incited his sense of grievance.

She considered whether he could be an outsider, whether he only entered one particular neighbourhood in order to commit crimes. That seemed bizarre — too much detachment, too much self-control in what appeared to be obsessive behaviour. She remembered what Stevens had said, that Cipasso was the type of small-time hoodlum that the gangs might have recruited if he had been of a different type. But the gangs themselves would be put off by his obsessive nature, his absence of redeeming features and, in particular, his lack of malleability. He wasn't a corporate man. He knew only one track to run on — his own.

It was true that, given its shifting demography and complex social undercurrents, Venice was a good place to hide. But if he were the calculating type, why would he commit crimes on his own doorstep?

She looked at the parade of victims — middle-class women, paragons of stability and civic virtue. How did he select them? Did he study their behavioural profiles? Did he plan his attack with the meticulous attention to detail of certain criminals, or was it a spur-of-the-moment thing, some mingling of temptation and opportunity? Sometimes it seemed like that. The fact that he could lie low for several months before committing another crime, then two, maybe three, in one week suggested some kind of cyclical behaviour. In crime detection they sometimes called such behaviour the werewolf cycle.

How, in particular, did he manage to melt back into anonymity? He must have some disguise, something that lifted him clean out of the mainstream.

What was the farthest distance you could get from being a young, violent male? A paraplegic? Something occurred to Cynthia that hadn't occurred before. What was the furthest that a man could hide from the image of a physically brutal rapist? Wasn't it as a woman? She thought of the wig in the drawer, something the police suspected was connected to Cipasso, though without physical proof. Other things began to move around her mind. Venice had a long history of bohemianism. Amongst other things, it had a fairly sizeable transvestite community. It was also a part of town well known for its exhibitionism. Maybe Cipasso resumed his disguise afterwards. Suddenly another thought occurred to her. Maybe he didn't have to "resume" the disguise; maybe he was in it all the time.

Was there anything in his profile that indicated any kind of emotional or sexual exoticism? The enormity of his crimes tended to suggest that everything about him was unusual. But that acted to disguise the fact that certain aspects of his personality might be perfectly unexceptional.

Was there something dysfunctional about his relations with older women? Was he taking revenge on his mother for leaving him when he was young? Were all these victims substitute mother-figures — objects of his disappointed rage? And if so, in some twisted but at least barely comprehensible sense, was his revenge not the worst possible violation of the mother-son relationship?

In the background, Cynthia heard Gore Emhard talking about his new pencil-holder to Hal Barton, the deputy editor. Sometimes in the swelter of a big office you heard odd snatches of conversation from distant parts, conveyed by currents in the newsroom like those layers of water in the ocean that carried whales' voices over huge distances.

"Odd ramifications," Emhard was saying, "some fascinating reverberations."

"Ecologically incorrect, of course," she heard Hal Barton comment admiringly.

She could see through the glass of Emhard's office that he and Barton were standing side by side, staring down at the pencil-holder. She heard Emhard say quite clearly, "Couldn't resist it. Had to have it right there and then."

Every man was an obsessive, she knew. Every male gene was a potential locus for trouble.

6

White gold decor, white table-tops, white minimalist walls. And a whole bunch of drag-queens on show, raising dust on the small stage, the faint mist of sweat and outraged perfume rising through the fogged stage lights.

Cynthia Lelague liked the place. It had the strange ambiguity of somewhere outside normal time, or perhaps of time suspended. It was off the beaten track, and she liked that too. In physical terms, El Greco's had the ambience of modern techno, part Eastern ascetic. There was a Japanese simplicity to the strong wooden tables and chairs, and to the food that was served — large bowls of nourishing soup.

The barman, too, was Japanese. He was dressed in motorcycle cap and leather boots. He moved down the length of the bar and stood opposite her, viewing her with his slanted eyes. She was fascinated to see he used eyeliner. The cheekbones and eyebrows reminded her of Greta Garbo.

"Like something to drink, maybe?" he asked.

"A beer. A big one."

"Sure." He drifted to the cooler at the back, filled a glass with ice, put an empty glass beside it, then snapped open a can and set it down beside the two glasses, watching to see how she'd drink it.

She poured the beer into the un-iced glass and took a heavy gulp. She looked towards the stage.

There were maybe a dozen of them hoofing on the boards, kicking their legs like the old Rockettes or the girls at the Crazy Horse, their eyes massively overmade, pancake layers thick. She had wondered at the ambience, expecting some odd, almost sentimental obeisance to the feminine, but was surprised by its opposite. Instead the performers seemed to aim for grotesquerie, for monstrousness, for an absurd or knowing parody of the feminine.

Listening to the affected squeals of the artists and watching the rising legs, Cynthia remembered something about the paintings on cave walls, in which the images of animals were used to expropriate and control the creatures' souls. It occurred to her that perhaps a similar ritual of expropriation was taking place now.

"Tell me something," she said. She put down the glass.

"Depends," the barman replied.

"When those guys go off the stage, do they all go back to being lawyers and accountants? Or do some of them live like that?"

"Most of them go back to their normal lives. One or two stay like they are."

She nodded and drank. She wiped her lips with the back of her hand and smiled back at him.

He said, "You a fag-hag?"

She saw it was a perfectly ordinary question, a technical question, no malice intended.

"I guess I'm more of an interested observer."

"That so?"

He was about to remove the empty can and the unused glass, when Cynthia said, "Just one more thing. If you were trying to work out who keeps their female clothes on afterwards, who doesn't change out of them — how would you tell?"

"Why would I want to know?"

"Because you're curious."

"Why would I tell you?" he asked.

"Because you know."

He looked at her with his slanted, beautiful eyes. "You think they're strange?"

"A little strange, maybe. But that's not why I'm asking."

He looked at her eyes, directly and carefully. "Strangest person in here," he said simply, "is you."

"That's two strikes against me," Cynthia said amiably. "Now you owe me one."

He turned his slanted face towards the stage and considered the hoofers. After a while he said, "Look at their shoes."

She took another drink.

"Their shoes?"

"The ones that have comfortable-looking shoes are the ones that will keep their clothes on afterwards."

She nodded. "Makes sense."

"Sense," he said, nodding again. "I leave you now."

He drifted away up the bar towards two new customers who had entered and placed their studded leather elbows on the bar. They looked like motorcycle outriders, but then nothing here was quite what it seemed. She turned towards the stage and looked down at the shoes. There was something to be said for the information he had given her. Most of the artists wore high heels, on which they teetered and tottered. Other shoes she could see were exceptionally tight-fitting, she guessed to make the men's feet look small, more like women's. When she went through the line-up again a couple of times, there were maybe two with sensible shoes that looked as though they wore them all the time. One was six and a half feet tall, black; he could have been a minor-league basketball player. The other was a head shorter, Latino, not far off Cipasso's height. He wore a black wig that went with his dark eyes, plenty of eye-shadow. He had a boy's body, a dancer's fluidity. She looked at him more closely. Though slender, there was an implicit strength in the shoulders.

She had been visiting drag bars in the area for several weeks, but now something inside her floated upwards, like the first effect of alcohol.

After the artists had gone backstage, Cynthia paid the barman and walked out the front door, then swung left into a small alley. She was looking for a side door but there were only heavily barred windows down that length of the building. A tall wrought-iron fence topped with iron spikes separated the side from the neighbouring empty building lot.

She backed out and walked along the front of the building. The long lights of a car came down the road, causing her shadow to climb the building vertiginously. There were two men inside, staring straight ahead. The car seemed to slow down. Maybe they were thinking of accosting her. Maybe they thought she was a streetwalker. She felt cold and ready. But when the car halted, idling beside the curb, a man got out and walked into El Greco's and then the car pulled off and accelerated away. She waited until it was out of sight before she turned into the street that ran alongside the building and walked to the small parking lot out back. There were a few old pieces — an elderly Studebaker and several more upmarket cars, a Mercedes, a couple of Cadillacs, an Aston Martin, a classic Buick Riviera. The lawyers, she thought, the accountants, down here slumming it.

The back door of El Greco's flickered and someone with long dark hair and jeans moved across the parking lot, as lithe as a cat. She heard the door of one of the older cars slam and then heard the rough kick of the motor of the old Studebaker. The headlights went on. Almost in the same moment the Studebaker swung out backwards, kicking gravel. It shimmied once, slid into forward, fishtailed briefly, then came straight toward her.

She shifted sideways and the car moved close by her, and she saw the eyes under the dark wig and knew something then as the car swung up on the sidewalk and halted, engine running. She was certain she was being casually studied in the rear and side mirrors. After a few more steps, she leant against the fence and breathed out as though in fear and exhaustion. Once she'd been to acting classes and she tried to think herself into the role, tried to feel or imagine fear in her whole body.

He could have put his foot on the accelerator and that would have been the last she'd see of him for some time; he lived on instinct and he'd know in his heart if something was wrong. As it was, the engine was in neutral and he was gunning the accelerator slowly, as though thinking to himself.

Cynthia stood upright, tried to gather herself, imagined herself attempting to put up a show of fearlessness. She knew that a fearful person would deliberately not look into the car.

She walked to the other side of the narrow alley and tried to sidle by the static, idling vehicle. She was almost past and decided he had maybe given her a miss when she heard the faint click of the door-handle. Then suddenly he was out so fast the door struck her hip and almost simultaneously he hit her in the side with his full weight. A hand like a claw clamped over her mouth and he was pulling her, as easily as a doll, through a gap in the iron fencing onto rough ground on the other side. His hand was across her mouth and he was whispering in her ear, "You say anything I'm gonna kill you right here." She felt the pull of the fence on her dress, the force of his pivoting tug, a rip of material. Then she was being hauled, winded and breathless, into the waste ground.

She had seen once, on a TV programme, a trapdoor spider snap out and pull an insect into its lair. She knew a little about how the victim might feel. He must have pulled her a hundred, maybe a hundred and fifty yards until the streetlights were just a glimmer in the deep night. When he reached a clear piece of ground, isolated by old packing cases, it seemed he knew where he was going to have her and humiliate her. He shifted his grip to throw or drag her down, and it was then, when he least expected it, she struck her fish.

She had been waiting for the moment when he shifted his grip from her throat and mouth. She had tried to lull him into complacency by her own compliance. When his hands shifted off her for half a second to change his grip and throw her down, she punched him so hard in the stomach she felt him roll and shimmy with sudden sensation.

He was in superb condition. As if by instinct he had managed somehow to anticipate the first movement of her counterattack and to swing away from it. She hadn't fully winded him, though on the instant of her strike he was still gripped by surprise. She used the half second or so of initial astonishment to break his grip on her head and mouth by wrenching his hand and wrist. Pivoting, she kneed him in the groin and caught him a full punch with the heel of her hand on the side of the face. As he went down he spun onto his back like an eel and she took the opportunity to drop her full weight on one knee into his solar plexus, taking all the breath out of him. He jack-knifed in agony and flicked onto his side, hoarse and rasping for breath.

While he was kicking in pain, she worked fast and ruthlessly. She undid his belt and pulled his trousers down and tied the heavy belt around his knees, wrenched the buckle up real tight. A man in his condition would take maybe twenty or thirty seconds to recover from being completely winded. She ripped the first three buttons on his shirt and pulled it backwards over his shoulders and used the sleeves to tie his wrists in a rough bandage while he sucked in breath. Regaining something of his composure, he began to flail his body.

She punched him hard, aiming between the neck and jaw, so hard that for several seconds he was quiet. His wig had fallen off. Beneath it his head was shaved bald.

Maybe it takes a predator to know that his position is helpless. He started to hiss and scream imprecations at her. She picked up his wig and began, with considerable patience, to stuff it into his mouth. He clenched his teeth but at each scream of outrage his jaw loosened and she wedged in a little more. As she forced the wig in farther his screams became fainter, then seemed to disappear, like a train going away in a tunnel.

She took a tape from her handbag and ran it round his neck and mouth to keep the wig in position. He was breathing through his nose now, snorting with shock or indignation like a stag.

She looked down at his trussed figure, taking in strong lung-fuls of air after her exertions. She released him sufficiently to shimmy onto his back to look up at his assailant.

"You want to fuck women against their will?" She planted her feet down on either side of him, taking her time. "Want to hear their screams?"

He looked up at her. The wig protruded from his mouth like moustaches.

She said "I could tread you into the ground like a beetle."

He tried to say something, but it didn't come out as anything coherent.

Cynthia said, "Maybe it's good for you to see what it's like, what it's like being completely at someone else's mercy."

7

In the offices of the *Angel Times*, the early shift had just come into the building. Cynthia was working at her laptop when a folded copy of the *Gazette* was thrown down on her desk with considerable force.

She followed the trajectory back to its source. Gore Emhard was standing beside her, looking down at the newspaper which was now splayed open at the front page, reposing like a victim who has fallen from a great height. "So who is this Fuckwoman?" he said. "What kind of a goddamn nut is she?"

She leaned forward to take in the title and the first few lines, then looked back up at him.

"Looks like the story got away from you, Cynthia," Emhard said.

He pointed down at the front page of the *Gazette*. The headline read:

F-WOMAN STRIKES AGAIN

Emhard reached up and switched on the television screen above Cynthia's desk. An announcer read out a news item. Whenever "Fuckwoman" was pronounced, there was the now familiar electronic bleep across the first syllable.

The announcer said, *"The vigilante who styles herself 'F-woman' has hit out again — this time at a convicted multiple rapist and felon called Pablo Cipasso. Cipasso, who was on the 'most wanted' list of criminals, was found last night bound and wounded in a wasteland building lot in downtown Venice. Police believe he has been responsible for more than half a dozen violent rapes of women in the area, but have been unable to track him down for more than three years. It looks as though F-woman got there first."*

"Goddamn," Emhard said.

"Following the apprehension of the suspect, police sources reveal that traces of make-up and a wig, along with woman's shoes, had indicated at previous crime scenes that Cipasso might have been a female impersonator. Police believe he may have been one of the impromptu performers in nearby transvestite bar El Greco's. They also suspect that F-woman may sometimes deliberately act as bait for rapists, setting herself up to appear vulnerable."

Emhard said softly, almost to himself, "Some sassy bitch."

"Cipasso is thought to have seen F-woman not long after leaving El Greco's and got out of his car, an old Studebaker, with the intention of attacking and raping her. Police found signs of a struggle near his abandoned vehicle, and the tracks of a person being dragged into the empty building site. After hauling his apparently helpless female victim into the shadows, in the process of attempting

to rape her, Cipasso experienced the surprise of his life when the woman now known as F-woman fought back, managed to overcome him, tie him up, and then left him for the police to pick up."

"Crazy vigilante," Emhard said.

"Cipasso, who police believe was tied up with his own belt and shirt, also suffered the indignity of having his female impersonator's wig stuffed into his mouth. He is apparently shaken and bruised, but his condition is said to be stable."

"Jesus," Emhard said. "I don't know who is crazier — that rapist or this goddamn woman. They shouldn't put this stuff out over the air."

"There is a further bulletin, and a psychological profile of F-woman, over on our sister Channel 26."

They both reached simultaneously to turn over to the station on Channel 26.

"Speculation intensifies about F-woman herself. Aware that a substantial and increasing proportion of the populace are in favour of the rough justice F-woman administers to her rapist victims, police psychologists are trying to work on a profile of the feminist vigilante that would help to identify her. Dr James Holocenter, a psychiatrist in LAPD's Special Profiles department, has recorded this interview."

Dr Holocenter talked softly and easily, with a natural authority. It seemed to Cynthia that maybe because he felt he was on his own territory now, or perhaps because he was making the running, he was a changed animal compared to the curt and nervous figure she had seen a few days before. Then he had been defensive about LAPD's failure to apprehend rapists or catch the vigilante known as Fuckwoman. Now, he fielded a couple of initial questions smoothly, then said, *"My guess is that she's someone who bears a substantial grudge against the male sex. She may have suffered abuse of some kind as a child. I'm being speculative here, of course, but we have to start somewhere."*

The announcer said, *"Dr Holocenter also cited the clues she leaves behind as indications of her personality."*

Dr Holocenter had settled down now, and almost seemed to be reading off a prepared text. *"One of the more interesting features of these crimes is that F-woman appears to model her exploits on Superman and other comics. I'm empowered to inform you that she habitually leaves behind a specific reference to Superman or one of the other comic strip heroes. In this most recent case she left a note saying, 'Is it a bird, is it a bee?' On one level, it's a classic homage to Superman, of course. But it also seems to be an arcane reference to the birds and the bees, or the sexual crimes of the alleged rapist."* Dr Holocenter paused as though for emphasis. *"We're dealing with a sick mind here. We believe the essential constituents of F-woman's personality are adolescent emotions combined with a substantive paranoia. She needs psychiatric treatment and maybe some strong chemical abreaction therapy."*

"Love those instant prognoses," Cynthia said softly.

"What?" Emhard asked.

"Just mumbling to myself."

They continued to watch.

The announcer said, *"Members of the public have their own views on the self-styled vigilante. Asked who or what was the identity of F-woman, a local superstore manager had this response."*

A white-coated middle-aged man with his hair in a ponytail directed his thin face towards the camera: *"Could be an alien, for all I care. What I do know is that goddamn alien is doing a lot better job than the Los Angeles police."*

The announcer said, *"Another opinion came from Taco Fujimori, the barman at El Greco, where Cipasso was thought to have performed in one of their impromptu transvestite dance shows. Asked about F-woman's identity, Mr Fujimori stated, 'My own guess is she's a diesel dyke from Orange County.' Mr Fujimori has helped police with a photofit likeness of a woman who visited the bar last night and was asking suspicious questions. Mr Fujimori's photofit image of the woman appears below."*

There was a picture of a being that looked like an anthropoid ape in a wig. On one level at least, it seemed to Cynthia as though the feelings of suspicion between her and the bartender were mutual. On another level, it was a relief not to be too easily identified.

Cynthia said, "My guess it's the orang-utan from Griffiths Park zoo."

"What?" Emhard asked.

"Nothing that bears repeating," Cynthia said. "I guess there's a lot of confusion over who she might be."

"One maniac is as bad as another," Emhard said. He turned off the TV set and stretched out his long arms. He had a crick in his neck. Massaging his vertebrae with his fingers, he stared up at the ceiling. "In my youth, on Saturday nights we younger journos used to cruise downtown to The Busted Steer in our pick-up trucks and our Fords. Then we'd drink ourselves stupid and play a little poker and swap jokes. Other times we'd quarrel and beat the hell out of each other. That was good clean fun in the American way. This weirdo stuff turns my stomach."

He flexed his neck a little more and then moved off. Cynthia watched him go back to his office. She wondered whether he'd console himself with the aesthetic charm of his bison's penis pencil-holder. Maybe it was the only thing he had left that connected him to a sane world.

She turned back to the computer screen and began to file her copy for next day's paper.

8

Cynthia visited the Aztec Health Club on 3rd Street after hours, when everything was a fraction of the normal price. If you were careful to avoid extra charges, you could use the place economically. If you bought food or had a drink, or a massage, or the hundred other beauty treatments they offered, the prices were astronomical.

They had good weightlifting equipment, benches and presses. She worked out every evening for one and a half hours, then she swam forty lengths in the Olympic pool. She found swimming loosened the muscles, gave her body a certain sleekness.

She had trained herself not simply for power, though she could apply more power than anyone had a right to suspect. She trained her body to think for itself, to move economically and fluently, to assume its own independence. Those who came up against her were rendered suspicious and then fearful by her relaxation, by the way she gathered herself almost languidly to strike. She would feint and then hit them with unexpected force.

Her assumptions about her opponents were simple and clear. Physically, they were stronger than she was. It was largely chemical: they were loaded up with testosterone and other hormones; they had the typical pattern of male musculature, with higher proportions of strong muscle striations. But their bodies didn't have her own relentless self-respect, her sense of freedom. She trained herself to be loose and rangy and lithe, and to accept punishment, because she knew it was temporary. But there was always something to follow. She would slide around the edges of their attack and strike back at them. She found that by gathering herself calmly behind her intent, she could hit harder. That frightened her opponents the most. They were disconcerted by the way she patiently endured their physical attack. But the deepest damage was psychological. In some part of the male psyche, her opponents didn't believe any woman would counter-attack. They didn't accept that any woman could enter a violent confrontation in the cold expectation of pursuing the confrontation to its fearful outcome. When that first incipient doubt or fear came into their minds it was her experience that their confidence began to unravel. They became bunched and fearful. All their tensions began to fight against one another. That was when the confrontation entered its final stage, when one of the opponents seemed to grow and the other to shrink.

On two nights a week she practised Judo with a Mexican called Juan Cortez. She would let him throw her and pin her down and then do her best to get out of it. Her whole mind was focused on the single task of removing herself from his hold. If she couldn't get out using one method, she'd try another. She'd attempt to lull Juan and then throw her full weight into something unexpected. If the unexpected thing wouldn't get her out of the hold, sometimes it disconcerted her instructor enough for him to shift to counterbalance it. Then without warning she'd put all her force into the expected attack, which was now wholly unexpected. Juan was frequently surprised and sometimes astonished at her concentration and detachment, by the laconic speed with which she could shift her concentration.

That evening Cynthia visited the Aztec Health Club shortly after midnight, walking up the stairs to the impressive entrance and reception kiosk. Without looking up, the attendant behind the glass said, "Sorry, we're closed." The shadow continued to hover outside the glass. He glanced up, his eyes wide behind glasses. "Oh, Miss Lelague."

Cynthia said, "Hi, Matthew. Sorry, I can only afford this place after hours."

"Who gave you that low-price deal, Miss Lelague?" Matthew said. "You got friends in high places?"

He pressed a switch and the doors opened. "'Fraid the air conditioning's been switched off. Only night lighting inside now, too."

Cynthia smiled. "That's why I get a low price."

She walked through the open doors into the big central hallway. The night-lights were dim. She moved softly down the long corridors, turning right past a long swimming pool, steaming milkily in the night. She liked to move quietly, hearing her soft footsteps on the tiles. At the end of the hall she pushed open another door, breathing softly.

The gym, like the rest of the building, was only half lit by overnight lighting. She moved her gaze past the lifting presses and other equipment to an open space, at the centre of which was a wrestling mat. She stared past the wrestling mat into the darkness on the other side.

At the other end, almost entirely hidden in the obscurity, was a single figure. She could not see his face. He was so still he seemed like a piece of the furniture. Every few seconds a cloud of white breath emerged from the darkness which housed him.

"Hi, Juan," Cynthia called out.

"Hi, Cyncy," Juan said. "You late."

"Sorry, Juan. Had to put in some extra work for the late edition."

Juan Cortez did not move. The plumes of his breath continued to emerge from the obscurity. Cynthia took off her tracksuit top and bottoms. Underneath she was in a wrestling leotard.

She moved towards him, advancing into the middle of the wrestling space. She stood on the centre of the mat. Plumes of breath moved out from her.

Deliberately, she turned around so that she faced away from him. She sensed, over her shoulder, Juan's breaths in the darkness. Suddenly, his breathing stopped. She heard the faintest drubbing of feet as he sprinted across the distance separating him from her.

Just as he was about to reach her, she side-stepped, so that he caught her a glancing blow on the shoulder. At the same time she seized his wrist and threw him over her own shoulder onto his back. Then she brought her knees and calves down on his shoulders, pinning him to the mat.

"Not bad," Juan said.

Deftly, with his shoulders pinned down, Juan raised his legs. The legs approached her, as though under their own volition. They took hold of her neck in a scissors lock, and pulled her over onto the carpet.

He pinned her down neatly. She struggled, but could not break his hold.

Juan said, "You give in?"

Slowly, Cynthia relaxed. Her toes extended. Her arm spread out in apparent submission on the mat, her fingers relaxed. Cautiously, Juan took deep lungfuls.

He gasped once, suddenly, as Cynthia bucked her legs, and he tried to ride the enormous force applied to him. Almost instantaneously she bucked her midriff, attacking him on a different axis, destabilising him. Before he had had time to adjust his balance again, she switched her full force back to her knees. At each movement Juan seemed to lose some purchase on her. Then she drove up unexpectedly with her stomach so that he lost his hold and simultaneously he was thrown face forward onto the mat.

She pinned him down and forced his arm up his back. They lay parallel like lovers.

"Goddamn, Cyncy," Juan said. "You fight like cat."

Cynthia swallowed. "Sure, Juan. Always fearful, always ready."

"You frighten rape, Cyncy?" Juan said. "You have bad nightmare?"

"Just a professional interest, Juano."

She relaxed her grip and rolled away from him, lying on her back.

"Like every day you expect to meet your man." Juan said.

"That's not far off the truth."

He rolled slowly on his back and stared at the ceiling. They were both covered in sweat from their exertions.

After a while Cynthia raised herself to her feet. "You swimming?"

Juan smiled noncommittally.

Cynthia stepped through the open doors of the gym into the swimming hall. She dived in neatly, then began to do a fast crawl down the middle. Juan watched her form disappearing into the milky white, the two trails from her legs like tendrils. At the other end, so far in the dark he could hardly see her, Cynthia did a racing turn.

Afterwards they walked back to the changing rooms. He was covered in sweat, she in water drops. Juan turned for the door marked MEN. He watched her as she paused at the door marked WOMEN.

"See you next week?"

He nodded. "Sure."

Cynthia undressed in the women's changing rooms. Beyond the wall she heard Juan splashing in the shower. She paused for a moment to listen to him, then turned towards her own cubicle.

The water was cold at first. She turned the temperature control a little higher. The needles of hot water touched her shoulders, neck and back. She felt the soap float cold and pure down across the skin of her belly and thighs, a moon against her sun. These days this was her only embrace, it seemed to her, the only foreign touch her body knew. For a while now she had sensed some movement outward from her own centre towards Juan, like a centrifugal force. But some part of her mind always shied back, as though the very thought of it impinged on her privacy. It was as if her will set up an equal and opposite force that was centripetal, closing in upon itself.

She turned around, raised her head, and felt the hot torrent against her throat, shoulders and breasts, the steam rising off her like a cloud.

9

Outside, Matthew said, "Goodbye, Miss Lelague."

He was sitting in the kiosk reading something. When he saw her coming out of the building he put it under the desk. Cynthia caught sight of a magazine cover, with two men standing together, leaning casually against a wall. The men were both naked except for thongs which, if anything, seemed to emphasise their sexuality. She had guessed before that Matthew was gay. That didn't alter her liking for him one way or the other.

No sexual activity frightened her, except perhaps the outer fringes of sado-masochism. She guessed that was because any expression of power or violence between men or women seemed to her inherently political. The black leather garments reminded her uneasily of fascism, and she wondered why people needed to flirt with the darker forces of domination and submission to get their kicks. She wondered too at the tangle of relations between men and women that led to such strange ceremonies, such odd rehearsals of aggression.

On one level at least, the gay scene interested her because it provided a basis of comparison. One of her gay male friends had suggested to her that relations between men were much easier than between the sexes, that the particular thing each wanted was much clearer. According to him there were fewer boundaries to be crossed than between the sexes, fewer barriers of differing expectations, fewer political negotiations.

She crossed Burlington Avenue and walked through the dark streets in the hot night, moving quietly in her sensible shoes on the paving stones that were still warm with the day's sunlight.

In Union Avenue several hookers were leaning quietly against a wall. Most of them had drug habits. They had pale faces and when they moved they had that peculiar deliberation of people whose minds are somewhere else. On Second Avenue a couple of drunks stumbled past her, drinking out of plastic bottles and weaving their way down the sidewalk.

In Valencia Street she saw, projecting beneath a triangle of deepest shadow, the trouser legs of three men leaning against a wall. Their upper halves were entirely obscured. Something about the disposition of those legs — the way they announced the men's presence while withholding their identity — suggested to her that maybe they would try a move on her. She guessed they knew she had seen them and were calculating her response. She had a sense of their focus on her. They were watching for signs of fear, because it was fear that interested them, that excited them. A fearful woman could attract predators and scavengers out of the dark as a wounded antelope would attract hyenas or lions out of the African night.

She knew the three men would be watching her advance towards them, without moving off her track, until she passed no more than a few feet away from them. They could have reached out and touched her, they were that close, and her presence dared them. She might just as well have gone up to their faces and looked them in the eye. She had fear, certainly, but her fear was under her control, not theirs. That was the difference. In the darkness she passed by them without incident.

She opened the door of her apartment and turned on the switch. The light seemed to bisect the bare angles of the room.

The flat consisted of a single main room, empty, almost monastic. There was a small kitchenette and a shower compartment adjoining. The divan doubled as a bed. It took her a few minutes to open it up and set down clean sheets. The flat had no air conditioning; it was formerly a painter's garret and it faced north. There were no paintings on the walls now, though, just whitewash. She liked the room's bareness and clear, open spaces. If she was sympathetic to any religion, it was Zen Buddhism. The flat reflected that sense of austerity and ascetism.

She turned off the light because she liked to undress in the dark. She could open the curtains and the window and not feel observed by anyone. In the darkness she lifted her dress off her shoulders and hung it up in the single wardrobe. Then, naked, she lay down on her bed and stared at the ceiling.

Sometimes, at certain times during the night, she considered the strangeness of her life. It was like a personal theatre, a theatre of the absurd. Each one of us reacts to our circumstances in his or her own way, but her life seemed to have unfolded with its own peculiar logic.

Sometimes she thought of her upbringing. She wondered whether there were other lives she could have led. But if she thought about what she was and what she might have become, they seemed to her increasingly unreal, as unreal as the relation between lived life and what you saw in the movies.

10

A few days later, somewhat unexpectedly, she received a letter from her mother, enclosing a newspaper article from the *Pasadena Post*:

Dear Cynthia,

How are you, darling? We haven't heard from you for a few weeks now. I hope your work isn't draining you too much, and that you're eating well.

I'm writing this note partly to enclose something which I think may amuse you. Have you been following the strange career of the vigilante who calls herself "Fuckwoman"? When I first read about her, I thought she must be some eccentric young female from a caravan park with a serious psychological problem, maybe some grievance against her absent father or something like that. She reminds me of some of the young women that turn up to our psychology unit's open days — defensive and angry and searching for some outlet. But more recently there have been signs that she has quite a specific, even highly developed, ideological stance. I'm not saying that makes her any better or worse, it just adds another layer to the character.

We have a good local reporter here in Pasadena called James Blender, a young man in his twenties who I suspect will end up with one of the big newspapers in due course. His articles are usually well researched and deal with their subjects more fully than most. In deference to his talents, the Post *sometimes gives him room for larger pieces. The enclosed article by him carries a certain coherence, though who can assume any real authenticity in any of the mass media about such an odd figure?*

Cynthia darling, I sometimes have this odd daydream or nightmare that "Fuckwoman" could be you. I know it's ridiculous to think that of one's own daughter, but there are certain aspects of her character, at least as reported, which remind me of you. And if I attempt to provide "Fuckwoman" with some form of rudimentary psychological profile, I have to say it seems to fit you quite well. It's not just the apparent confidence, the occasional arrogance, and the thirst for instant justice that call you to mind. I am also reminded of how you deal with crises, with that alarming boldness and counter-attack which I suspect makes you such a disconcerting opponent. To give only one example, I remember when you were in your teens and the Entwhistles' son Harry cheated on his line-calls at tennis just a couple more times than you thought were necessary. You walked around to the other side of the court, lifted him up and suspended him by his tee-shirt from one of the metal brackets on the corner poles. I remember you strolling back to the other side of the court in one of your calm rages while he hung there with his arms and legs jerking helplessly. Then you carefully served out your game and left the court, leaving him dangling incoherently in space. I had to ask your father to help me lift him down because you were insistent that he should remain there for a while longer. I recall your father's helpless laughter as we assisted the little squirt down and had to pretend that we were shocked by our Amazonian daughter's behaviour.

I always knew you were strong, but I didn't know until then that you were quite that motivated. It wasn't just physical strength that suspended young Mr Entwhistle up there. Something seemed to come over you, like Popeye eating spinach or the Incredible Hulk. I know what happens when some sense of injustice seems to animate you.

Cynthia, darling, when you next put pen to paper, to place my mind at rest, please write me your news with just a little line to say you are definitely not and never have been "Fuckwoman".

Lots of love,
Fernanda

Her mother always signed herself by her Christian name, the clear and beautiful signature that showed her character as transparently as a window.

Cynthia put the letter down and looked at the newspaper article. It was headed:

THE CASE OF TARANTINO'S POODLE, by James Blender.

The article began:

In the newspaper accounts of the vigilante who calls herself F-woman, and who is fast becoming some kind of contemporary icon amongst certain minority groups, there have been reports of several high-profile engagements which have been much commented upon by the media. These have involved our eponymous heroine tackling some rapist at large, immobilising him, and subjecting him to the humiliation of being captured and detained by a member of the sex he so hates or despises.

But a more recent report has shown that there is another dimension to F-woman's character, one which might provide some form of insight into her motivations.

This particular episode, the Jim Rivers case, perhaps caused the LAPD more consternation than the others. The background would appear to be as follows:

Female holidaymakers and casual visitors in the Griffiths Park area found themselves pestered and occasionally threatened by a man calling himself "a disciple of Quentin". Several women made direct complaints to the local police that they had been harassed by a person who boasted that he was a devoted fan of Quentin Tarantino, the famous film director and enfant terrible. *His attempts at conversation seemed sincere, but a number of the females he approached were not impressed, and we understand that more than one such visitor, when approached, said that they didn't admire Mr. Tarantino or his films. The notion that anyone in their right mind could not admire Tarantino apparently enraged the man, who then became abusive and called them dumb bimbos and uncultured assholes and sometimes even exposed himself to them.*

It appears that F-woman hunted down this molester and subjected him to her own rough code of justice. An individual later identified as Jim Rivers, the avant-garde *film critic and proprietor of the magazine* Style is Everything *(sold in France as*

La Surface est Toute) *was found recently hanging alive but deeply embarrassed from a bridge over the incoming traffic where the Golden State Freeway crosses Ventura Freeway at the Northwest corner of Griffiths Park. He had been suspended by a kind of leather brace from one of the concrete uprights on the bridge over the west-going traffic on Ventura. His lower half was naked, and some form of message had been written on his buttocks in blue indelible ink, though it was difficult to work out from the roadway the full contents of the message. The police had to stop the traffic while safety nets were spread out below him and a team set to work to lower him. He was sweating and shaking when he approached the blacktop, and his rescuers put aside the safety nets and set him down on a mattress. Then they unclipped the leather brace, untied his hands and arms, and put a modesty blanket over him.*

Mr Rivers claimed that he had been hanging for half an hour while the traffic rushed below him, and that some cars and trucks even honked, while other drivers raised their fists in good-natured salute. They thought it was a joke, that it was part of the collegiate rag from UCLA, or that he was mooning to the morning traffic from Encino. It was amazing, Mr Rivers said, how some people misunderstood primary narrative.

It was only when Mr Rivers had recovered some degree of equanimity that he informed the police he had been captured and subjected to this indignity by a woman who referred to herself as F-woman. In his statement he described her as "a tall, rangy bitch in a blonde wig, who spoke in some kind of a weird, highly disguised nasal voice as though she came from another planet. I mean," Mr Rivers added, "at first I thought she was just a typical Valley girl." It appears that his humiliating exposure to rush-hour drivers moving into the San Bernadino valley was considered by his captor to be sufficient punishment for his alleged improprieties with women.

As the fourth known victim of F-woman's depredations, Mr Rivers achieved notoriety of a type he did not actually welcome. An aesthete, film critic and cultural commentator, he had until then enjoyed a small but select following for his outspoken championship of Tarantino movies as examples of high culture. As part of this avocation, he had achieved something of a reputation for chastising Hollywood film-makers for their lack of social realism, and was famous or notorious (Mr Rivers wasn't concerned which, attention seemed to be the thing) for advocating Tarantino's most violent work, with its streetwise slang and cool, as a realistic model for modern behaviour.

Unlike F-woman's other victim, Rivers had no rape convictions, and so far no other convictions have been pinned on him. In the absence of such evidence, students of F-woman came to believe that in his assailant's eyes, Rivers' "offence" was largely ideological. In support of this view, when police officers cut down and lowered the figure of Mr Rivers, they found that the message which had been inscribed across his buttocks was the following piece of doggerel:

There's no more social realism
in Quentin Tarantino,
Than in *Wizard of Oz*
Or a Travolta Latino.

Mr Rivers complained to the LAPD that he was subjected to further humiliations when, after taking him back to police headquarters for questioning, they insisted that graphologists and cryptographers should examine the writing minutely for clues as to F-woman's identity. In addition, various psychologists, psychiatrists and even literary experts were asked to study the somewhat acerbic message in order to "decode" it. Rivers objected further when the text was widely published on police WANTED posters, with its original background in the form of a black-and-white photograph of his rear end, in the hope that members of the public might come forward to identify the handwriting.

When Mr Rivers had recovered some of his customary sang-froid, he claimed that the greatest atrocity committed against him was F-woman's writing style. To attach a piece of doggerel to him which didn't even scan properly, he claimed, was a style outrage surpassing even the physical humiliation he had suffered at her hands. Nevertheless acquaintances reported that, following the incident in question, Mr Rivers did not leave his house during daylight hours and that he armed himself with several high-velocity rifles and a trained Alsatian. Even now, these sources claim, he lies awake at night in case his chief critic returns.

Since then, it is understood Mr Rivers has been provoked further by an additional piece of doggerel which was sent to the Anaheim Gazette, postmarked from Canoga Park, with no return address and so effectively untraceable.. Purporting to be from F-woman, it added another element to the somewhat unorthodox dialogue between Rivers and his assailant regarding film theory. At first police detectives were suspicious that the letter was a hoax, but handwriting experts have confirmed that it came from the same pen as the original verse on Mr Rivers' rear end. The message was written in the same indelible blue ink, but this time on a piece *of white notepaper which could be obtained from most stationery stores. The message read:*

There's nothing wrong with romance,
Or with fantasy either.
But when geeks start to claim
That infliction of pain
Is balm to the soul,
And can laugh like a drain,
At a movie so vain
As *Pulp Fiction,* I claim
To prefer my romance
from Bogart or Hepburn.
If violence is cool,
And rape is just fine,
Why don't we all drool
Over Rivers' *derrière*?

The latter, clearly a reference to the widespread publication of the original verse on Mr Rivers' nether regions, appeared specifically designed to inflame the amour propre *of the celebrated cultural critic and aesthete. There was a further outbreak of publication in the popular press of the original black-and-white police photograph of Rivers' rear end, and considerable heated public debate over the contents of both messages. Mr Rivers was asked for his own view of the most recent missive. His only comment was that F-woman's verse technique had not improved.*

Even so, it is reliably reported that he bought several more rifles, some additional cases of fast-burning high-velocity ammunition, and a Doberman Pinscher to reinforce the Alsatian. He told his wider circle of acquaintances that the Doberman was just to provide company for the other dog. To his intimates he confided that the three of them were waiting for the next round of film discussion with F-woman and looked forward to some "meaty, sweaty, primary narrative, with a secondary context of casual violence."

The story continues.

11

Cynthia could see why her mother might be alarmed by the article. If she really was "Fuckwoman", her mother would believe that some crazy was holed up in his digs somewhere, nursing grievances and ready to fill her with lead at a moment's notice. On the other hand, if she wished to put her mother's mind at rest, how could she explain that a typical Tarantino fan was essentially a harmless geek? That he was a showcase of male complexes and insecurities, masquerading as their opposite?

No doubt she'd alarm her mother even further if she told her that in hunting Rivers down, she'd staked out a certain area of Griffiths Park on the north side. After several nights of unrewarding patrol, she'd finally seen a figure who resembled Rivers accosting some young women in the same area where his previous incidents had been reported. She was inclined not to intervene because she didn't want witnesses. But after one particular altercation, when he'd said something insulting and the girl had turned away in disgust, Cynthia had followed him home to his apartment, which was set on a sloping hillside overlooking the park. The apartment was part of a fine older building, converted to new flats. Rivers' accommodation appeared to be on the ground floor, with its entrance directly on the street. She caught a glimpse of the inside from one of the windows facing the road, and gained an impression of minimalist decor and one or two fine pieces of furniture.

Having taken down the apartment number, she drove back to her flat for a night's sleep. Woken by her alarm at five in the morning, she showered, dressed, had a cup of coffee, and drove out again in the calm pre-dawn darkness to Griffiths Park. She took one of the deserted side-roads and pulled into an empty lot. Making sure she was not overlooked, she got out of the car, set up her torch facing the car so that she could see reasonably well, and carefully changed to false numberplates. Then she drove on towards Rivers' apartment and cautiously parked a couple of streets away. By the time she reached his apartment and knocked on the painted wooden door, her watch said five fifty-three.

Almost immediately after her knock, a flicker of light appeared in an upstairs window as the lamp in the bedroom came on. Then she thought she heard someone descending the stairs. She guessed he would be sleepy and confused.

The lights came on downstairs. She heard the faint squeal of a drawer being opened inside and she deduced he had picked up a firearm. After a while the downstairs lights were switched off and she heard footsteps come to the door. She knew that turning off the light inside was supposed to reduce the target offered by the householder. Rivers' obsessive precautions indicated to her something about his state of mind. It was clear that he was alarmed by the knock on the door.

The locks were drawn and the door was cautiously opened. A face appeared in the darkness. Rivers said softly, "Who the fuck are you?"

"Fuckwoman," Cynthia said.

There was an agreeable silence, lasting perhaps three or four seconds. Cynthia said, "Why don't you just step forward so I can identify you?"

He didn't move. His figure seemed pale as a ghost in the gloom of the interior. There was just enough light from the last of streetlamps for her to make out the shape of his face. His eyes behind their steel-rimmed spectacles seemed to grow larger. The two of them were perhaps a couple of feet apart, and they examined each other as best they could in the half-light.

Rivers said, "The fuck I will."

She knew the word "fuck" was emblematic, a virility symbol, a badge of cool realism, Tarantinoesque. But that didn't mean she liked to see it used in that way, as mere decoration.

He appeared to be hesitating about whether to slam the door and lock her out. But instead, in a tone of patient condescension, he said, "OK, lady. Let's straighten this out. Just tell me what the fuck it is you want."

"You say 'fuck' again," Cynthia said pleasantly, "and I'm going to remove your balls."

There was another nice silence while he considered this possibility. As her eyes grew more accustomed to the light she could see the faint raze of stubble on his cheek, the Japanese pattern of his dressing gown.

After a while he said, "Why are you doing this?"

Cynthia said, "I intend to see you punished for accosting women in Griffiths Park."

He gave something like a derisive snort of laughter and then with surprising swiftness (he seemed to have fully recovered now from being woken up) he snapped the door closed. But she got her foot in promptly, and after that it was simply a matter of holding on.

The next few moments reminded Cynthia of a former boyfriend of hers during her student years. They used to wake up in the early hours. Once each knew the other was awake, they used to fuck fervently and silently, with only heavy breathing between them. That was what it was like now. She and Rivers moved backwards and forwards for a while, comically and intimately, neither one saying anything, both breathing in occasional brisk gasps with the effort. The door was like a seesaw between them. It was at that point, still trying to push the door closed, that he must have reached into his dressing gown pocket and taken out the gun.

The artillery piece was an interesting new element in the narrative. It came out through the crack in the door calmly, the barrel blue and shiny as rail lines, pointed directly at her head. She examined it carefully. It was a .32 calibre pistol, similar perhaps to the pieces used by Pumpkin and Honey Bunny to hold up the restaurant in *Pulp Fiction*. It was elegant but — to her tastes, at least — perhaps a little arty.

At the same time Rivers felt moved to speak. In a voice calm with controlled rage, he said, "Get the fuck out of here, you fucking asshole, or I'm going to spread your fucking face across the entire fucking street."

At this point in a Tarantino movie, she thought, the other guy realises he's in a spot of trouble, on account of one "fuck" and three "fucking"s in a single sentence, which fact suggests ineluctably that the owner of the handgun has had enough and means business and the best thing for anyone to do is to remove himself from the vicinity. Added to this, the almost Latinate cadence of the sentence, the rolling threat delivered with several "fucking"s like thorns on a rose stem, bespoke a man of literary means and a certain masculine lucidity. That was the theory, anyway. Unfortunately it was Cynthia's considered view that the narrative in Tarantino movies wasn't realistic — all those mannered little sermons about hamburgers and things which a certain type of film critic seemed to admire — and so she felt moved to ignore entirely the quaint homily Rivers had just propounded.

"Listen, sweetheart," Cynthia said. "You've just taken one hand off the door and put it on a firearm. You know what that means?"

There was no reply.

"Let me help you. It means that you can't apply your full weight to the door any more. I'm not sure that Tarantino understands things like that — those little points of detail which women tend to notice. Now, as far as I am concerned, that simply loads the dice against you, because I'm still here and I've got two hands free."

"Last chance," Rivers said. "Last chance or I spread you."

He had his foot jammed on the door, and he put his other hand on the gun. Now he was two-handing her, the barrel was his final argument.

Cynthia said, "The way I see it, that's just throwing good money after bad."

She allowed a few seconds to go by, while she cheerfully squared up to the task of pushing open the door. Then she applied full pressure, and heard the soles of his slippers squealing on the elegant bare blond pine floorboards inside as he tried to resist her. It was another intimate moment between them, another episode in that little dance which so easily and appropriately might be called the early morning doorfuck. They moved backwards and forwards in a kind of concentrated, muscular silence. He was breathing more agitatedly now, almost as though he were coming, but her own breathing was low and smooth and full. That was how it was with men, she thought, less staying power than a woman. Slowly she edged the door open and pushed into the room. Then she was through the door entirely, backing him across the floor and through the solid darkness of the room until he came up against the furthest wall.

For several seconds they were silent, both breathing heavily.

"Now," she said, "why don't you just put down that gun. You might hurt someone."

But some final residue of resistance caused him to disobey her. He was shaking and fearful, but he swallowed and continued to hold the barrel to her head.

"Your last chance," he said. "Then I spread you."

His finger hardened on the trigger. She could sense that finger tightening and she didn't like it, but she wasn't much moved by it either.

"Do I have to get unpleasant?" Cynthia asked.

Face to face in the darkness of the flat, the coldness of the barrel on her forehead above her left eye, she reached down below his waistline into deep darkness and separated the folds of his dressing gown carefully with her hand and took hold of his balls. She squeezed a certain amount until he started to shiver, then she squeezed a little more.

The gun was starting to shake. She could feel the faint vibrations of the barrel against her forehead. She applied some more pressure until, with a sound somewhere between a groan and a manly sob, the firearm dropped nervelessly to the elegant Turkoman carpet.

Rivers subsided to his knees. He crouched over, clutching himself with both solicitous hands. At the same time he whispered, *"Fuck, fuck, fuck..."*

Cynthia let him have his say. Meanwhile, for his own safety, she kicked his artillery into a corner. Standing in the gloom above him, she waited calmly for him to recover.

Her mother, no doubt, would have been alarmed at her behaviour. It might have looked as if Cynthia were tempting fate, breaking into a man's apartment and squeezing his balls mercilessly while he held a loaded firearm against her forehead. But she knew she was as safe as houses. She couldn't tell her mother that to a true Tarantino fan a handgun is a fashion accessory — that is, a pure style accoutrement — and about as real a menace as a feather duster. She fervently wished she could tell her mother that the possibility of a Tarantino fan actually pulling a trigger at close range and being faced with real blood and pain as opposed to fantasy blood and pain was sufficiently small to be worth the risk.

That, at any rate, was how she took Rivers hostage.

After his bluff had been called, there was something rather touching about the way that Rivers became entirely reasonable and subservient to her wishes. She said, "Put some clothes on. Then you're coming with me."

She waited for him while he dressed. Afterwards they went out into the dawn and walked down through the empty streets to the place where she'd left her old Ford. They got into the car and she drove through the early morning towards the Golden State Freeway before the sun was up. She liked this time of the day. Rivers was silent beside her. They halted on the shoulder where it crossed Ventura Freeway, and got out. There were cars going by, but their drivers must have guessed or assumed that the couple standing at the side of the road seemed engaged in peaceful discussion and no one thought any more of it.

When Rivers realised she wasn't intending to harm him but to suspend him as safely as possible from the bridge, he almost fainted with gratitude. He allowed himself to be bound up and attached to the leather harness. For his own peace of mind she permitted him to inspect the safety of the attachment point.

The only unexpected humiliation was when, bound in the leather harness, she insisted on removing his trousers and turning him round so that she could write her message of film criticism in indelible blue ink on his buttocks.

"What does it say?" he asked.

She read it out to him.

"Oh, neat," he said. "Real neat."

Then she lowered him unresisting over the parapet and into the rosy dawn above Ventura Freeway.

12

While Cynthia was lowering Rivers over the parapet, she suspected he was making his plans for a face-saving public gesture of defiance. She guessed that, even then, he was concocting his story to the police about how he'd been surprised in his bed and dragged out at gunpoint and then driven to an unknown destination. There he was ordered out of the car and brutally suspended above Ventura Freeway by some huge, enraged Amazon who had threatened him horribly. Only his astonishing calm and mesmerising reasonableness in the face of her madness had enabled him to escape with his life.

It had come as no surprise, either, when he claimed that, far from Fuckwoman being merciful towards him — given her usual proclivities towards her chosen victims — it was entirely his own presence of mind and persuasive powers which had caused her to be unusually considerate towards his physical wellbeing. "She was holding this gun at my head," he said to his police rescuers. "It was starting to get confrontational." He nodded. "Yeah, it was starting to go down to the wire. I guess I'm just fortunate in being a tad more authoritative than most."

As for the subsequent reports about the rifle and the Alsatian and the Doberman Pinscher and the hoped-for reunion with her, that seemed to Cynthia like more empty gesturing, and she even wondered whether the widespread accounts of the dogs and additional artillery were another imaginative fantasy. Maybe he was playing to his audience of Tarantino fans. In her view, he was no more likely to use a rifle than a handgun.

That was why she had decided to send in another piece of doggerel to the *Anaheim Gazette*. It was her way of warning him that he'd behaved unacceptably.

There was also an element of experiment in her somewhat unorthodox verse submission — a small and additional exploration of the components of the male psyche. It seemed to her that any reasonable person in Rivers' position would accept that he had survived an embarrassing episode and would do his best to place the incident behind him. He wouldn't try to lie to himself and attempt to rewrite history. If her worst expectations were confirmed, Rivers would do the opposite. He would dwell upon the incident, brood over the wounds to his psyche, and, worse still, build a new life around it.

She was fascinated, in short, whether the fabrications about the nature of his assailant that Rivers had given to the police immediately after his capture consisted of a short-term ploy or arose from a deeper motive. Could the desire to save face drive an entire personality, taking precedence over all other motivations?

Speaking for herself, she didn't expect anything more or less from a devoted Tarantino fan and cultural aesthete. As the title to his French magazine suggested, so in life — *La Surface est Toute.*

13

When Gore Emhard walked into the main office carrying a newspaper, he seemed to be pushing his thoughts ahead of him like grief. People stepped aside so that he could pass. He moved past them without acknowledgement, locked into his own compass. When he reached Cynthia's desk he halted without greeting her and switched on the screen above her. An announcer came into view.

"Look at this," Emhard said. "This is really sick. See what Fuckwoman has started now."

There was a brief item on the forthcoming meeting between the American and Russian presidents over further nuclear weapons limitations, another on the perennial subject of the uneasy relations between the two countries. Emhard was silent, standing in front of the television's radiation like a tall, lean isotope. Then the announcer said, *"In Los Angeles yesterday a woman was raped in the Civic Center area. This is the third rape that has taken place in the neighbourhood in the course of the last year, and police investigators are finding a sinister pattern. The area houses the municipal buildings of the Los Angeles City administration. In each case the rape victim has been one of the female employees of City Hall. Things have got so bad that female personnel refuse to go out unaccompanied. Terror has caused woman employees to be nervous of even facing long, empty corridors inside the buildings."*

Cynthia said, "Another maniac."

"No, it's not the same," Emhard insisted. He nodded briefly towards the screen. "Listen."

The announcer said, *"The most recent rape took place in broad daylight in one of the small parks or quadrangles between the municipal buildings. The rapist was so effective in suppressing the screams of his victim that no one was alerted. Some initial details of the most recent rape have been given out by LAPD. The identity of the woman concerned remains anonymous. Following the case, we interviewed LAPD psychiatrist Dr James Holocenter."*

Holocenter was sitting in his office, with a wall full of reference books behind him. His bony, ascetic face was solemnised with a natural authority. He had removed his jacket, and his red braces emphasised his informality. There was something curiously old-fashioned about braces, but also unconventional and disarming. He spoke to the camera more plausibly and confidently than Cynthia had seen before. She noticed that on his appearance other reporters and researchers in the main newsroom switched on their screens or drifted towards other screens. It was difficult to put a finger on the subtly changed alchemy of his appearance. Maybe it was something to do with the conjunction of the image with the frame itself, as though the subject lived naturally within the frame. Whatever the causes, it seemed to Cynthia that she was witnessing the complex and largely inexplicable evolution of a media personality.

Holocenter addressed the camera directly: *"The most disturbing feature about these recent cases is that the City Hall rapist seems to be obsessed with the self-styled vigilante F-woman. According to his victims, he constantly reiterates sentences such as, 'Tell F-woman I want to meet her.' At other times he is reported to have said, 'I want a confrontation with F-woman. F-man meets F-woman.'"*

"That is sick," Cynthia said.

Emhard nodded, as though confirming a melancholy truth. Then he turned and left, carrying his burden of thought with him. She watched him depart, and turned back to look at the screen.

The announcer was saying, *"Mayor Frank Dally said this morning that the real tragedy was that vigilantes like F-woman excited the public appetite for violent retribution, and the result has been an escalation in the activities of disturbed men like the City Hall rapist."*

"God," Cynthia said softly to herself.

For the next few seconds she hunted through the newspaper on her desk, looking for further references. There seemed to be no additional coverage that she could see. Given the controversial nature of the case, the information emerging from the authorities appeared to be unusually tightly controlled. She reached up, turned down the volume on the screen, and picked up her phone.

"Officer Stevens, please." She looked at the soundless images while she waited. There was a click, and then a man's voice said, "Stevens."

"Hi, Cynthia Lelague here."

"Why, Miss Lelague."

Stevens sounded affable. She wondered whether he'd told his colleagues about their little confrontation in the filing room. She said, "Do you have anything of interest on the City Hall rapist?"

"Zilch," Stevens replied, without hesitation. "From that point of view, this is the worst case we have ever seen. He leaves no traces of himself at all. It's like the victim has been attacked by a machine."

"Any file material worth a visit?"

"We have nothing. Like I say." Stevens paused. Then he seemed to switch into another gear. "You're welcome to come round any time you like, though, Miss Lelague. Show me a couple more wrestling holds. What'd you call that last one — the *double entendre*?"

She couldn't help smiling, despite herself. "The double standard."

"I gotta get me a copy of that feminist wrestling manual of yours. Gonna give it to my girlfriend Emmylou. She's a wild and adventurous woman — though maybe not as wild and adventurous as you, Miss Lelague."

"Is that so?" Cynthia said. She was not quite sure what to make of this unexpected playfulness. It seemed like flirtation to her.

Stevens said, "Perhaps you'd be kind enough to give me the name of that feminist wrestling manual?"

"The Theory and Practice of Ball Bearings."

Cynthia heard a brief snort at the other end of the line. While speaking, she continued to study the television monitor above her desk. There was an outside shot of City Hall and a picture of Mayor Dally walking up the main steps. It looked like a lead-in for an announcement by the mayor.

"Thanks for your help, Detective Stevens. I have to go now."

"Goodbye, Miss Lelague. Any time."

She put down her phone and turned up the volume.

On the television monitor, the announcer said, *"Mayor Frank Dally has been speaking about the City Hall rapist to our senior reporter, Myron Overbear."*

Myron Overbear was the chief reporter of TVLA. He looked like a little like the young Sydney Poitier. He was ebony black and one of the handsomest men Cynthia had ever seen. In his attempts to extract statements from various interviewees, with his unfailing courtesy and perhaps an odd sense of distance or irony, he appeared as cool as a mountain stream. She heard that he had originally entered television journalism, as many actors did, hoping to be seen by producers and casting directors. The offers of film parts came in, but quite unexpectedly he had fallen in love with the life of a news reporter. After a while he dropped his film agent and took to the news full time. He dressed well but soberly. It was unusually cold for October, and he had on a black linen suit and white scarf. Sometimes Cynthia noticed how, when he came on, the faces of several of the female staff seemed to become blank for a little while, as though involved in their own thoughts. A few reporters gravitated towards the screen, one or two still talking into mobile phones while they studied the image.

The camera was floating behind Myron Overbear's shoulder, doing a slow dolly towards the mayor's face. Addressing his subject directly across the hand-held microphone, Overbear had the refined diffidence of certain tall men.

"Mayor Dally —"

Cynthia tapped the volume switch up two notches so she could hear the words.

Frank Dally was a sleek man too, though of a different kind. In his early forties, he had the animal presence of a politician and some of the self-regard of a successful lawyer. His grey suit was immaculate, his hair coiffured. Like many short men, he seemed inclined to compensate with a little more force and vitality than one might otherwise expect. When addressed, he had a way of listening that was almost aggressive — head up and slightly to one side, his stare directly on the interlocutor.

Myron Overbear said, *"Mayor Dally, you recently said that you believe vigilantes like F-woman actually increase, rather than decrease, the incidence of violent rapes. Isn't that something of a controversial statement?"*

Dally half smiled, as though in acknowledgement of the calmness of the delivery, the way the directness of the question contrasted with the almost languid detachment of his interviewer. Then the initial smile closed down and his professional face came on. He began to enunciate his answer clearly, illustrating his theme with occasional precise sweeps of his hands.

"I think we have to look at the evidence here. We have to try to put ourselves in the mind of someone who's somewhat disturbed. He sees someone like F-woman take the law out of the hands of the police and away from the due process, and he sees that authority

placed in the hands of the violent." Dally looked over the interviewer's shoulder and directed his face towards the camera as though to add to his statement's rhetorical force. *"Isn't that an example to others to behave similarly? Isn't that a direct incitement to lawlessness?"*

"Are you saying F-woman is directly responsible for this man's attacks on innocent women?"

"That's exactly what I am saying. He keeps talking about F-woman to his victims, tells them he wants to meet her. That is the reason why he is committing these crimes. I believe if we look into the social causes of these particular crimes, the real culprit isn't this man."

"Who is the real culprit, then?"

"I would say that the real culprit is the person who incited him."

"Goddamn," Cynthia said softly to herself. She looked around at the other small groups in the newsroom who had gathered around the television sets.

"Mayor Dally —" Myron Overbear was speaking again — *"isn't that exactly the kind of reasoning that says that a woman who dresses up sexy incites a man to rape her? I mean, isn't the idea that a particular person incites a crime a dangerous principle? Shouldn't we blame the criminal, not the so-called inciter?"*

"I'm not proposing a general principle here. I'm talking about a very particular and specific case. You only have to listen to what the rapist himself has said. He says he's doing these things in the hope of a confrontation with F-woman. When people support this type of behaviour of someone acting outside the law, I think they should consider the consequences. That's the sickness at the heart of these

vigilante actions. As a society, that's what we have to face up to."

Myron Overbear paused, seemed to nod. But that was when he was at his most dangerous. His voice moved to flat, almost monotone. *"Are you saying, Mayor, that if it came to a trial, we should try the vigilante, not the man who perpetrated the crimes?"*

Cynthia watched Mayor Dally flinch, roll with the punch, adjust his balance. *"I'm saying when we catch the perpetrator and we try him, we should think about the wider context."*

"The wider context?" Myron Overbear said, as though tasting the sound of the phrase. *"I thought you said we shouldn't speak in generalities, that this is a specific and particular case."*

"I said exactly that. But everything also has a context. The wider context in this particular case is the people who support the vigilante."

"Are you saying we should put them on trial, as well?"

Dally himself was fast, too. He'd seen this one coming. *"I believe that in some subtle but significant manner, those who support vigilantes are also on trial. That's what has happened here. A man has been incited by a vigilante's actions to conduct rapes against innocent women. I believe that when we look to causes, we should start by looking at the vigilante's behaviour, and we should also look at the people who support that vigilante's actions."*

Myron Overbear knew that sense of significance when some kind of challenge is issued, when a border is being crossed. He said, *"It will be interesting to see how this case develops."*

Mayor Dally nodded. The senior reporter turned towards the camera.

"This is Myron Overbear returning you to the newsdesk."

Cynthia switched off the set. She breathed in deeply and

walked to the large north window. The atmosphere outside was grey and overcast. She stared out at the smog that was covering the sky from Van Nuys to Encino.

14

Cynthia sat on the floor of her small apartment in a meditating position. Her eyes were closed. She was like that for almost an hour, conducting her contemplation in darkness.

After a while her eyes opened.

She stood up and walked to the window and opened the casement. If you looked out at the city the great skyscrapers and landmarks were like the vital organs of the physical body — solid, luminescent structures in the night. The flow of traffic between them was like the stream of blood through veins and arteries. Fast-moving traffic across the expressways was swifter, arterial blood; slow-moving traffic through the town centre and suburbs, halting at innumerable red traffic lights, was like venous blood. She looked out upon the spectral torso of the city.

After a while she turned and went to her wardrobe and put on a halter top and leggings. In the half-light, she glanced at herself in the mirror. She resembled someone who was on her way to an aerobics class. It was important, this evening at least, that she purvey a certain sexual attraction, so she took her clothes off and put on a kaftan instead. It felt more in character. She liked kaftans because of their implicit range of expression. Under normal conditions the material hung reasonably loose, did not cling to the shape of the body, and was therefore chaste. But when you moved, it showed up the free movement of the limbs beneath the cloth so that — depending upon the disposition of the body beneath — it could purvey a certain subtle sensuality. But appearances in themselves were peripheral. The important thing tonight was that the garment allowed her limbs unimpeded movement. That was what she wanted above everything else.

Carefully, leaning forward to the mirror so she could see the planes of her nose and cheeks, she put the final touches of make-up to her face, using much more powder than usual, plenty of eye-shadow, a bright slash of vermilion lipstick. In the single full-length mirror she examined herself briefly. She seemed as spectral as the city. When she smiled at herself, spreading her mouth wide, she looked like a whore — exactly the way she intended.

She let herself out of the door and set out towards downtown.

A golden dust of lights lay across the precincts of the city. At first the streets were bright, and there was a flow of pedestrians past her. Then, as she continued to walk, the streets became darker, less well lit, more sinister. She made her way through deserted areas, without lights, with trash bins spilling over, and past solitary drunks and hookers.

She continued to walk for another quarter of an hour, past the billboards, down silent walkways, across deserted spaces where cars were parked haphazardly, as if they had been abandoned. At the end of Baton Rouge Street a gang of men were standing in the shadows, leaning against a stained, concrete wall. As she walked past one of them a pebble was flicked out in front of her, and a voice said softly, "Hey, chickie, chickie."

Cynthia ignored the call. She walked on. But then another call rang out of the shadows, louder and more assertive — the voice of a gang leader. "Hey, hooker, you got to pay your dues."

The voice had authority but she continued to walk. She swayed her big hips softly. Her body felt loose and tigerish beneath the kaftan. As she walked, she heard footsteps behind her. After a while she guessed there were perhaps a dozen men following her.

She felt good and supple and rangy. She enjoyed the walk, nursing the sense and feeling the outrage of it, the way they believed they could intimidate her by just following her. They'd done this dozens, maybe hundreds of times, before, making a woman's stomach melt with fear before they did what they intended to do.

They followed her the length of Baton Rouge, and there one of the men called out casually, "Hey, nice ass."

Cynthia thought it was time to halt.

The men gathered around her loosely, easy and lax, like flotsam around a rock. They drifted around her as if in a dream. They wanted to look her over before they did anything to her. One or two reminded her of Juan, and she felt a sly flutter of tenderness. They might have been his brothers and cousins.

She said, "Which one of you brave men commented on my ass?"

There was general sniggering from the pack. It moved backwards and forwards, like a ripple in a tank of water. She was fascinated by their collective mirth, the way it seemed to feed on itself. When everyone had sniggered enough, one of them said, "Doesn't matter which one of us said it. We all like your ass, sweetheart."

Cynthia nodded, as though she were establishing a legal principle. "So you all take responsibility for that remark?"

That movement again — of a ripple of general mirth between them, passing round a sneer like a bottle of beer, so everyone could take a swig. "I guess we all do."

She looked at their faces, moved her concentration across them one by one as they gathered around her.

She said, "If you cease your threatening, and apologise for attempting to accost me, I am prepared to forgive you. All young males have got to learn to deal with hormone problems. Testosterone is a known cause of violence and other forms of anti-social behaviour."

They watched her as if she came from another planet. It was always so difficult to communicate with the male psyche. Cynthia tried again. "I guess you people are annoyed that I'm not responding in the way you expect. That forms a vicious circle with your own body's chemicals, and you rush into things you can't control. Sometimes, self-awareness of these problems can help you to come to terms with things. Speaking for myself, I would like to forgive you for what you think you are about to do. After all, you can't help being male."

There was a brief silence. Then someone at the back said, "Did you say something about hormones?"

"I believe I did."

"The only *whore moans* we're gonna hear," the same voice said, "are your own."

"I'm sorry to hear you say that," Cynthia said. "You see, if you attempt to touch me, you will have to answer for the consequences."

Cynthia started to move off, but two of them casually blocked her way.

"Bad move," she said.

Her arms hung loosely by her side. By swinging her torso slightly, left shoulder forward, she could prepare to hit with the right, and at the same time disguise her preparation. Without any obvious preliminaries, she punched the man facing her in the solar plexus, so that he doubled up. Then she savagely brought her knee up into his face. She felt his nose splinter beneath the impact.

She knew that in that half second of astonishment, there was a surfacing realisation. Beneath the depth of their complacency, they would begin to know that she was going to fight them to the death. But they didn't know the precise dimensions of that quite yet. It seemed to run against every final expectation of how a woman should behave. Instead, with the odd sense of watching a plate fall off a table, floating timelessly towards the waiting tiles, they observed their companion stagger backward out into the street, clutching his face. They saw that life was leaving him, that even while he was standing he paused for a moment in a peculiar stillness. They watched the light go out of him, limb by limb, his crumpling legs, and then his collapse onto the sidewalk.

How long did they stare? How long did they watch his prostrate body? They realised he was out cold. They sensed that the terrible impact behind her knee was real and then they worked back carefully from effect to cause and so back towards Cynthia Lelague, standing there without moving, waiting calmly in the dark for them to come to her.

There was a time before things began to accelerate, before they started to move out of control.

15

It seemed for a while that everyone was dreaming. As they came to, it appeared their surfacing had special force. When it occurred to them, in their collective awakening, that this woman had almost casually knocked one of them out, had performed the act with a cold deliberation and precise intent, something odd happened.

If it had been a man they were facing, perhaps they would have brought out knives and maybe guns. Perhaps that was part of being a woman that saved her from that particular fate. If so, it was not so much chivalry that sustained her, but the residue of that deep complacency which reasoned that if there had been one lucky strike against a single man, the gang could handle her collectively without recourse to other means.

At last they seemed to find their collective will. They closed in like a pack of dogs on a doe. And she, for her part, did not attempt to run, but waited for them, as though not only expecting but inviting this second stage of violation and possible annihilation.

At first it was not difficult to engage with her, she did not seem to resist, and so they closed in on her and seized her by whatever arms or legs came to hand. And at first she allowed them, allowed them to take hold of her by whatever means, permitted them to reassert their complacent hold over women's flesh. They seemed undecided whether to follow one of two courses; to beat her to a pulp, or to gang-rape her first. For a few seconds the matter seemed to hang in the balance.

"Let's fuck the shit out of her," a voice said.

"No," another voice said, "We cut the bitch up first."

She allowed them to sense, for a heady moment, the central decision over her life was theirs, although to her mind the decision was never more manifestly her own.

Perhaps they enjoyed that moment of decision too much. Perhaps they prolonged it a little too copiously in thinking of it. It didn't make much difference. It was her own decision which, given only a few inches of latitude of movement, caused her to punch her left elbow softly and almost invisibly into the solar plexus of a man behind her. It was her decision which prompted her to raise her right knee — one of the few parts of her which had not been seized or invaded — softly but devastatingly into another man's crotch, causing another grip to loosen. And it was her decision when — this manoeuvre hardly having finished — she raised her calf behind her and hit another of her assailants in the genitals with her heel. A third man lost his grip as his mind swerved and shifted to the pain at his centre.

During those few seconds when the pack around her seemed

secure, but not yet decided about her fate, other events took place beneath or outside their collective knowledge. It was then, with all the time in the world to consider her particular fate and manner of leaving this world, when they seemed to be pulling in different directions, that damage was already being done, methodically and carefully, to the individuals who composed the mass. While they considered her future, their own grip on events was being loosened piece by piece; she was preparing the ground patiently and scrupulously for what would follow.

Even with several collapsing through pain, they were still packed around her as tightly as bees swarming around a queen. But the relentless and invisible work was continuing. The fact that several pairs of hands were loosening gave greater freedom to her own arms. A few more inches, and several others felt the odd queasiness and demoralisation of being hit in the solar plexus. It was hardly noticeable, almost decorous. Their soft sighs of astonishment were like sexual gratification. Perhaps they only noticed then — when a man to the left of her started to sink and collapse towards the paving with a soft grunt — that her left arm was now fully free of impediments. The man in front was trying to rape her, had unzipped his cock and was pressing it up between her legs. To celebrate her freedom, she punched the heel of her hand straight into his face in a blow that sent him perhaps seven feet across the road and into a sprawl against the kerb.

It was a ferocious hit, delivered onto the bridge of the nose and the eye. Until then, they had been attempting to confine her. Now they wanted to strike her in retaliation. But, before striking, one has to release. The several men on her right side seemed to reach the same conclusions simultaneously. They released her right arm in order to strike at her.

"Bad move," Cynthia said softly.

She hit with a left and a right, with maybe half a second between punches. Two more were reeling back across the road.

Now she was kicking and fighting, delivering blow after blow. She was building up something like a rhythm of destruction. She knew that fighting is imbued with the work ethic; you set down and do it and do it well and thoroughly. Whatever was in front of her she demolished. Whatever was behind her she threatened with elbow sweeps and back kicks until she could turn and deal with it directly. In the meantime she set out to destroy whatever was in her path.

It was solid work, performed with zeal. It seemed to move from stage to stage, from phase to phase. She wasn't just holding off her attackers, or merely attempting to clear a little space for herself. Now she began to select individuals and hunt them down. She was like some terrible predatory insect. The punches were delivered with the heel of the hand, or at close quarters with the forearm and elbow. She remembered her favourite phrase from Milton, about "the two-handed engine at the door." She was the two-handed engine. She was Death, destroying in the dark. After a while most of the gang were down on the paving stones, or reeling, clutching their faces or their stomachs or their genitals.

She struggled with her heaviest assailant. It seemed to her he came rising out of the black shadows towards her like a walrus out of the water, the muscle bulging from his thick neck into his face. He hit her hard with a body tackle that winded her, and forced her back against a wall through sheer mass. Her retaliatory rain of punches seemed only to annoy him. He drove forwards using his full weight to lock with her and close her down so that she could not punch. She adopted a strategy of patience, allowing herself to be driven back again towards the wall. With a final heave he flung her at the wall backwards, expecting to wind her again and for her body to bounce back into his arms, where he could crush her at leisure. But she turned in the air like a cat and struck the wall with her left shoulder. Her spinning turn seemed to take the energy out of the collision, so that she bounced back oddly and unexpectedly and came out sideways. She dodged his final rush to pin her, and then from her advantageous position of being at the side of him rather than in the full face of his rush she struck him so hard on the side of the head that for several seconds he seemed about to fall. He turned towards her, though by now he was groggy. With a series of counter-punches she started to drive him backwards across the street. She pinned him against a wall and her hands closed over his throat. She stared into his fearful eyes. She squeezed his windpipe and watched his eyes glaze.

"Tell me something."

He gave out a soft gasp like a sigh. She tightened her grip further.

"You know anything about a character called Fuckman?"

He tried to speak, then said hoarsely: "Don' know nothing about Fuckman."

She tightened her grip on his throat. He struggled, appeared about to say something. She eased her grip just enough for him to speak.

"If there was some guy called Fuckman, we'd know." He struggled again for breath. "Ain't no Fuckman in our locality."

She looked into his eyes, trying to work out whether he was telling the truth. She decided he was, and contemptuously released him.

He slumped slowly down to the pavement.

She felt tired, and oddly lonely standing in a street full of groaning bodies. After a few seconds she had gathered together her composure. Her shoulderbag lay in the street, open and violated and robbed as they intended to violate her. She didn't know which one of them had gone through it while the rest had attacked her. It didn't matter. She picked it up and closed it, then she turned towards the upper end of the street and walked on.

She felt no remorse. It seemed to her that what they intended for her was unspeakable, and that was the reality that she would carry away with her.

At a payphone she put in a call to the emergency services. When a patient, slightly harried male voice came on the line, she said, "There has been an accident on Baton Rouge Street."

"What sort of an accident?" The voice at the other end sounded slightly cynical.

"A gang of men attacked a defenceless woman. It's difficult to tell how many are down. There are ten, maybe a dozen casualties."

There was a pause at the other end of the line. It seemed to her as though the call was being put through to someone else, perhaps a supervisor. Another voice said, "May we take your name, miss?"

"Why do you want my name?"

"We sometimes get hoax calls."

"Yes, of course," she said, watching the reflections of the traffic moving in the glass of the telephone booth. "My name is Fuckwoman."

There was another pause at the other end of the line.

"You serious?"

Cynthia said, "A lot of people are hurting and in pain."

"Are you saying there are maybe a dozen casualties? Forgive me for asking, but what happened exactly?"

Cynthia was suddenly tired of repeating herself. A police car was moving in the dark air of the street, its lights whirling as it passed her. It cut a corner and drove down Baton Rouge. She saw the car swing sideways as it tried to avoid the bodies that lay all over the road. The sudden turn caused it to rise up on two wheels. She heard the tyres squeal as it mounted up the sidewalk, and the soft crumple of its right side against the nearest wall. Two officers got out of the undamaged doors. The first covered the scene with an automatic, the second was summoning assistance through a radio.

She put down the phone.

16

Did Cynthia feel any kind of remorse?

She remembered a story Gore Emhard had told her, as part of his campaign to annoy her with his lewd man-to-man jokes. A desert wanderer and holy man, moving from oasis to oasis seeking peace and tranquillity, found that wherever he stayed in his journeys he encountered camels — individual camels who occupied the shady places beneath trees, or camels in noisy, quarrelsome herds. At night, he was woken by their bad-tempered rumbling and roaring. Anywhere he went, the camel population had expanded out of control.

But one particular oasis he visited was blessedly free of the quadrupeds. He asked a local man how they had managed to limit the camel population. The man smiled, tapped his nose, and said, "Meet me here tonight, I'll show you how it's done." In due course they met as the man suggested. "Say nothing, and follow me," the man said, and proceeded to creep through the empty oasis until they found a single camel standing beneath a date palm. It was clearly a male, because as they approached the holy man could see its testicles suspended between its legs in the moonlight. The man whispered, "Watch." He carefully picked up a large flat stone in each hand, crept towards the camel, and when he was within range, he brought the two stones together with maximum force on the animal's private parts. The camel gave a great roar of pain and thundered off into the night. "That's how it's done," the man said. "Practical contraception."

"But," enquired the holy man, "doesn't it hurt?"

"Not if you keep your thumbs out of the way," the man replied.

That was how Cynthia, adapting Gore Emhard's joke for her own purposes, felt about those men she had battered and beaten senseless. Did it hurt? No. Not if you kept your thumbs out of the way.

17

The following morning Gore Emhard emerged from his office and walked into the main newsroom as though in a trance. The air conditioning was already humming and Cynthia could sense the faint ozone and the layers of cold that the air conditioning produced. Her desk was in a position next to one of the ducts in a pleasant river of coolness.

Out of the corner of her eye she observed Emhard traverse the length of the room and turn down the main aisle. He seemed to orient himself in her direction, then finally walked towards her.

He placed the knuckles of both hands on her desk top and looked down at her.

"Hear what happened?" Emhard asked.

Cynthia looked up at him.

Emhard said, "Last night Fuckwoman went bananas. Took on a whole gang and busted the hell out of them."

"Any casualties?" Cynthia asked.

"Some of them have been hospitalised. Two are on life support machines."

She tried her best to make her surprise real, but Emhard didn't seem directly interested in her response. He turned on the screen above Cynthia's desk. "God, I hate getting my news from the TV or the goddamn net. Why can't this damn Fuckwoman do her profane deeds during the early part of the evening, like a decent person, so we can cover them for the following day?"

The screen came on. An announcer said, *"Ambulances were clearing away the wounded today from a commercial area of downtown Los Angeles. Shortly after midnight last night the vigilante known as F-woman engaged an entire gang in physical combat, and the shocking toll was recorded by our roving camera team as police cordoned off the area."*

On the screen parked white ambulances stood among police cars, their red and yellow lights flashing. Stretcher-bearers carried bodies away.

Emhard said, "What kind of person could do damage like that? Goddamn, this is frightening."

The announcer said, *"Our chief reporter, Myron Overbear, was on the spot this morning, taking the temperature and asking local residents what happened."*

Myron Overbear appeared on the screen facing the camera. Over his shoulder the red lights of the police cars flashed, lighting the side of his face and his cheekbones in an almost homely fireside glow. He looked more than ever like a movie star.

"The scene of carnage has largely been cleared. Little remains of the ferocious battle that was fought on this spot last night except some bloodstains and the forensic teams who are currently combing the area for further evidence. The battle was fought at the junction between the appropriately named No Exit Street and Baton Rouge Street. I asked local shop-owner Ku Fung Wa what he thought of last night's events."

Mr Ku had a loud red tee-shirt and dark glasses, and seemed approximately as wide as he was tall. He spoke unexpectedly softly against the confusion behind them. *"Best thing that ever happened here."*

"Don't you think, Mr Ku, that violence only leads to violence?"

Mr Ku leaned towards the microphone, like a man taking a bow. *"Too damn right,"* he said. *"Violence has been leading to violence for too long. First one gang, then another, fighting it out. This place is full of violence. Finally they got their medicine right here. Never seen it so calm as it is now. First time I ever come out on street at night without packing pistol."*

"So what is your verdict on F-woman?"

The Korean leaned towards the microphone, and spoke his soft words again, moving his lips carefully to enunciate each word. *"She f**ked them good."*

"Well, on that emphatic statement, this is Myron Overbear returning you to the newsdesk."

"Thank you, Myron. There have been further extraordinary scenes this morning following last night's incident. In the four or five hours since the event took place, an unruly mob has gathered outside the Los Angeles City Hall and is shouting slogans in favour of F-woman for Mayor."

There was a shot of the entrance to City Hall. A ragged but nevertheless substantial and increasingly truculent crowd was chanting, *"Fuck, Fuck, Fuck!"*

Emhard said, "This city has gone mad. That woman is releasing demonic forces."

The announcer said, *"Inside the beleaguered City Hall administration building, the Mayor has summoned senior staff for wide-ranging consultations about what appears to be a developing crisis. The meetings are being conducted in private and off camera. Meanwhile, senior police psychiatrist Dr James Holocenter gave us this statement."*

They cut in on Dr Holocenter, sitting in his study in front of his impressive array of books. He looked pale, but paleness suited him. As always, he gave the impression of an East Coast academic temporarily out west. The announcer said, *"Dr Holocenter, what is your interpretation of these escalating events?"*

"I believe that this latest incident shows more clearly than ever the true nature of the vigilante who calls herself F-woman. Her actions demonstrate, if further demonstration were necessary, the acute nature of her psychosis. Unwilling to face up to her role in inciting the City Hall rapist, she has clearly lost control and attacked, for no apparent reason, a bunch of city youths loitering in one of the neighbouring precincts. There is no evidence so far that they even belonged to a gang. Until we hear to the contrary, we are obliged to assume they gave no offence. I would like to make an appeal, on behalf of the LAPD and all good citizens, to the woman known as F-woman to give herself up now and so bring an end to this terrible campaign of violence and counter-violence."

Cynthia breathed out. Inside she felt strangely clear. Maybe she had become used to assertions that seemed to have nothing to do with the subject in hand. Holocenter appeared to be using every single incident he could find to focus on her. She swallowed her anger and attempted to sound reasonable. "Do you believe Fuckwoman started all that violence?"

"What exactly are you saying?" Emhard said, distracted.

"Well, it seems to me there was a certain amount of violence around before she came on the scene."

"Maybe she didn't start it," Emhard said. "But she's opening up the hatches and letting the rats out of the sewers. That shrink is the only person who's talking any sense about this business. I want you to go over and interview him."

Cynthia felt her astonishment bank and rise a little further. "You want to give him extra space in our newspaper?"

"You heard me," Emhard said. "Get as much as you can on the City Hall rapist. I don't want to see the screen news ahead of us again. Let's get on top of this story."

Cynthia watched Emhard walk away to his office, his long, slightly stooped back, his striped shirt like an old-style newsman. Several people approached him to give messages or reports; he inclined his ear to them, out of indulgence, but he kept walking, as though moving through a cloud of his own thinking.

Cynthia picked up the phone and dialled.

"City Hall? Cynthia Lelague here, *Angel Times*. I would like to arrange an interview with police psychiatrist Dr James Holocenter. Thank you." She waited while the phone was tried. It rang twice and was picked up immediately. A voice said, "Holocenter."

"Dr Holocenter? Cynthia Lelague, *Angel Times*. We're interested in the briefing you gave this morning concerning the vigilante known as Fuckwoman. My editor believes that what you said makes sense and he wants to cover it in tomorrow's newspaper. Would you mind if I came over and interviewed you?"

She heard him say in his carefully enunciated, cold voice, "You'll give this matter prominence?"

"Sure. We'd give the interview special billing. I've been commissioned directly by the editor."

She waited several seconds while he considered. She could hear his firm, precise breathing, and could sense his mind moving through the options.

"What's the time now, Miss Lelague?"

"Ten twenty."

"Eleven thirty suit you?"

"Eleven thirty?"

"I've got other things before and after."

"OK," she said. "I'll be there."

His phone went dead.

What was driving him, she asked herself? Personal ambition? Vanity? He didn't seem vain to her, at least in the accepted sense. The impression she gained was of a strange sense of coldness, of a personality so much under control that you couldn't begin to fathom the emotions that drove him. He seemed like someone with a mission, yet someone who would express nothing, as if his mission was private to himself.

Cynthia put down the phone and walked to one of the west-facing windows. She looked out towards Watts, Downey, Whittier, La Habra. She wondered how many gangs were out there tonight, whether her hospitalisation of an entire chapter had any effect, or whether they'd be out in force tonight. Male vanity, she thought, might bring out every small gangster and hoodlum there had ever been out on the street. Maybe Gore Emhard was right, maybe she was releasing demonic forces.

18

The act of putting on her overcoat made her realise that she had bruises all over her body. The bruises were concentrated on the upper parts of her arms and thighs and also her stomach. It was the result of being the centre of the gang's attention for only a short time. She did not care to think what would have happened if she had been their focus for several hours in the shadows of that deserted street, a lonely female victim. In the light of what they would have done to her, her act of violence against her attackers seemed to her like an act of cleanliness. The bruises reminded her of her own mission. It was strange how, after less than twenty-four hours since the fight, all the faces of her assailants seemed to be resolving into one archetypal face, into the flat, concentrated planes of the LAPD senior psychiatrist.

As she approached the main foyer she looked upwards at the building of City Hall. It was one of the great buildings of Los

Angeles. She knew it both in reality and as a myth because it was the "Daily Planet" building in the classic Superman Series in the 1950s, replays of which she had watched avidly as a child. George Reeves, as Clark Kent, went in and out of its doors as often as he did telephone booths.

Officials walked briskly backwards and forwards, carrying papers. It seemed a hive of activity. Phones could be heard ringing in the recesses.

She swung right through a set of heavy wooden swing doors, moved into a second corridor. A hand-painted sign in gold lettering said, "Police Administration Staff and Supplementary Services." At the foot of a flight of stairs an elderly uniformed officer stood on duty in an armoured glass case with an open front. Amongst the chaos and bustle he looked avuncular and kind and happy in himself, and she wondered briefly whether maybe that was because he'd lost the bug of ambition and settled for what he had.

"Cynthia Lelague, *Angel Times*. I have a meeting with Dr Holocenter at 11:30."

"Your identification?" He smiled at her apparent hesitation. "Sorry, lady, we get some unusual types visiting the criminal psychiatric division."

None more unusual than this one, Cynthia thought to herself. If only you knew. She showed her press identity card. The officer pointed to a flight of stairs opposite.

"Up two flights, second on the left."

"Thank you."

She pushed through the fire doors and, out of sight of the elderly policeman, glanced back to make sure no one was watching her then took the steps two by two in quick bounds, touching the banister only lightly with her hand.

At the top of the stairs she turned left and followed the green-painted corridor until ahead of her was a sign in white lettering: *DR J HOLOCENTER*.

She took a deep breath and knocked on the door.

Footsteps approached. The handle was swung deliberately. The green door opened in a precise, cold sweep.

As she expected, Dr Holocenter was a tall, somewhat cadaverous man, though she had not calculated for the peculiar force and austerity of his presence. His whole body seemed resolved into verticals. Even the lines on his face seemed hierarchic. He stood sideways on, regarding her from behind his spectacles, as though sighting her with a rifle.

"Miss Lelague?"

Cynthia nodded.

"Won't you come in?"

He stood aside to let her through. Then he closed the door behind him deliberately and leaned against it, considering her calmly.

The room was long and narrow. Light fell through the tall window against the adjacent wall.

"Is that a French name, by the way?" Dr Holocenter asked. He had remained silent for some time, so that she was almost surprised when he spoke. His pronunciation was precise, even pedantic.

"Lelague?" Cynthia answered. "French Huguenot, I believe. It's a corruption of Lelage."

"Ah yes," Dr Holocenter said. "The Huguenots. An interesting ethnic group. Historically speaking, a somewhat persecuted minority."

They were both still standing, he leaning casually against the door, she in the centre of the open floor. The room seemed to be soundproofed against all external noise, as if they were in a vault.

While he studied her, she took the opportunity to glance around the room. The whitewashed walls were entirely bare of any decoration. There was a single certificate on the wall, from the Institute of Psychiatry. The effect was a prevalent austerity. Some part of her approved the lack of decoration.

"Won't you sit down, Miss Lelague?"

She nodded and sat down on the tall chair he indicated. It was like all the other pieces of furniture in the room, simple and cold and vertical.

Calmly, he placed his own long frame on the chair opposite her. He smiled, though he did not take his eyes off her. She noticed the eyes didn't smile.

He said, "Well, Miss Lelague, do you have a question you'd like to start with?"

Cynthia said, "Yes, I do."

Dr Holocenter smiled again. "Be my guest."

"I guess the question many people would like to know is why do you appear to be so hostile towards the vigilante who styles herself 'Fuckwoman'?"

Dr Holocenter paused. The smile grew to a shadow, then the shadow disappeared.

"Hostile, Miss Lelague? I hardly think hostile is the word. I happen to be a psychiatrist with nearly thirty years of practice in police and criminal matters."

She wrote down his reply in her shorthand. In her experience people reacted oddly to being recorded on tape, and were either intimidated by it or were unnaturally voluble. By contrast, the rhythm of writing down an answer before framing the next question slowed the tempo of the discussion, and gave it a kind of weight.

She finished writing and said, "What point are you making?"

"My diagnosis of Fuckwoman as a mentally abnormal sociopath is based on many years of such diagnoses."

"And also, I understand, on the fact that you've never met her."

Dr Holocenter considered her, and smiled.

"That is true. On the other hand, I have examined her actions very carefully, more closely in fact than many people with whom I am personally acquainted."

"Nevertheless," Cynthia insisted, "you've been making prognostications about the internal thoughts and motivations of a person you've never even met. Perhaps you will forgive me, but isn't that somewhat unusual practice?"

"In what manner?" Dr Holocenter asked. He seemed inclined to indulge her.

"I thought that psychiatric practice was based on the classical direct interview, not on second-hand information or indirect guessing."

"There are patterns of behaviour, Miss Lelague, which are common to certain types of psychosis, and which in turn are highly indicative of a particular psychological state."

"Indicative to whom, Dr Holocenter?"

"To a trained psychiatrist."

Cynthia said, "Isn't that argument somewhat circular?"

There was something else in his smile this time, something both interested and calculating. Perhaps he sensed an ideological opponent, or at least something a little unusual in his interviewer. "In what sense, Miss Lelague?"

"You say Fuckwoman's mental state is obvious to a trained psychiatrist, not because it's true, but because he's a trained psychiatrist."

"I don't think I quite understand the direction of your questioning."

"I am suggesting that the bottom line doesn't seem to be the truth or otherwise of the facts, but the authority of the psychiatrist."

Dr Holocenter nodded, not out of agreement, but in acknowledgement of a line of questioning. It was courteous, almost chivalrous.

"As I believe I mentioned, in the course of clinical duties, one builds up a base of experience, and one uses that base of experience in the consideration of other cases."

In her view, there was another advantage to transcribing answers in shorthand as opposed to recording: you could ask aggressive questions while you were writing. Because your body language was unchallenging, because you weren't staring the interviewee in the face, because you didn't have a microphone like a phallus in front of him, you weren't physically intimidating or inciting him to counter-aggression. The effect was sometimes disconcerting. As Cynthia finished writing down his reply she said, as casually as she could,

"Doesn't that just mean you've been saying the same thing for thirty years?"

There was another long silence. Dr Holocenter moved in his chair and considered her more carefully, as though he had just discovered another species.

"Well, well, Miss Lelague. This is refreshing."

"You haven't answered my question."

The faint trace of a smile again. "It is also a matter of cross-checking with colleagues, who in the same circumstances would reach similar conclusions."

She wrote down his reply, nodded and, without looking up, aimed another casual hand-grenade. "Doesn't that just mean you back up one another?"

"Why, Miss Lelague," Holocenter smiled indulgently. "Do I detect a note of hostility towards me? Or would that be towards the authority of psychiatric practice itself?"

"Why don't we keep to the subject, Dr Holocenter?" Cynthia suggested.

"What subject is that, Miss Lelague?"

"We're discussing the basis of your authority in diagnosing the mental state of a person you've never met. Now you're attempting to shift the focus to my own mental state. Doesn't that imply you aren't able to answer the question?"

Holocenter smiled. "Your own mental state strikes me increasingly as of interest."

"In what sense?"

"Because it seems to be setting the agenda in your questions."

"Are you suggesting that I'm disturbed, perhaps?"

"Are you disturbed, Miss Lelague?" Holocenter asked softly. It seemed to her that he almost murmured the question. "I'm merely following your question."

"Perhaps I am, Dr Holocenter. But while we're on the subject of one's mental state dictating the agenda, couldn't I just as reasonably ask the same question of you?"

"In what way?"

"Presumably I'm disturbed because I have the temerity to question your authority as a psychiatrist. That would seem to fit in nicely with your methods of operational practice."

"Is that perhaps your Huguenot ancestry speaking?" Dr Holocenter murmured again.

She allowed his question to move around in the empty spaces of the room. He sat calmly opposite her, watching her with his cold, direct eyes, a faint smile playing on his face, as though the tone of her questions conformed to a certain pattern that he found particularly interesting. There was an emotion there, she knew, and in some manner she suspected it confirmed her innermost fears. She knew too that she must continue to draw him out, must find some point of engagement.

"As we're speaking of psychological states, Dr Holocenter, where would you say your hostility to women comes from? Is that environmental in nature, or would you call that a sociopathic trait?"

"I beg your pardon?"

Cynthia said, "Did you have a problem with your mother, or are you hostile towards women in general?"

"Miss Lelague, these questions are very amusing, but..."

"What is it about Fuckwoman that so excites your animosity?"

She was writing fast now, so fast that one question followed another.

"More to the point, Miss Lelague, what is it about Fuckwoman that excites your sympathy?"

"Why should that interest you?"

"In my experience, people who come from a specific background, for example a French Huguenot background, repeat the experience of their own culture in subtle, even subconscious, forms. Which persecuted minority are you sympathising with now?"

Cynthia said, "Raped women, actually."

Dr Holocenter smiled. "Raped women? How interesting, the same obsession as Fuckwoman."

Her pencil, poised to take notes, had been active until now, but she wrote down carefully in her notebook in her clear hand, *I think he's taken the bait.*

After a while Dr Holocenter said, "I seem to recall that Superman, on whom Fuckwoman builds her sociopathic persona, also worked as a reporter, in the form of the mild-mannered Clark Kent."

"There's one important difference between Clark Kent and a reporter such as myself, Dr Holocenter."

"What's that?"

"Clark Kent was a man."

Dr Holocenter smiled.

"I admire your powers of observation, Miss Lelague. That's what makes you into a reporter, I guess. Perhaps you'd permit me a small indulgence in speculation. The thing is, if I were to build up a detailed psychological profile of Fuckwoman, I'd lay on strong odds that being a reporter would be part of her detailed recreation of the Superman persona. And if I were to add a little extra layer of personality, why, I think she'd probably come from a background which would include some kind of a heroic persecuted minority, like the French Huguenots."

She finished transcribing his last sentence, then wrote down in her notebook, *Let him think he's outwitting me.*

He seemed content to study her while she wrote.

Cynthia said, "Anything else you'd like to say about my background?"

"Why, yes. I think the personality of the vigilante known as Fuckwoman is constructed upon the assumption, explicit or implicit, that the best means of defence is attack. That's very clear in the psychological profile we've been building of Fuckwoman herself."

"And what does that prove?"

"It does not prove anything. But it does suggest at least that if Fuckwoman had been annoyed by my attempts to diagnose her condition, she is likely to take certain forms of action."

"What forms of action might those be?"

Dr Holocenter paused, and said, "Her character is such that I would perhaps expect a visit from her — in one form or another."

She transcribed his sentence carefully, then wrote in her notes: *He's hooked.*

She closed her notebook and slipped the pencil into its holder. It seemed to her the interview had ended, and what she wanted to say now was personal, between them and no one else. She looked up at him directly, sitting opposite her.

"Why don't we stop being obtuse, Dr Holocenter? Are you suggesting I'm Fuckwoman?"

"Well, Miss Lelague, now that you mention it, the thought had occurred to me."

"If you think I'm Fuckwoman, why don't you arrest me?"

It was interesting the way the silence appeared to increase at that point. It seemed to pour off the walls in a solid, palpable mass. Cynthia waited, wondering whether he'd take up the challenge.

"At the present moment," Dr Holocenter said, "we lack final proof of Fuckwoman's identity."

She paused a little, to give what she would say next more emphasis. "That doesn't seem to be any kind of disadvantage, given your methods."

"We all work on hypotheses, Miss Lelague," Dr Holocenter said, apparently unperturbed. "Have you ever read Karl Popper, by any chance?"

"Yes."

He half smiled at her, as though impressed.

"Then you will know that at the centre of his philosophy is the view that you cannot prove or disprove a theory until it is expressed. It has to be formulated first. Only after that comes the burden of proof."

"As a matter of fact," Cynthia said, "I have read his views about proof. And in my reading he constantly points out that absolute confirmation of proof is impossible. You don't find out the truth of things by looking for confirmation. You find out the strength of a theory by trying to refute it. I have to say, I don't see much sign of that here."

"My, my, Miss Lelague. You certainly believe in getting onto the attack. As a matter of...ah...professional interest, would you say that you actively identify with Fuckwoman?"

"That's an interesting hypothesis, Dr Holocenter."

"I would say, Miss Lelague, that your obvious hostility to me and my methods is another indication of your own mental attitude. Perhaps I could say that seems to be another likely point of similarity with Fuckwoman."

"I wouldn't say I was hostile, Dr Holocenter, though I would just like to make what seems to me a technical point."

"What might that be?"

"I think the task of finding out who or what Fuckwoman is would be better served if you stuck your tendentious, self-proving theories up your own capacious asshole."

"Well," Dr Holocenter said, nodding as though in confirmation to himself. "I guess that brings our interview to an end."

"I guess it does."

"I will of course lodge a formal complaint with your editor concerning your interviewing techniques and your obvious lack of objectivity."

Cynthia said, "That seems entirely consistent with your authoritarian methods."

Dr Holocenter stood up and smiled down on her as if, from his own point of view, the interview had been entirely satisfactory. He held out a hand. "It has been an interesting experience, I'm sure."

Cynthia considered the proffered hand but didn't take it. After a while Dr Holocenter withdrew it. He seemed unoffended, as though her behaviour was in character. He nodded at her, then walked carefully and deliberately towards the door; there he set his hand on the handle and swung the door open.

"Whatever you may say or imply, Miss Lelague," he said, "I do believe that in certain particulars we understand one another rather well."

19

S he was about to walk through the door when Dr Holocenter added, somewhat unexpectedly, "May I suggest something *apropos*?"

Cynthia stopped. His voice was oddly conciliatory.

"What, exactly?"

He seemed to swallow, half nodded, then said, "Might I propose, perhaps, that we should have a real discussion now?"

"A real discussion?" Cynthia asked.

She stood still for several moments.

Holocenter said, "You've played the role of the aggressive reporter, and I've played the role of the senior psychiatrist, jealous of his reputation. If that's all you wanted — a couple of professionals playing their accorded roles — you're welcome. We can end it there if you wish."

She hadn't expected this change of tack at all. It suggested greater flexibility in his character than she had suspected. More than that, she found herself frankly curious about what he might say next. "What are you suggesting?" she asked.

"Speaking for myself, I'd like to continue this discussion in a less…contentious manner."

The dangers were obvious. The more information she gave about herself, the more she helped him. But she was also intrigued about what he might reveal about himself. On balance, her curiosity outweighed the dangers. She considered a moment or two more, then nodded.

"Won't you take a seat again?" Holocenter said, with every indication of courtesy.

She sat down. But this time, though he sat down opposite her, he didn't remain seated for long. After a while he said, "Forgive me," and rose to his feet again, as though some inner compulsion caused him to assume his natural, vertical state. He walked calmly over to the other side of the room and stood for a moment in silence, facing half away from her, as if considering what to say.

His appearance confirmed what she had seen and sensed before, but now her impression seemed, if anything, heightened or amplified. She had never in her life met someone so upright. Even his spectacles were austere, metal-rimmed. In the gloom specks of hard light reflected from their rims, drifting around them like fireflies.

She had time to consider him more closely, and perhaps this was part of what he wanted, some form of acclimatisation between them. He wore a white coat like a lab technician, with a single pen in his pocket. His shoes were well-made leather and she could see grey, conservative trousers with turn-ups protruding beneath the coat. He stood with his hands at his sides, the palms turned inwards, the long fingers curved in towards his body while he considered something private and perhaps incommunicable.

The room, now that she looked at it more carefully, was also vertical, the ceiling almost double the height of normal ceilings, a kind of gallery let into the roof above. Even the windows were vertical — tall panes arrayed like soldiers in the side of the wall. They were above head height, so that although they let in light, one could not see out. Perhaps that was their function — to emphasise the purpose of his office as a place of mental concentration, utterly lacking in any distractions. On the white ceiling above her was an old-fashioned single fan with blades made of laminated wood which sent its soft beats of air down upon them.

He reminded her a little of Gore Emhard, but whereas Emhard seemed to carry the world on his shoulders, Holocenter's height mysteriously entered or penetrated the air above him, as though the very atmosphere about him was charged with it, as around a church steeple. Where Emhard smoked and drank to excess, in Holocenter those same habits would have been considered a weakness. He was, in all his outward habits, an ascetic. There was not a single sign of indulgence or gentleness in him.

She lived in a city where image was everything. But it seemed to her that no actor would have been able to replicate or mime the full dimension of Holocenter's austerity. It came out of his nervous system, and she had to admit, against her inclination, that that particular part of him at least was genuine.

Holocenter was still standing sideways on to her, looking upwards toward the light, when he said, "You know what, Miss Lelague? I can't help feeling a certain liking for our feminist vigilante."

For the second time that morning, she found herself caught off guard.

"Liking?"

"Admiration, esteem, perhaps even respect," Holocenter said. "That surprise you?"

"A little."

He was still standing sideways to her, staring into some private dimension of his own. "You want to know why?"

"I suppose so."

"Because she knows what she wants. She has great intelligence, she has courage, she has tenacity." He paused. "Yes, if you wanted to score points off me, you could say I am fascinated, perhaps even somewhat obsessed with her. Again, would you like to know why?"

She nodded cautiously. He must have caught the movement of her head out of the corner of his eye because he continued calmly, "Do you ever read crime?"

"Read?"

"Crime novels. Patricia Cornwell. P. D. James. Elmore Leonard. That kind of thing."

"Not much."

"I would agree that it's a somewhat formalised genre, though it has its expert practitioners. Perhaps you remember *The Silence of the Lambs?*"

Cynthia nodded cautiously. She wasn't quite sure where the conversation was moving. She had been conducting an interview. Now they were heading off on a tutorial about literature. He seemed to guess her thoughts.

"I hope you don't mind my diverting a little. I'm interested in certain stereotypic views of the criminal, expressed by the popular crime writers."

Cynthia observed him on the other side of the room, standing still and silent, as though waiting. He continued, "In crime fiction at least, there's very often some kind of criminal mastermind. The character in question often occupies a pivotal role in the narrative. He — it's usually a he, I notice — often possesses high intelligence, considerable personal discipline, a sense of control over his deepest personality traits. He occasionally strikes up some sort of relation with the investigator — who is often a woman. As often as not, there appears to be some kind of additional emotional *frisson*, not necessarily explicit, but implicit, in their relationship. The point is that, even in a putative emotional relationship, the investigator is nervous of being manipulated or controlled by the criminal mastermind. She suspects that — given the opportunity — he would be prepared to use even her own feelings against her."

"What point are you making, Dr Holocenter?"

Light seemed to pour down on him, as in a cathedral. "The point I'm making is that fiction seems to favour a confrontation on all fronts — not only in terms of the professional ability of the investigator, but also perhaps in terms of emotion too, and character."

"I still fail to catch your line of thinking."

"Leaving aside the emotional aspect — let's grant the writer a little poetic licence to amuse the reader — it is the constant, almost formal reiteration of that type of character in fiction which I regard as significant."

"The criminal mastermind?"

"Precisely."

"Why does that interest you?" Cynthia asked. She had the sense of his mind running ahead of her, picking out grounds for discussion or lecture.

"For this reason. Because I've never met one outside fiction."

She was intrigued, despite herself. "You never met a criminal mastermind?"

"No. I've met intelligent criminals. I've met enormously cunning individuals of both sexes. I've simply never met any individual criminal who I believe could function well outside crime. In my experience, people tend to enter crime for negative reasons — because they perceive no viable alternative."

"I am still not following you."

"Dennis Nilsson, the British serial killer, said that that type of character portrayed in fiction — the Hannibal Lecter figure, the serial killer mastermind — is nonsense. 'Bunkum', I think was the word he used. He said criminals were almost invariably damaged, that people turned to lives of crime mostly because they couldn't function in society in other ways. Perhaps they don't have the patience or self-discipline to hold down a normal job. There is often a preference for instant gratification, for taking unnecessary risks, for ignoring the rules. What I'm saying is that we criminal psychiatrists very rarely, if ever, meet a mind or a personality we can actually admire."

Cynthia said, "What are you driving at?"

Throughout their discussion he had been staring slightly upwards at the light, so that it poured onto his pale face; the whiteness of the light and the paleness of his flesh made them seem like one element. "Our female vigilante is the opposite of the weak or damaged case. She gives the impression she really could make her way in any sphere she prefers. She could hold down pretty much any kind of a job she chooses — my guess is she does just that. I'd also suspect that she's pretty good at her work."

"So?" she asked in the silence that followed.

"There's a certain amount of irony in what she does — you'll grant, perhaps, that irony is nearly always a sign of intelligence, of being able to see things from more than one perspective. There are other signs that she's not only intelligent, but well-adjusted. She seems to be objective about her acts. She treats the persona of Fuckwoman almost like a writer might treat a fictional character — as something that came from inside her, but which also exists outside her, like an invention. She seems to be able to maintain her objective distance from the role she plays. In that way she's almost the exact opposite of the obsessive who is driven by interior compulsions. The notes she leaves are complex riddles aimed at embellishing this almost fictional creation which exists outside her."

She had a sense that he was flattering her for a reason, that it was part of a plan.

"What are you saying? She has an integrated personality? She's creative? I thought you called her a psychotic."

"There are various kinds of mental aberration. Einstein was a neurotic. Darwin was an obsessive — if you read his copious daily diaries, you'll see he had more psychosomatic ailments than you could shake a stick at." He smiled. "Occasionally, just occasionally, we'll meet someone who is on the other side of normality — whose psychoses, if they exist, seem to strengthen their character, make it function better. It's a form of privilege to meet someone like that."

She waited for him to continue.

"As I say, those unusual beings are possible, but they're very rare. And they don't often belong to a criminal background. They might be ideologues, or sometimes terrorists, say; or maybe both." He turned his head a little more towards her, not fully but halfway. "That's why they are of particular fascination to someone in my profession. We spend most of our lives trying to put together broken lives, and that's rewarding in its own way. But just occasionally we have to treat someone whose life isn't broken at all, someone whose life has been put together perhaps just a little too well."

He paused. She was content to wait for him. At last he said, "What I'm trying to say, Miss Lelague, is that these are people we can learn things from."

She said, "What kind of a thing could you learn from her?"

"Ah," Holocenter said. "Perhaps you'd allow me to approach that question somewhat obliquely. Can you imagine, for example, what sort of a room she lives in?"

She shook her head, not so much in answer to the question, or to hide the fact that she of all people would know, but rather as a means of inviting him to continue.

"Shall I describe it to you — hypothetically, of course?"

She waited for him to continue, and he said, "It's a room not unlike this one. I don't mean in the layout or furniture, but rather the absence of contents. She's an ascetic. I doubt if there's any ornamentation in that room at all. A bed, a shower maybe, a place to cook her solitary meals. She's driven by a single vision; she has pared her life down to a single ambition."

Cynthia turned her mind from her own room, though she was rendered nervous for a while by his description. She thought he would glance directly towards her now, to assess her reaction, but if anything he had turned further away and was once again facing calmly upwards toward the light. "Does that sound plausible?"

"Is that what this is? An exercise in plausibility?"

"I don't think so. I prefer to believe it's a tentative exercise in objective truth."

She waited for him to speak again. In the meantime he had not shifted his position, and was continuing to stare into his own private universe. She was aware of the silence again, like an objective fact between them. He said: "Do you remember what Camus said in *L' Étranger*? If a man has only one day of experience, he can spend the rest of his life in prison? That's what dedication is, Miss Lelague, it's the solitary mind feeding off its own experience. It needs very little food. It isn't deflected. I believe this woman has made herself into something like that, that she is, so to speak, *sui generis*. And I believe she has that quality of self-reliance which will make her enormously difficult to catch."

"You make her sound quite heroic."

"Do I?"

Cynthia paused. "If you admire her so much, why don't you let her alone?"

For the first time he turned away from the light, swung and faced her fully and directly. His hands were held at his sides, and now he clasped them behind his back. He seemed spectrally thin. "Why should I do that?"

"I mean, if you respect her own views."

"I didn't say I respected her views. I said I respected her dedication."

"But not what she believes."

"It's a very serious matter to assault and hold someone against their will."

"Isn't that what you do when you incarcerate someone?"

"You may like to pour scorn on the conservatism of our profession, Miss Lelague, but in the psychiatric fraternity we have developed a powerful set of rules, a set of meticulously evolved procedures which have been subject to the most rigorous analysis..."

That was when Cynthia started to laugh softly to herself. She couldn't help it. It was like an insight. She felt the recognition of it spreading through her and she just had to let herself go.

"Dr Holocenter, I do believe I see at last what you're getting at."

"Do you?"

"You think she's like a fellow psychiatrist, except perhaps one who has gone to the bad. She's out there, practising the sort of therapy you would like to practice yourself, without constraints, without the trammels of...accepted procedures. And I think you're envious. I don't think this is social criticism at all. I think this is a case of high-flown professional jealousy."

He was still standing on the other side of the room, locked in his own silence. She thought he was going to remain there without moving. But a smile had appeared on his face.

"Why, Miss Lelague, isn't that strange. That's exactly the

type of insight I'd expect from Fuckwoman. It may or may not be true — like much psychological explanation — only time will tell. But it has a certain directness, a capacity to cut to the core. I have to say, I am impressed."

20

They were facing one another directly now, and appeared to be in some form of confrontation again. But it seemed to her that he had other purposes — at least for the time being.

He turned away and started to walk slowly backwards and forwards at the other end of the room, as though thinking matters through.

It gave her time to do a little thinking on her own. She tried to work out why he seemed familiar to her. She guessed she had seen him a couple of times beside the Mayor at press conferences. But in that milieu he was curiously outside his element, a professional animal of an entirely different nature to the Mayor, caught unexpectedly in the spotlight of politics. It wasn't that Holocenter couldn't function in the political sphere — it was just that with a microphone, in front of a pack of journalists, there wasn't that easy, fluent communication with the pack that politicians quite naturally possessed. As his involvement with the case of Fuckwoman had progressed, as further media messages became necessary, she observed him decide the background by insisting he was interviewed in his study, where he held sway over books and learned tomes and, by implication, could invoke the authority of psychiatric practice. When he set himself in the context of authority he blended in perfectly, settled into his environment with ease and equanimity. Likewise, there wasn't any sense of unease here, in this room, where he consulted his patients.

Though he wasn't watching her directly, she had the sense that he was still observing her closely, that his restless pacing was part of the mechanics of his observation. He seemed to be hunting in his mind for traces of her, for those aspects which perhaps would link her to the vigilante.

The harsh, clear overhead light ricocheted off the black and white tiles and the chrome fittings. At the other end of the room he continued to pace. He was like a wolf moving silently in his cage; the glint of light on his spectacles, the eyes with their abstracted expression, the hierachic lines of his face, all seemed part of this same intensive, concentrated focus. He epitomised a kind of hunger, although in his own case it seemed to be a hunger for knowledge, or at least for rational explanation. She recalled a painting by Francis Bacon, one of those howling popes where the subject's face and arms and torso are all nervous system. That was what Holocenter reminded her of — a pure nervous system, nothing else.

Partly to distract herself from his casual pacing, she tried to guess his age. He might have been in his mid-fifties, but in other respects he was ageless.

After a while Holocenter said, "While we're on the subject of fiction, perhaps you'd permit me to consider another fictional construction." He waited for an objection and, receiving none, continued. "I hope you don't mind if our discussion takes a slightly comical turn. Let's take, as a more extreme fictional example of a master-criminal, the fictional notion of a vampire."

"Why a vampire?" Cynthia asked. Something about the idea slightly alarmed her — not the absurd, lurid idea that Holocenter himself might be something akin to a vampire, but rather the impression that in his hunger there was something otherwordly, something that related to an older, purer archetype.

"It could be anything. I'm just using the vampire as another extreme example of the criminal in fiction."

"Go ahead," Cynthia said. "I'm listening."

"The vampire is another classic outsider. He is not only outside society, preying on society: his particular constitution, his particular physical being, demands that he lives outside the pale. He is a criminal, so to speak, right down to his genes. Now, tell me this, if you will. Suppose a vampire is also, to some extent, *conscious*. Suppose — if you will allow me to take the metaphor further — he is conscious of what he does at the same time as not being able to stop doing what he does. Do you follow my meaning?"

Cynthia shrugged. "A post-modernist vampire?"

A faint smile passed across his features, as if in acknowledgement of her irony. "In a manner of speaking."

"I still don't quite see what you're driving at."

"Don't you, Miss Lelague?" Holocenter murmured. "I'll see if I can express it another way. Perhaps our own sense of liberty is itself a fictional construction. Perhaps we do what we do because we are compelled by forces in our character — psychological rather than physical forces — over which we have little control."

"What are you saying?"

"You asked me a little while ago whether, acting out of my respect for Fuckwoman, I would consider letting her go unmolested by the law."

"That's what I asked."

"That would be impossible," Holocenter said.

"Why?"

"Just as she appears compelled to act in the way she does, I am compelled to act in the way that I do."

"What way is that?"

"I am compelled to hunt her down," Holocenter said.

He was waiting for her response. After a while, Cynthia said, "So in that respect you and she — whoever she turns out to be — are actually a couple of obsessives, after all. It doesn't matter how intelligent you both might be. You can't help circling one another."

"Succinctly put, if I may say so."

She had forgotten to take notes. Now she turned a page and wrote down: *Is this on the record? Could I ever write about this and be believed?*

21

Standing in front of her now, Dr Holocenter appeared almost avuncular. He seemed even to have accepted as a reasonable hypothesis her assertion about his own motive. He said, "There may be many things on which we do not agree, Miss Lelague. But perhaps you may concur that we have a better understanding of our respective positions."

Cynthia nodded cautiously, then closed her notebook and put it in her shoulderbag.

She was rising to depart, when he said, "If you will be kind enough indulge me one last time, Miss Lelague, there is perhaps one final subject I'd like to raise with you."

The sense of tension returned. There was something purposeful, almost teasing, about his casual assertion. She said, "What subject would that be?"

"The final matter, so to speak, of Fuckwoman's motive."

"You think she has a motive — I mean a single, driving motive?"

Holocenter smiled. "I'd like to propose a theory about the genesis of her particular *persona*. Of course, I fully understand if you're fatigued with too much discussion. And as I say, I'm satisfied that we've clarified some of the differences between us — without, of course, resolving them."

It was a challenge to her, she knew, to subject herself to some further and perhaps final analysis. She suspected, too, that by refusing him, she'd always wonder what he else he might have had to say.

She had already risen from her chair and was facing him. She noticed the odd colour of his eyes, almost violet. She knew she could have shaken hands with him, and he would have accompanied her to the door, and she would have spent the rest of the days that followed trying to work out, despite himself, what he was going to say. He appeared to her both mature and childish — another facet, perhaps, of his peculiar personality. Her intuition, standing in front of him while he surveyed her calmly, was that he'd saved the most important thing until last.

"I hope this is going to be good, Dr Holocenter."

"Oh, I think you'll be interested, Miss Lelague — if you'd be kind enough to just allow me to approach the subject at my own speed."

So for the third time that day she found herself sitting down in that room, putting her shoulderbag on the floor beside her. She crossed her legs, leaned back in the chair, and prepared herself to listen.

He had returned — almost unconsciously, it seemed — to his striding again, walking up and down the room, lost in thought. After a while he said, "Before we proceed, there is something

I wanted to ask you concerning analysis itself. Something you said about psychiatric method. If I understand you properly, you say that psychiatric analysis is mainly tautologous — argument in circles. Assertion is followed by 'verification' of a prognosis — that is to say, confirmation by a small circle of colleagues. Whatever they happen to agree upon is therefore the truth. Is that an accurate summary of your views?"

At some level she had ceased by now to be surprised by him. She said, "That's pretty close to what I suggested."

"Good," he glanced at her and away again, while he continued with his pacing. "If the psychiatric system supported itself in the way you say — autonomously, so to speak, and without reference to the external facts — there would be little capacity to make predictions, predictions that could be proved true or false. Isn't that a logical consequence of what you're saying?"

"I guess so."

Holocenter smiled again briefly. "Then perhaps — as a means of demonstrating that is not entirely true — you would allow me to suggest putting a few things to the test?"

"Regarding Fuckwoman?"

"Exactly."

"Before you do…" Cynthia said.

"Yes?"

"How can you verify these observations if you don't know her?"

"Oh, we'll find her in due course," Holocenter said, with perfect equanimity.

"But you said that she wasn't like a normal criminal. She created herself. Isn't it going to be difficult to catch someone like that?"

"It will be difficult, but we have a strategy, which we will apply in due course."

"We?"

"Myself and the LAPD."

"But if you claim, as you do, that she doesn't have any clear or obvious weaknesses..."

"We'll concentrate on her virtues instead."

"How?"

He stopped for a moment in his pacing and looked towards her. "I believe you are becoming a little too precise in your questions. Miss Lelague. Suffice it to say that we will exploit her virtues, and perhaps you'd leave the detail to me."

Cynthia said, "A moment ago you claimed you could demonstrate your predictions."

"It is possible to do that at least without uncovering our plans for her eventual entrapment."

"How?"

"I believe, for example, I could make a guess at her family — the structure of her family background."

Cynthia felt a slight chill pass through her. She had an inkling of where he might be heading. She began to understand what he had meant by opening up the discussion between them, even perhaps the purpose of his odd and incongruous introduction of certain types of fiction in which one personality is pitted against another. Perhaps this was what his so-called test would amount to. He was proposing to bring in her family in some way she could only guess at. He was going to use her family to close the circle on her.

"I'm listening," she said.

She was aware of the silence of the room again, as though it were an extension of his character. In the midst of his pacing, Holocenter turned towards her calmly. One eyebrow was slightly raised in quizzical enquiry. He said softly, almost to himself, "I believe you are, Miss Lelague."

He didn't seem to be making a rhetorical point, merely a neutral observation. Now he turned away and looked up again at the light streaming through the windows, as though gathering his thoughts. He said, "Contrary to popular belief and myth, most social revolutionaries — and I would classify Fuckwoman as a social revolutionary — do not emerge from either the working class or the underprivileged. Almost invariably they come from the middle class, and usually from a specific sector of the middle class: the well-educated middle class. Marx and Lenin are classic examples; Castro and Che Guevara, Ho Chi Minh, Pol Pot, Chou-en-lai — there are plenty of others. Mao is one of the few exceptions; he came from land-owning peasants. To talk vaguely or vehemently of social revolution is one thing. Putting it into practice is another. That requires a high degree of confidence, a degree of intellectual confidence or even arrogance, and the sense of belonging to a radicalised elite."

She waited in silence. "What precisely are you inferring?"

"My first point is that she comes from an educated, middle-class background."

"Aren't you just speculating?"

Holocenter nodded. "Of course. The point is, though, how true is it?"

Cynthia said, "You have no way of knowing for sure."

"Perhaps not. But I believe what I am suggesting is borne out by the evidence in certain subtle ways. The public is always so surprised when the terrorist or revolutionary happens to come from the more comfortable strata of society. Patty Hearst, Ulrike Meinhof, Leila Khaled — I could name half a dozen others, whose background you could check if you wished — shocked contemporary society largely for that reason. Presentable, upper class or middle class girls, engaged in violent insurrection."

"Please go on," Cynthia said.

Holocenter paused and smiled. "My second point is this. The social revolutionary is usually an only child, or, at the very least, a child who has been raised apart from his or her siblings — a lonely child. That also happens to be the kind of child who dreams, who manufactures his or her own world."

He was talking fluently and calmly now, as though his thoughts were propelling him forward. "Point Three. That child is likely to be the product of parents who are of a radical disposition. Very often, the social revolutionary merely takes the radicalism of his or her parents for granted, so much for granted that he or she feels entitled or enabled to place force behind those beliefs. There's often a kind of inheritance at work here. The parents may have to work towards their beliefs, but by the time they're adult and raising children, those beliefs are often strongly formed and part of the family environment. The child in question is reared in conditions of secure belief in radical solutions. Thus, if I may draw a conclusion, it often happens that a social revolutionary merely places strong-arm tactics at the service of deeply ingrained radical beliefs learnt at the parental knee." He halted for a moment and glanced towards her. "I hope I'm not being too obtuse."

"No," Cynthia said. "What you say is rather intriguing." It seemed important to her, at that stage at least, to appear at ease, even though her mind was scurrying over the territory, attempting to follow the line of his reasoning, checking out the deductions. "You certainly spin a nice story."

"Why, thank you, Miss Lelague," Holocenter murmured. "I take it you won't mind if I continue a little further along this... ah...fictional incline?"

"Please do."

He seemed wholly immersed in his thoughts now. "Let's look more closely at Fuckwoman herself. She's a feminist, is an obvious deduction. More than just a feminist, I think — a highly confident feminist. I'd assert with her kind of confidence, so militantly displayed, she learned her feminism at her mother's knee. I'd surmise that the likelihood is that her mother commands considerable respect in society at large. Of course, her mother's influence over her might just be a case of effective parental relations — certain people are strikingly good at influencing their children, just as other people are strikingly effective at other things. But my guess would be that respect for her mother's beliefs is reinforced by widespread social respect for her mother's views. I'd go so far as to say that her mother is qualified, an academic perhaps, possibly a senior sociologist or social psychologist — something of that nature. I'm building up a picture of an influential woman, a woman who commands considerable respect in society at large. She bequeaths this confidence to her daughter. It seems to me that the person who calls herself Fuckwoman is herself so confident of her own beliefs she can even afford to be playful, almost satirise those beliefs — hence those literary *bon mots* and intellectual games. She can construct the elaborate, almost cinematic structure of the persona of Fuckwoman upon deeply held foundations. That's my fourth point, then. Fuckwoman's mother is in all probability a highly educated and respected academic figure."

She waited in silence for him to continue.

"Point five," Holocenter said. "Let's attempt to explore a little further the background that would give Fuckwoman such confidence. My guess is that not only is her mother a feminist, but perhaps other members of her family are feminists. That type of inherited feminism, I'd say, is likely to be matrilineal; it follows the female line. Maybe she comes from a dynasty of feminists, if 'dynasty' isn't so masculine a term that it makes for an apparent contradiction of meaning."

"Why wouldn't she just follow in her mother's footsteps?" Cynthia asked. "Why become militant?"

Holocenter paused, and it seemed to her he was thinking deeply about something.

"A good question. There's something distinctly matriarchal about Fuckwoman. It's almost as though she models herself upon an Amazon, a tribe of Amazons. She assumes a degree of feminine militancy which is quite breathtaking."

Cynthia said, "You didn't answer my question."

"No," Holocenter smiled. "You're right, I didn't answer it directly. I wanted a little more time to think about it. To me it stands to reason that the inheritors of a tradition generally want to extend that tradition further. That assumes a certain confidence in that tradition, and in the capabilities and confidence of the subject. But let's go back to your question. Where does she find her militancy? Allow me to posit a guess — a little jump in speculation. My guess is that she has a father who is a militant or a former militant. She grafts her father's militancy onto her mother's feminism. There we have, so to speak, the complete persona — the feminist with militant capabilities. I'd say that together those two features pretty much generate the character we know."

He had stopped sideways on to her, staring upwards into the light from the windows, his eyelids half closed. Maybe he was no longer watching her directly. Maybe he had formed such a clear impression in his mind of her — of the notional abstract of her — that he was simply considering the object of his creation.

She waited for him to speak further. But she also knew that silence and absorption were as much a part of the process to him as any other of his prognostications. She guessed he had said pretty much everything that he wanted to say, and now he was waiting for her to speak.

Her intuition was that he was listening to her right at that moment with as much intensity of concentration as anyone was capable. She knew that sometimes a person could listen so hard that his waiting almost turned the very air into a living force. She sensed he was listening in particular to her silence, wondering whether he'd hit the target. She was having difficulty in formulating a reply.

"It'll be interesting to see how much of that is right," Cynthia said at last. "I hope you don't mind if I note some of this down — for my own interest."

"Not at all, Miss Lelague."

She opened her notebook and began writing there, taking her time, determined not to appear ruffled. She summarised the points; one, two, three, four, five, and then a sixth, about her father. She gave Holocenter six out of six, with maybe a slight wobble on point five. It was impressive, she had to admit.

She wondered if he had any chance to investigate her background before she came to the interview. But it was her strong impression that he'd only made up his mind about her candidacy for the role after he'd met her, which was during the meeting. And since he hadn't taken any time off to make phone calls or consult police computer files in the course of their discussions, there seemed to her no way he could reach those conclusions without deducing them directly.

And then there was the rationale, the movement from speculative point to deduction, circling back to check the logic, looking for cross-references, checking to make sure the picture seemed coherent. She guessed that now he was on the track of her, he would start to investigate her background as soon as she left the room. And what would those police files and public records tell him? That her mother had maybe a couple of parking tickets in Pasadena? There'd be little to find. But it wouldn't be that which would interest him, not once he knew her mother's identity. She knew it would be easy enough to find out that her mother was Professor Fernanda Lelague, a leading sociologist at UCLA. As he looked more carefully at the evidence, he'd find a picture of her family background which increasingly suited his speculative construction.

And then there was her father. He had been a radical at Berkeley in the 1970s, part of the final wave of student militancy that came out of that university in the aftermath of the Vietnam War. It would take him a while to find out about that, and fit it together with her father's subsequent integration, if you could call it that, into the capitalist system. But once Holocenter began to find other factors fitting into place, who might say where his investigations might lead him?

"What do you think of the general reasoning?" Holocenter asked calmly. He had lowered his glance from the height of the window and was looking at the wall, an expression of slightly bemused concentration on his face.

"I'd be more impressed if you caught her in the act," Cynthia said.

He half-smiled and nodded to himself. "Maybe so. I believe I have spoken enough now. Have you any questions you particularly wish to ask of me?"

Cynthia said, "You said that you wanted to make this a real discussion."

"That's what I said, yes."

"May I ask you a question about something you said earlier?"

"Of course."

"You said that Fuckwoman is an intelligent woman who chooses to express herself in terms of irony. But in an earlier interview you said that you would catch Fuckwoman because of a particular weakness she exhibits. According to you, she likes publicity." She glanced over at him, hoping for a reply, but he was standing silently, waiting for her to continue.

She waited a little longer for him to respond, but he remained silent, at least for the time being. Cynthia said, "If I may quote you directly, you said, 'I believe that like most psychotics, she has a personality flaw, and that's what will give her away.' In addition, and I quote, 'She feeds on publicity. When she captures a suspected rapist, she leaves little notes behind, giving her identity, like a kind of signature. All the attendant media coverage that follows these acts seems to serve the same psychological purpose — she seeks some form of approval from the public, or at least from certain members of the public.'" She closed her notebook and looked up at him again. "How does that square with your view that she is independent of public opinion, that she follows her own mind? They can't both be true."

Holocenter remained still. After a few seconds he said, "Exactly what question are you asking?"

"If you think that she has no obvious character weaknesses, why would you assert that she's a publicity-seeking psychotic?"

Holocenter turned towards her and smiled. It was a longer smile than the earlier faint traces of amusement. This time it was a smile of purpose. He said, "Why, to provoke her, of course."

He was standing still, regarding her directly. She was surprised at his candidness, but something inside her wanted to press ahead, even so.

"Why would you want to provoke her?"

"In the hope that it would sting her into some kind of response."

"What kind of response?"

"My assumption would be that one day she would approach me to take issue with me over that statement."

"Why would you think that?"

"Because she's confident, and intellectually sure of herself, perhaps even a little arrogant."

"And so you think she'd approach you directly."

"Yes."

"As you think I am doing now," Cynthia said.

"Precisely," Holocenter said, "as you are doing now."

His words seemed to hover in the silence, as if they were at some distance from both of them.

"And then what?" Cynthia said.

Holocenter smiled, almost apologetically. He coughed, and swallowed once, and she saw the long movement in his throat. He seemed to be choosing his words carefully.

"When she did," he said, "I would know, finally and for certain, that it was she."

22

They agreed, almost by mutual consent, to curtail the interview there. It was a sanguine moment, strangely poised. They were both still somewhat guarded towards one another, though their goodbyes were a little more amicable this time. Cynthia stood up and they shook hands formally. Holocenter's palm was dry, without a trace of moisture, and it confirmed to her that he was at home in his territory, that it was some deep inner drive that caused him to want to hunt her down, that he felt no contradiction or self-doubt.

In the corridor outside she paused. It was a short moment to reflect. She felt relieved that she had carried out her mission. At the same time, she experienced that strange light-headedness of knowing that the die had been cast, that certain things were irrevocable.

There was an odd moment in the corridor when she thought that he had closed the door, but instead sensed his presence in the frame behind her, like a column of still air. He had been watching her in silence, with something of his customary vigilance. She guessed then that perhaps he wanted to say something further to her, perhaps some parting word, some distillation of what had passed between them.

For her part, Cynthia had enough to think about. She pretended not to notice his continued presence, and set off briskly down the corridor. She kept walking, determined not to exhibit any kind of response while still in his view. As she walked she felt, or sensed, his cold eyes upon her until she reached the end of the corridor and was about to turn the corner. For some reason his surveillance didn't bother her. She guessed that his interest was technical — that maybe he was trying to work out, attempting to calculate, from the movement of her physical frame — whether she could have taken on and despoiled a gang of a dozen or so men in open combat.

The corridor was long, perhaps fifty yards. She was about to turn the corner when Dr Holocenter called out after her in his cold, clear voice, "Goodbye, Miss Lelague. Pity you can't catch the City Hall rapist."

23

It was only when she was back in the newsroom, when some of the strangeness of her interview had settled, that she asked herself why she was determined to provoke Dr Holocenter. Why did she feel obliged effectively to break her cover? She had known, even before meeting him, that he was waiting for her like a large spider, and she flew directly into his web.

But she was aware too of certain wasps who would fly into spiders' webs, even allow themselves to be entangled, in the hope that the spider would emerge from its ambush place and attack them, and so allow them to press home their own attack. Once the spider was paralysed with a sting, they set about cutting themselves free of the web, so that they could carry the spider back to their lair for their young to feed on.

It was part of her compact with herself not to duck, not to hide, not to run away. In that at least Dr Holocenter was right.

She would go out and show herself to him and dare him to fight. She would challenge him, in effect, to arrest her.

She knew that if he had taken the initiative, and ordered or commissioned her arrest at the interview, there would have been certain types of circumstantial evidence which would have indicated that she had been present at the fight with the gang the previous night. There was the bruising on her upper body which a search would have revealed, in addition to some odd half moon imprints where the nails of certain gang members — during the brief frenzy of their possession — had dug into her flesh. There was the fact that she had no strong alibi at the time of either the incident with Jim Rivers or the recent imbroglio with the gang. But then, even to risk the possibility of a false arrest in such a highly sensitive case would have been damaging to a police department whose reputation was already highly fragile.

She knew he had to wait. And she knew too, that he knew he had to wait. It was part of the game between them.

As it happened, a wasp flew in the window and hovered between the verticals of the panes. A fragment of biological knowledge came back to her from her high school days. Wasps belonged to the order *Hymenoptera*, which included ants and bees. They were called *Hymenoptera* because of their non-reproductive or "virginal" worker and soldier castes. She liked the *Hymenopterans* not least because, apart from a few drones, they were all females. From the queen to the workers and soldiers — the entire nest was a matriarchy, a matriarchy of Amazons.

Still thinking of Holocenter and what he had said, she

opened the window and herded the wasp carefully towards the frame. It seemed complacent, undisturbed. Maybe it sensed the open air. She watched it fly out, towards Van Nuys and the lowering smog.

24

The curious thing was that in the days after the interview with Dr Holocenter Cynthia felt she entered a kind of limbo. In certain respects the nature of their confrontation had been resolved, or at least defined. They had observed one another as opponents at close quarters. She was impressed with his powers of observation and deduction. He had suspected she would attempt to meet him and confront him. And he had been sufficiently alert, when that meeting occurred, to know that he was facing his opponent directly. It seemed to Cynthia, in retrospect, that Holocenter must have known who she was almost immediately she entered the room, and the entire interview had been spent in attempting to establish some kind of contact with her.

There was an element of intimacy in his analysis, the professional intimacy of wrestlers who face one another across the mat.

She lay in her narrow single bed thinking about something that Holocenter had said, that you are conscious of yourself and aware of certain compulsions, and at the same time you are compelled to act out those compulsions even though you yourself know the final conclusion.

There was another factor which she knew would play its part. They were both denizens of Los Angeles. The trouble with that crazy city was that at its heart was the movie business — the business of dissimulation. You got down to the heart of most big cities and you usually found the smoke trace of some heavy industry — in Pittsburgh, steel; in Detroit, motors. Maybe in other cities, as in Chicago, it was a little more complex, a big railroad centre and trading city perhaps darkened by the scent of old crime. But at least you had a sense of working down to the bedrock, to the real substance beneath. Here in Los Angeles it was the other way round; here, as you excavated downwards, you came to the professional manufacture of illusions. Underneath the physical fabric of the city was another city, a city of trick-shows and lights. In that way at least Los Angeles was the opposite of other cities, of other urban traditions. The deeper you mined, the more ephemeral and illusory things became.

That was why, at a certain point, she liked being among eccentrics, amongst people who seemed out of place in that city, because their sheer cussedness protected them from the central delusions of the city itself. Perhaps Holocenter was saved from the ephemeral heart of the city by being from another culture, an eastern seaboard culture, with old notions of good and evil. Perhaps the same was true of Gore Emhard. Maybe his annoying adherence to a traditional masculinity was his own method of self-protection from the illusions of Tinseltown. He also seemed to exist outside the central preoccupations of the city.

There was another character who seemed to have found his own life on the periphery: Myron Overbear, it was widely rumoured, had turned down the chance several times to make it big in movies, and had chosen instead the life of a journalist. Recently, she had been forced to think a little more about Overbear because of an incident that occurred unexpectedly in the course of her daily work as a journalist. A couple of days after her interview with Dr Holocenter, she was covering a political fund-raising convention for the Democratic party and standing in a corner with some other hacks, drinking coffee. Around her were several of the television staff from LATV, taking a break from filming the speeches inside the hall. As it happened, Myron Overbear, that prince among reporters, came walking past her. She guessed he was heading towards the radio interview booths on the other side. As he traversed the centre of the hall, he turned and directed his eyes vaguely towards her.

He was walking over the parquet, not fast but almost floating. She was standing in a group of other reporters, just standing and talking. He looked not precisely in her direction but upward, over the top of her head, as if he could see something there. And then an odd change came over him. He seemed to pause, as if struck by some interior thought, then became restless, casting about him as though searching for someone who wasn't there. Then he began to move again, almost as though he were hunting the local area, as if some unseen part of his intelligence was tracking something down. She observed him drift towards her, and in some part of her thoughts she suspected that he wasn't hunting with his eyes, but with some other sense that she couldn't see. He came on, calmly and relentlessly.

The truth was, he was not alone at the time, which made the whole thing seem stranger. There was this small guy at his shoulder, talking to him, moving his hands; Overbear was listening to him, turning his head politely towards him occasionally, nodding at certain points. But at the same time Overbear's feet were sliding and shifting, as if under their own compulsion, towards the group of reporters that contained her. The little guy was following, walking alongside, talking incessantly, but a part of Overbear's mind was clearly on something else. The little guy seemed to be some kind of financial accountant, talking nine to the dozen about some new tax rule about a shift in immunities over certain allowances. Overbear was listening, coming closer, never looking at her, until right at the point when he was standing in front of her, when something happened and he said directly to her, without introducing himself, just said straight out, "Forgive me asking, but who the hell are you?"

The whole group in the area around Cynthia — standing at odd angles with their coffee cups, a few of them smoking — stopped talking. The little guy was left with one hand articulating a point, making a kind of arrested chopping motion in the air.

She felt Overbear's eyes on her. "Cynthia Lelague. Reporter, *Angel Times*."

"Didn't ask what you *do*," Overbear said. "Asked who you *are*."

"I just told you."

"That so?" Overbear said. "You don't look like any kind of reporter to me."

"What do reporters look like?"

"Don't look like you," Overbear said.

The group around them had got over their first astonishment, but none of them started to talk again. It wasn't just Overbear's presence — his charisma was like a tide — it was the calm intensity of his interrogation. Now Overbear was saying, almost casually, as though he were talking to himself, "Reporter's someone who moves around the edges. Reporter's someone on the periphery. Reporter's someone on the *outside*. You ever look outside through the rain and see someone talking into a payphone, someone standing on a deserted corner on his own? That's a reporter."

"Maybe that person in the phone booth is me."

"No, it isn't. You aren't living on the outside like that. You're living on the inside."

She didn't know what to say, so she just smiled stupidly. "Maybe I should be branded."

"You are branded. That's my point." He paused, regarding her with that familiar objectivity with which he approached his interview subjects. "One day we're going to see who you really are." He didn't smile. "When that happens, I'm going to be there."

Everything he said was calm and serious. But having spoken his mind, he seemed to lose interest in her. He turned and walked away. The little guy at his shoulder started talking again, chopping his salami, and Overbear drifted off, saying listen, why can't I do this, why can't I do that. You might have thought that Overbear had never even said what he'd just said, because in one sense he was already far away. Cynthia watched him leave, the same way he had come, still talking with the small guy.

One of the other people there, a bright girl called Fay Renton, said simply, "Wow." She wasn't referring to what Overbear had said so much as the way he'd said it. It seemed as though Fay Renton treated his approach — his sudden and unexpected interrogation of Cynthia — like a performance, like a marvellous impromptu act, an example of Los Angeles gothic, which is to say, for its appearance, not its content. And then — more or less precisely at the point when Overbear had reached the radio booths, and was pausing there for a few final words with his hand on the door of one of the cubicles, nodding goodbye to his colleague — only then did the conversation around Cynthia start again.

It began desultorily at first. People gave her a few odd sideways glances, as though only partially interested in the sort of person who'd be the recipient of that kind of attention on the part of a big-time media star. But, like Fay Renton, that wasn't what interested them — what interested them was the theatre of it all, the performance.

The coffee break came to a slow end; they put down their plastic cups and went back into the conference, and Cynthia thought the show is over, folks. That was when she knew that she was safe for a little while longer at least, that they'd remember the whole outer accoutrements of Myron Overbear's hunting scene — the way he was quartering the turf, the way he seemed to find her out. But what he'd said about her would soon be lost, mere talk, mere noise. The image would be preserved, but not the content.

Until, of course, the day it came true. That was what concerned her now. She knew that day was close, surprisingly close. That was what was eerie about Overbear's approach — he didn't only sense she was strangely different, he sensed she'd be emerging from her chrysalis soon.

25

After her encounter with Myron Overbear, Cynthia felt inclined to sympathise with one of those casual witnesses like Fay Renton who acted as though what they had seen was simply a species of cinema. In the reversed world of Los Angeles, it was like a scene they had all seen in the movies. Myron Overbear had looked beneath the exterior and caught a glimpse of something underneath — something rare and strange. It resembled the classic unmasking scene in a good *film noir*. But what exactly had he caught a sight of? Some deeper reality existing beneath a false surface? Or was it a little more complex than that?

The following day Gore Emhard came through the main newsroom, carrying his thoughts in front of him like a stormcloud. When he reached Cynthia's desk, he put down a photograph in front of her and said, "What do think of that?"

She glanced at it briefly and thought maybe he was up to his old tricks — that it was some photographic equivalent of the bison's penis pencil-holder, something designed to outrage her sensibilities and at the same time leave her as little room for manoeuvre as possible. It took a little while to assemble the true subject of the photograph in her mind.

A small, spry man in a black evening suit stood between two tall and curvaceous women. It looked like some kind of event, a gala or prize-giving or celebration. The photograph was taken from behind the rostrum, and in front of the rostrum could be seen the faces of the Hollywood elite, women in beautiful dresses, men in bow ties.

The position of the photographer was somewhat privileged. Hidden from the eyes of the seated audience, the man's hands had settled comfortably on the out-curving rears of the two women. The photographer's flash had picked out those white hands beautifully. They were like large moths. They were, so to speak, the main subtext of the photograph.

"So," Emhard said, "What do you think of our Mayor?"

"Mayor Dally?"

"Right first time," Emhard said.

She paused for a moment, then said, "What are you asking exactly?"

"Just wondered what you thought of the position of those hands. Precisely what are we talking about here — mild salacity, somewhat questionable taste, or outright molestation?"

Cynthia licked her lips. She said, "I'd say we were moving towards outright molestation."

Emhard nodded.

"Spoken like a true feminist," Emhard said. "So, how do you

think we should treat Mr Dally? Real harsh, I hope."

Cynthia knew now where Emhard was headed. Although Dally was a right-wing Republican, he had assiduously cultivated the female vote by supporting a raft of legislation in favour of higher representation of women in the upper echelons of politics and business. Positive discrimination might have been outlawed in the state by referendum, but it hadn't stopped him fighting through several laws which were strongly in favour of women's rights.

"We're in your hands, Cynthia," Emhard said, as though echoing her thoughts. "Are we gonna nail the lecherous son-of-a-bitch, or we gonna let him go? I mean, personally, I'd like to pin his boleros to the wall."

Cynthia felt her mouth go dry.

Emhard said, "I hope you're not going to be soft on the guy, Cynthia. I'm looking for some hard-edged decision here. I want to know I have the backing of our leading feminist in getting this guy behind bars."

Frankly, she'd have liked to nail Emhard's boleros to the wall for putting her in that position. But it didn't alter the fact that her emotions were almost perfectly balanced between mild outrage at a gratuitous and mildly lewd gesture on the part of the Mayor, and a small but not unconsidered debt of gratitude to Dally.

She was silent for a little longer, and after a few more moments of deeply enjoyable consideration of her plight, Emhard raised the photograph from the table.

"Well I'll be damned," he said. "For just a moment, I thought I saw signs of real human conflict there."

Without another word Emhard walked back through the newsroom and closed the door behind him.

In the silence that followed, Cynthia felt a blush of roseate warmth rising up from her neck into her cheeks. She knew that Emhard had done it again, that he'd managed to rile her without apparent consequence to himself. It was another crime that was going down in the files.

There were several other reporters who had been within earshot of their exchange. She could feel their appraising eyes on her, not so much directly on her as upon the circumstances in which Emhard had left her. After his departure she sensed the remnants of their smiles sliding away, as the newsroom settled down again to its work, like fishes moving to deeper water.

26

The ramifications of the Dally photograph continued to haunt Cynthia for a while afterwards. It reminded her once again of Hollywood, of the difference between what was on the surface and what lay beneath.

One of the reasons she enjoyed *film noir* was the simplicity of its primary assumption that beneath the exterior were darker undercurrents, and as you moved further under the surface, things got blacker still. It was based on the formula Darker Equals Deeper. What made her uneasy was the reverse equation, that Deeper Equals Darker. In *noir*, if you wanted to go deep, dark was the sign that you were being profound, significant, truthful. Actually, when she thought about such things more closely, she came to the conclusion that the assumption was just as likely to be pure nonsense, like so many cinema conventions. People could have a dark surface and be light underneath. Just as often, you could scratch the surface of a bad guy and find a good guy under the skin. There were often good reasons for being dark on the surface, but different underneath. Al Capone liked everyone to know he was a killer. It kept people in line. He didn't want everyone to know how much he loved and admired his mother, or that he was a considerate family man. Adolf Hitler was a vegetarian who was kind to dogs. It suited him to keep that side of his personality as obscure as possible.

In his own way, Holocenter had pointed out something like that to her about the nature of revolutionaries. In line with conventions of cinema, people expected that when the truth about terrorists like Patty Hearst or Ulrike Meinhoff was brought to light, something monstrous would be revealed. Instead, as often as not what they found were pretty, middle-class girls who came from stable backgrounds and had loving parents. It was a species of revelation which seemed to shock no one more profoundly than the parents themselves.

Noir was another highly artificial construction, another form of opera, driven by equally artificial assumptions and constraints. By contrast, in her view Los Angeles was genuinely *noir*: underneath the shiny surface of the entertainment industry, dark emotions ruled — personal vanity, power, the lure of celebrity, and commercial greed. And so *noir* didn't reflect profound truths about the world so much as the nature of the film industry itself.

In Los Angeles you became used to the fact that the surface was the opposite of what lay underneath. Take Mayor Dally, for example. In certain ways Dally was pure Hollywood. He was a master illusionist in a city where the central industry was illusion. You had the impression you were dealing with a tough son-of-a-bitch, a young lawyer who'd risen up through the city's sewers and hard streets, someone who'd fingered criminals and psychopaths and who'd come through unsullied, though not unscarred — someone you should respect and also fear a little. It was an image carefully fostered.

Cynthia remembered this when another aspect was carefully added to Mayor Dally's image. Out of curiosity she followed up the photograph that Emhard had put on her desk. It had been taken at a big Hollywood film gala. The guests came in limousines and wore anti-AIDS ribbons. Mayor Dally hosted the occasion with his chief assistant Miss Aureole Tarzanna. They were raising funds for ADEPT, the Association of Departmental Police Training. The scheme aimed to train policemen and policewomen in greater sensitivity towards racial, sexual and other minorities. Dally's chief assistant, Miss Tarzanna, had the idea of inviting celebrities and the moneyed classes to screenings of great *noir* films at five thousand dollars a ticket. Miss Tarzanna came from a PR background, and was wise enough to know that in that town money created its own exclusivity. People would fight for the privilege of paying through the nose to sit in tuxedos and long dresses and watch a film that they could see on cable any day. At the end of the showing Dally would go forward and stand in front of the screen behind the lectern set up by his City Hall aides. The press and reporters would gather round to take notes and photographs as Dally gave a speech thanking his rich audience for giving so generously to a favourite charity. And then he would hand out an award from ADEPT to a Police precinct that had distinguished itself over the last year in relations towards minority groups.

That year he was flanked by not one but two striking-looking women. On his right was Miss Aureole Tarzanna herself, in a beige suit with white pearls. On her left was Lieutenant Lila Dimitri, an officer of the Silver Lake precinct. The women were both in their young thirties. They both had curvaceous figures. There were photographers on all sides, in front and to the side and also behind. It was the photographers that were behind the platform — those in the most disadvantageous position — who were rewarded with one of the best and most evocative pictures of the year.

After Dally had given his speech and handed out a cheque of $780,000 for new recreational facilities in the West Hollywood police department, after some police captain had walked away to tumultuous applause, the Mayor's hands had floated down in calm symmetry through the electrified air and settled for a moment in friendly appreciation on the bodies of his two female colleagues. You could say that his hands rested on their backs, in brief stay. But the anatomical fact was, those hands were quite low down on the women's backs. His hands were right on that part of the back where the ass moves out from the lower part of the spine and hesitates before thrusting out into space. A photographer had caught his white hands right there, like two large moths stunned in a beam of light.

The photograph became a celebrated image, hovering between old-fashioned courtesy and a studied lewdness. That was pure Los Angeles gothic. That was the Mayor demonstrating his warm, sexual side. That was Dally playing his rough man-of-the-street card.

And what exactly was he thinking in that moment? Lustful thoughts? Maybe. Or was he thinking instead about his political image, about adding a little salt to the impression of the hardworking people's Mayor?

The following day there was a brisk competition in ironic headlines as the picture headed the front or second pages of nearly all the local city newspapers. *DALLY GIVES PERSONAL SUPPORT*, the *Angel Times* put down. *MAYOR TOUCHES HEARTS AND SOULS*. The editors loved their boy, the men saw a man's man and women someone who had true warmth towards women, even if it spread a little too far at times.

Dally had seen evidence in private polls that he was considered a little remote from the average citizen. And he'd done what Hollywood always did. He'd carefully constructed a diverting and popular illusion around a single sharp insight: the warmhearted man of the people, the man whose gestures sometimes reflected a little natural earthiness.

Cynthia knew or suspected that Dally had a dark secret. It was held close because it ran counter to the image he projected. The evidence for it was probably inside one of the inner breast pockets of his well-cut suits. Dark rumours circulated about the contents of that pocket, but Cynthia was pretty certain she had an idea what it contained. She suspected that inside his wallet, never to be seen by outsiders, was a picture of his wife and their two young daughters. This wasn't the Midwest, and family values wouldn't necessarily play well to a great liberal city. That snap of his adored family would never see the daylight of publicity. Instead the public would see Mayor Dally's generous hands posing on two gorgeous rears.

It helped set Cynthia's own life in perspective. She knew that if the image of Fuckwoman was a form of deliberate projection, it wasn't any different in kind from the projection of the Mayor, or any other senior official or player in the life of that city. She too had constructed a piece of Los Angeles gothic, and so — to that extent at least — she was an inheritor of the city's presiding tradition.

27

In that odd time of limbo, another incident occurred that reminded her of the strange existence she led. She was walking home in the dusk, and turned off and followed her usual path back to her flat. She cut into 3rd Avenue and then down into LeHoya.

Turning a corner she had a sense that a shadow had moved out of a wall, like an eel that had emerged from a dark hole. Someone in soft soles or moccasins was on her tracks. She continued down LeHoya Avenue with this same impression naggingly insistent inside her. Over the next few minutes she listened hard for the footsteps following her, but they were well disguised and faint against the traffic. Then in Veda Avenue she heard them more clearly. It seemed they were closing suddenly with her. She was about to whirl and strike when she felt the gun at her head. Instead she stopped, out of momentary condescension, listening instead to the silent, internal monotone of her own fear.

They were in a deserted part of the street now, and the first thought that came to her was that this was one of the chapter members she'd beaten to a pulp, or maybe one of his relations, looking to settle scores. But as the hypothesis spread out through her mind, her senses could find no signs of other members of the chapter. That struck her as strange.

The gun seemed steady on the back of her neck. She guessed that its owner was a loner, that he was driven by a fierce, private conviction, and so she waited for him to make the next move. The voice, when it came, was surprisingly educated.

"What do you think of *Jackie Brown*?"

In the following few seconds, she tried to hunt down the voice. She played for time.

"*Jackie Brown*?"

The barrel pressed harder against the nape of her neck. "The Tarantino movie, asshole."

She had located the voice at last. It was Jim Rivers, cultural commentator and social critic.

"Are you going to tell me you haven't seen *Jackie Brown*? What kind of an upstart film critic are you?"

"Yes," Cynthia said. "I have seen it."

The gun at her head pressed closer, out of some kind of private fervour.

"And?"

"And what?"

"What do you think of it, asshole?"

Cynthia composed herself to offer some cultural insights, a little intellectual stimulation, and perhaps see whether she couldn't induce him to become a fraction over-emotional and make a mistake that she might exploit.

"I think in that film Tarantino matured considerably," she proffered. "Gone are all those juvenile obsessions about violence — those arty speeches about hamburgers before someone shoots someone else for entertainment. I'd say there was a hint there that he'd left his earlier persona behind, and was settling into the role of a mature, mainstream director."

"You asshole," Rivers said. "You half-witted, dumbfuck bimbo asshole."

It seemed to Cynthia that she'd struck just the right note first time out. Perhaps on account of this she felt a part of her habitual confidence coming back. She was emboldened to continue her discourse.

"At the centre of the film," Cynthia said, "is a beautiful and sensitively handled love story. The emotional dialogue between the male and female protagonists is both exquisite and heartbreaking. This time, you can tell Tarantino really loves his main characters. He dotes on every aspect of Pam Grier, particularly. Speaking as a woman, with a woman's deep emotional needs, I haven't been as moved by any ending since *Witness*. You remember that wonderful aching feeling as Harrison Ford and Kelly McGillis say goodbye? The empty road waiting behind Ford's shoulder? That lump in your throat the size of a hen's egg? This is as good as that. I have to say I loved every moment of it. Felt my poor female heart being wrenched out of its frame."

"Goddamn," Rivers breathed out. "You total feminine asshole. You are just a mess of emotions. A person like you doesn't deserve to live. That has to be the sickest analysis of a Tarantino movie I have ever had the misfortune to hear. Now I'm going to tell you what has really happened."

"What's that?"

"*Jackie Brown* was a cynical aberration — a tactical ploy by a director who has outfoxed his mainstream critics once again. It's brilliantly designed to throw people like you off the track. The love story is bogus — just as all love stories are bogus. Tarantino is saying, "Look, I can do this as well as all the other assholes that do love stories." You fell for it hook, line and sinker. Look what he did next. *Kill Bill*, volumes one and two. He's gone back to the real thing — brilliant, iconoclastic dialogue punctuated by existentialist violence, and that's where he left you swooning, hormone-fuelled female assholes drowning in his wake."

"I think you might be deluding yourself," Cynthia said. "The beauty of *Jackie Brown* is that during that movie he turned into a hormone-fuelled asshole himself. The stifled adolescent finally came of age. He came out of the closet. Let's face it, Rivers, he let out his inner woman."

She heard something half way between a snake's hiss and the beginnings of a hysterical laugh. It seemed to her right to just keep rolling on. "In *Jackie Brown*, Tarantino finally got in touch with his feminine soul. Once that happens, you can't ever go back. You can try to hide it, certainly, but now it's there you can't put it back into the box. You can't go from maturity back to teenage geekiness."

There was a hiss of rage and an almost incoherent silence.

Cynthia said, "I bet you when he edited that movie he was weeping over the ending. The way I see it, there's a part of Tarantino that's becoming an old-fashioned romantic. Why, he's even started making chicks' movies."

The gun was starting to shake at the back of her head. She guessed she was making progress. "I think when all this hyper-fashionable violence is over, when he's grown from an immature geek into a full human being, he's going to become one of the great romantic directors — not entirely original, but a maker of glossy, entertaining productions for mainly female audiences. I always knew that under the cynical violence was a vein of deep sentimentality. I see him as the new Mantovani of cinema."

"Listen, if I didn't know you were trying to rile me..."

"You'd what?" Cynthia asked. "Fill me with lead? Face it, Rivers, one day Tarantino's going to leave you behind, he's going to desert you. He's cynically exploited you all with his early, testosterone-fuelled movies about violence. He made a grab for your arrested, pubescent male psyche in his early movies. He found an audience of emotionally deprived adolescents and he calculatingly used them to establish his career. But *Jackie Brown* isn't an aberration. He's searching for something else. You can see a perfect line of movement from *Reservoir Dogs* to *Pulp Fiction* to *Jackie Brown* — a movement away from violence and towards deep-seated emotion. I'd say the *Kill Bill* movies are just the last gesture of his adolescent persona, eliminating that old stuff from his system."

"What about his next movie? A group of Jewish vigilantes wiping out Nazis in the Second World War in a maelstrom of violence. You calling that a chicks' flick?"

"He's trying to repress his feminine side, but it won't work. *Jackie Brown*'s his greatest movie. It'll catch up on him."

"There's no violence in *Jackie Brown*?" She could hear the sneer in Rivers' voice.

"The violence in *Jackie Brown* is mature violence, understated violence — violence that expresses character and pushes forward the narrative. It's violence at the service of the emotional drama, not the other way round."

"That's what you just don't understand, asshole," Rivers said. "Our boy is hiding in there, waiting for dumbos like you to make your move. Then he's going to show his face again."

"If only that were true," Cynthia said. "The fact is, what you see in *Jackie Brown* is true violence, that is, violence between real people — violence which evokes your sympathy. When Robert de Niro kills Bridget Fonda in the parking lot after she's riled him, that's a wonderful study in pathetic male overreaction to being wrong. Don't you see what he's doing?"

"Who? De Niro?"

"Tarantino."

"Don't tell me about Tarantino."

"Tarantino is satirising people like you. Did that violence in the car park solve anything? No. It just created worse problems. De Niro is just the next one to die. Deep inside, Tarantino has turned against violence as decoration, violence as mere metaphor."

"Bitch asshole. Tarantino's a genius who you will never understand. Even to pretend to understand him is an insult, the depth and nature of which you will never comprehend. In *Jackie Brown* he was just coasting along with Elmore Leonard, hiding his hand for the next foray. That's all he was doing. I'm standing here listening to you spout off and inside I'm laughing."

"You're history, Rivers. Why don't you go and jerk off over *Reservoir Dogs* and remember the good old days of pubescent violence and cool remarks. You are going to join a pathetic, dwindling band of adolescent early Tarantino fans and you can spend the rest of your lives weeping over your hero and where he went wrong."

"I am gonna execute you now."

"Go right ahead, street boy. Play the Robert de Niro role. Put me down on the sidewalk because you can't stand being dissed by smart bitches. The police will be onto you so quickly you'll be in San Quentin before you can count to ten."

"They won't find me."

"The vendetta between us is public. It's a matter of public record. They'll just look up the newspaper files and they've got you. You know what they'll think of a cultured guy like you in San Quentin, don't you? They aren't interested in operatic violence and cute existential remarks out there. They're into the real thing. They'll be spreading your cheeks two or three times a day. I have a feeling you'll be a lot more popular in there than out here."

"You couldn't be more wrong, bitch. The police will think your killer is one of the gang members you attacked and assaulted. That's why I chose their area to waylay you. They wouldn't think that a cultured guy like me would do something like this — that's the beauty of it. They'll spend their time hunting down the local tough guys instead. That's their kind of narrative."

"Nice plot, Rivers. I hope it looks as good when you're in San Quentin and they're queuing up outside the washrooms for your ass. As things stand, I enjoyed talking to you. But our conversation's over."

"Time to go, asshole. Time to go to that great chicks' movie up there."

She had to keep him on the rails a little longer, try to disturb the pattern of his attempted execution. Killing is like love; it has its own rhythm.

"God doesn't just love chicks' movies," Cynthia said. "She is a chick."

She knew he couldn't resist epigrams. There was a pause, then Rivers said, "That's why I have no intention of going there."

"Going to descend to where all the bad boys are, down to those eternal mean streets? My, you certainly are romantic."

"Romantic is where we started, asshole. Romantic is where we end."

She sensed his finger on the trigger, and the will moving down his arm.

Cynthia said, "I'm just going to walk on home now. My advice is to go back to yours."

She stepped forward smartly, enough to be decisive, not enough to present a violent threat. After ten paces she heard his shadow closing up with her, the patter of his moccasins as he came up right behind her to execute her. Her interpretation was that this was the final pathetic means of causing fear. Maybe he still believed he could pull the trigger. The gun touched the back of her neck again, but she kept on walking. Then she turned a corner and was back in the bright lights of the boulevard, and she didn't have to look behind her to know that the film critic and cultural iconoclast had melted away into the cold lights of the downtown streets.

The one thing that surprised her was that after the dialogue with Rivers, she exhibited no signs of after-crisis panic or fear.

Her pulse rate seemed normal, her breathing regular. She went home to her small flat and ate a meal of beans washed down by iced mineral water. She reasoned that her body had a right to feel fear or at least a tremble of aftershock. But the fact was that as soon as she had homed in on Rivers' identity she had felt confident and in control. It occurred to her that perhaps she was a monster. Or maybe she was just someone who had a mission, and Rivers wasn't part of that mission. That was why she could just brush him off, not in some superficial sense, but because her spirit was impervious to him.

28

In her small flat that evening, Cynthia wrote:

Mother,

I'm writing to thank you, a little belatedly, for your recent letter enclosing the article on Jim Rivers and Fuckwoman.

You're so wonderfully generous. I know I must be a kind of horror to you, a terrible tomboy who has somehow lost the deepest female capacity for empathy with other human beings. In the past you've described me as an Amazon. It is true that I do flail and scream silently inside when I listen to some of the stupidities of men. But I suppose I consider myself a kind of joker or comedian, and my natural methods are not the civilised deployment of your own cogently expressed liberal arguments, but the application of some more overt form of shock therapy to the male psyche. I seem to lack your calm intellect. Instead I favour the example of those Zen masters who creep up behind their students while they are unawares and give them a sharp whack on their backs with a stick, in order to help them break through into the awareness of being.

God, I can see myself being arrested, and you and dad coming to pick me up out of prison on bail for some provocation, some joke that went wrong. I have this feeling that whatever I did, you would both back me up without hesitation. The strange thing is, as I get older and further away from your influence, I feel I am becoming more extreme, more detached, more capable of some grand or hopeless gesture. Isn't it awful the way the child of a liberal upbringing feels compelled to assert his or her own character by becoming illiberal?

That's the point I'm making now. I suspect you may hear in due course that the true identity of Fuckwoman bears a more than superficial resemblance to a rather familiar and largely dutiful daughter. And you will have to face up to the fact that your own offspring is a somewhat notorious figure.

This is entirely of my own making. It started as a kind of joke, but after a while a joke becomes serious. I really do have a capacity for detective work. I'm logical and methodical and I know how to follow clues. As you intimated, I am also physically strong and determined enough to overpower most men. Rapists are not the most powerful of men. They are angry and frustrated, in most cases men who regard themselves as failures, who have taken the lamentable course of expressing their self-hatred against women in a particularly brutal and repulsive way. If you can withstand their first attack, they start to break down.

I think of men as armoured beings. The armour isn't physical, so much as psychic. It is meant to protect them, but it also separates them from their own emotions, not least because it prevents their free communion with other human beings. I hope you will forgive me for being both metaphorical and fanciful, but sometimes I think my function is to break down this armour.

It's partly to do with the self-confidence you implanted in me and partly because I am what I am. Whatever it is, the role took over.

The last thing I want is for you to defend me by saying that I am your daughter and that underneath this character is a sweet being who wouldn't hurt a fly. I want you to let me do something on my own, and that means suffering the consequences of my own choices. So if you see me arrested I'm asking you both to stand back, not to interfere, and to let the processes of law or justice take their natural course. Let me do this, let me take the consequences without your help.

Actually, all joking aside, I'm proud of what I did. By catching several serial rapists, I probably prevented perhaps a dozen serious and brutal rapes of women by angry men, and I believe that's a good enough thing to do in this world.

Above all, I wanted to do something that would shock this strange society into thinking some serious thoughts about sexual roles, and perhaps about the way men's violence seems to infiltrate sex. Maybe when men hear about other men being subjected to the humiliation of being caught and immobilised by a member of the sex they despise, they will at least consider what it is like to be a victim.

As for me, I know that in this strange city, entertainment is everything. Life can be a comedy or a tragedy, but it always ends in death. There's no logic or reason in it. You get to a certain point when you don't plead for help, you accept your fate.

I'm at the final stage now. A few days ago I went to meet Dr Holocenter, the senior police psychiatrist at LAPD who is in charge of hunting me down. I actually interviewed him in his den, not least because I wanted a close look at my adversary. I knew before I met him that he is, to all intents and purposes, an archetypal authority figure, regarded as a brilliant man in his profession, one of its natural leaders. Yet what fascinates and perhaps horrifies me is that he seems to have subsumed his entire character into that role, which is his own specific form of armour. He likes to impose his will on people. He doesn't do it by hanging around on dark street corners or haunting empty parks hoping to meet his victims. He does it by means of psychological techniques, through the use of medical authority. But my suspicion is that in his case the impulse is the same as the rapists I have attempted to stop in my own (perhaps eccentric) manner. It's the impulse to impose your absolute power over someone else, to the point that it utterly controls your victim's personality.

In due course I know I have to let him do his worst, and then rise up and defeat him. When I met him, I spent much of my time daring him to arrest me. I taunted him and insulted him. And I could sense, more than anything, the impulse within him to exert that final control over me.

The next phase is approaching, and I know if I can get through it I can get through anything.

Please don't speak to me or try to see me until this matter resolves itself. Have faith in your daughter.

My fondest love to you both.

Cynthia

29

The following day Cynthia knocked at Emhard's door. When she heard the familiar growl, she turned the handle and considered the chaos of his office.

"Speak," Emhard said.

Cynthia said, "Mind if I look more closely into the City Hall rapist case?"

Emhard was seated at his computer and didn't turn round. "Any particular reason?"

"I wonder why there's so little information coming out of LAPD on it."

"This rapist's elusive, is all."

Cynthia said, "Even so, we usually get press briefings, initial attempts at photofits, et cetera — some indication at least of the way the investigation is going."

Emhard continued to tap at the keyboard. He nodded. "Sure, see what you can get."

She went back to her desk and lingered for a few moments before phoning up Detective Stevens.

"Cynthia Lelague here."

"Well, hi, Miss Lelague."

"I'm looking for any kind of update you can give me on the City Hall rapist."

There was a brief pause, then Stevens said, "I'm afraid I can't help you on that one."

"Any particular reason?" Cynthia asked.

"It's being handled by a special group within LAPD. There's a tight cover on it. I don't even know what their findings are at this stage. No information comes out to me."

"Isn't this all a little unusual?"

"Yeah," Stevens said. "I have to say I've never seen anything like it."

"Do you have any idea who's running the investigation?"

"I don't. And if I did, I wouldn't be at liberty to tell you. The department has been instructed to release no information on this case."

"That's weird."

"That's your word for it," Stevens agreed amiably.

"Tell me if I'm wrong," Cynthia said, "But as I understand it, the usual policy is that the public should be expected to help in finding a rapist — particularly one as elusive as this one. Accidental witnesses, prior suspicious behaviour at the scene of the crime — that kind of thing. But if that's so, the public needs to be informed of the time and place of the crimes. So why are they excluding the public's participation from this one?"

"Beats me," Stevens said.

She waited a little, then said, "Well, thanks anyway."

She imagined the conversation had come to an end, and was about to put down the phone, when Stevens said, unexpectedly and almost fiercely, "I am genuinely sorry I can't be of help, Miss Lelague. You have to understand that it would be more than my job's worth."

"That's OK. Thanks for telling me straight."

"Miss Lelague..."

She counted the beats. "Yeah?"

"Nothing," Stevens said. "You be careful, now."

She had the distinct impression that he wanted to tell her something else about the investigation, maybe precisely what the group was who were running it, but she had heard the impulse fading in the silence, or being wrested aside by stronger fears.

"Sure," she said.

She put down the phone and thought for a few seconds. Then she phoned City Hall administration.

"Cynthia Lelague, crime reporter, *Angel Times*. Who am I speaking to?"

"Helen Riddell. Administration."

Helen Riddell had an even voice, assured and helpful.

"I'm looking for any information on the attacks by the so-called City Hall rapist on administration staff."

"It's a horrible business, isn't it?"

"I presume you're not at liberty to disclose anything about the victims."

"No," the voice said firmly.

"You couldn't even confirm that the victims work or worked at City Hall?"

"I'm afraid not. There's an embargo on that type of information."

"Why do you think that might be?"

There was a silence at the other end. She thought she could hear Mrs Riddell sipping a cup of tea or coffee, while she considered her answer. At last she said, "I don't think it's my business to speculate about that."

Cynthia switched her point of attack.

"As someone who works there yourself, has the threat of the rapist altered your routine?"

"Women are not allowed to walk around outside the buildings unaccompanied, if that's what you mean."

"You happy about that?"

"No one feels entirely safe here at the moment, I have to say."

"Is this embargo helping any? Wouldn't it be better to disseminate as much information as possible?"

"That's not for me to say."

Cynthia prodded a little further, then said goodbye and put down the phone. She felt none the wiser.

If there was one advantage to the freeze on information, Cynthia decided, it was that the City Hall rapist's supposed obsession with Fuckwoman wasn't being constantly aired. At the same time, it began to occur to her that maybe LAPD were deliberately holding back information precisely so that the vigilante wouldn't be able to use details supplied to the public in order to get to the rapist first. Behind the information freeze she sensed Holocenter's strategy of control, maybe even an attempt to unsettle her. She knew he was capable of influencing

LAPD's efforts in order to keep her in the dark, to inflame her and keep her guessing. Increasingly, it seemed to her, LAPD's overall strategy on this particular case had the stamp of his overall authority. She also considered it likely that in the meantime they'd be feverishly working to bring in the City Hall rapist. That would be a double triumph: they'd have a suspect who was supposedly obsessed with Fuckwoman to the point of committing the rapes, and they would prove that in getting to him first they were ahead of the public's favourite vigilante. Considered from that perspective, it was all starting to fit together a little too well.

She tried other possible sources. The City Hall security system was equally tight in its information. A security guard repeated that he had no information on the case. She hunted around a little more, found no further traces and filed an interim report to Gore Emhard.

The case of the City Hall rapist continues to perplex outside observers. Despite the real and continuing threat to female workers in the Civic Center complex, LAPD have taken the unusual step of releasing no information to either reporters or the general public. According to certain inside sources, who cannot be named, the whole campaign is being handled by a tight group of senior police officers and personnel who are pursuing the case in a highly secretive manner.

This may be a move to ensure absolute secrecy and keep the City Hall rapist himself off guard. It is well known that high-profile offenders of this type are interested in personal publicity. At this stage, it is charitable to assume that LAPD are aware of this psychological predisposition in the individual they are hunting, and are deliberately starving the rapist of information on the progress of the investigation.

A less charitable interpretation might be that LAPD, having suffered in the past from F-woman's capacity to reach rapists first, have placed an embargo on any public information in an attempt to prevent that happening again.

Emhard read the brief report and said, "Good thinking. Keeps up public interest in readiness for when the case breaks again." He paused at the last paragraph. "I'll allow you a little feminist agitprop on Fuckwoman's behalf this time round. Don't see any harm if it helps to stir up LAPD."

Emhard had been surprisingly good to her for a while now. He approved her articles and gave several of them prominence. He hadn't even attempted to outrage her recently with some new politically incorrect object. She wondered briefly what lay behind this new policy of tolerance towards her, but turned her mind again to the subject of her report. Starved of even the smallest scraps of information on the City Hall rapist, she couldn't begin to form a psychological profile of him, or work out any form of possible campaign.

The whole of that following week she continued to experience the same odd sense of limbo while waiting for the case to break again, so she busied herself with routine reports and articles.

In the meantime, Emhard's newly emollient attitude towards her was causing her almost as much consternation as the behaviour of LAPD in regard to the City Hall rapist.

"Cynthia," Emhard said a couple of days later. "My wife and

I wondered if you'd care to come to a dinner party this Saturday. Short notice, I'm afraid."

She was frankly surprised. She had entered his office to check on the space for an article she was writing on the continuing growth in juvenile crime, and he had sprung this one on her unexpectedly. Sensing her hesitation, Emhard swung his chair round and regarded her from beneath his eyebrows.

"Guess you're suspicious of my motives. Think I'm going to ambush you."

"Well, Gore, it had occurred to me."

"Think I've got some new politically incorrect atrocities lined up for you to see at my house?"

"Now that you mention it."

"Hell, Cynthia, I think it's time we called a truce on that front. Way I see it, we have to get along together."

"We seem to have managed without that until now, Gore."

Emhard smiled. "You're such a cynic, Cynthia. I guess we men are just not so hard-assed as you women. We're sentimental and forgiving types, always hoping for a little kindness and attention."

Now she was convinced he was lying in wait for her.

"What time do you expect me, Gore?"

"Say, seven-thirty?"

"I'll be there," she said.

"In a highly suspicious state of mind, I can see," Emhard said, then went back to his work. After a few seconds he seemed to have forgotten about her.

"Thanks for the invitation," she said, closing the door behind her.

30

What is in a name?

The Emhards were rich southerners. Gore Emhard's grandfather had owned oil wells near Houston. His father had lived well on the inherited wealth and there was something left over for his son. Emhard, the scion of this family, inhabited one of the few older Spanish-style houses in Bel Air. He lived amongst his father's collection of stuffed animals with his aristocratic wife, Sarah, who seemed to be as fierce as her husband. To Cynthia's eyes at least, his wife was usually away on visits to odd places of the world concerned with conservation.

Cynthia was fascinated by the connection between hunting and conservation. It sometimes seemed to her as if hunting also arose out of a love of nature, though perhaps of an odd and immature kind. If it involved the same instinct, she was inclined to believe that it could direct itself into strangely different forms. She could partly accept that in an older generation the ancient, primitive love of nature was expressed, strangely, by killing everything in sight. She could believe — not least, because she assumed that was how love often manifested itself through the male character — in a love epitomised by death. It seemed to her a salient characteristic of a large body of men that they didn't nurture what they loved; instead, they raped and pillaged it. Maybe she took heart from the fact that these same killers, after pillaging the planet's wildlife for a number of generations, now increasingly hunted with camera instead. The so-called "sportsmen" who once bought from poverty-stricken third-world countries the right to kill beasts, these same in-dividuals now passed money into the resident hotels and rest camps whose income made game reserves viable enterprises. On another level, a more cynical level, it seemed to her they had massacred so much of the original wildlife that they reached a point of diminishing returns. Any more killing and the ani-mals they hunted would have died out altogether. Quite a few of them almost did.

As it happened, she went to dinner that Saturday at Gore Emhard's house in a state of some anticipation. Almost all the senior journalists on the paper were there. Hal Barton sat at Emhard's right hand, and there were several deputy editors and assistant editors. She wondered what she was doing in their company.

It was an odd occasion. Sarah Emhard sat at the other end of the long table and spent much of her time making fun of her husband's hunting activities. Emhard — surprisingly to Cynthia — seemed to take the badinage about his penchant for killing animals quite amiably. The evidence of this historic massacre was there for all to see. There were numerous animal heads lining the walls and hallways. Cynthia identified wildebeest, bongo, topi, gemsbok, sable, eland, dik-dik, roan, impala, kudu, and a smattering of predators — hyenas, leopards, cheetahs, lions, tigers — as well as some more exotic ones: striped hyenas, civets, lynxes, pumas. Beautiful creatures had been killed to satisfy the whim of a collector of stuffed heads with staring artificial glass eyes. The animals were mostly, though not all, from Africa — that continent beloved by men with hard-drinking habits and deep virility complexes. Perhaps, given Cynthia's own repugnance for the Hemingway tradition of big game hunting, what interested her most about the animal heads was that they all had more or less the same expression. By accident or otherwise, the glass eyes had somehow caught precisely the emotion that Cynthia suspected the animals felt as the high velocity bullet from a hunter's rifle entered the softer, more delicate tissue of their bodies — a kind of bemused astonishment, amounting to outright incomprehension, that anyone could be so stupid as to kill a beautiful, living, fluent creature in order to mount a stuffed head on a wall.

Apart from the parade of stuffed animals and the expected male badinage between Emhard and his male friends, leavened by a little teasing from Emhard's wife, the evening passed without incident. Cynthia wondered why Emhard had even bothered to include her. Perhaps his invitation was nothing more than the behavioural equivalent of the elephant toe ashtray: she had been asked to witness something of which he knew she would heartily disapprove.

So when she knocked on the iroko hardwood door of Gore Emhard's office the following Sunday afternoon (they worked Sundays to prepare the Monday paper), she knew it was business as usual. The glimpse of his intimate home life had only underlined the differences between them. She had resigned herself to the fact that Emhard was a man whose interior processes she would never fully understand.

Hearing his gruff call, she entered the inner sanctum and saw the familiar framed photographs of the great hunter standing beside the carcasses of magnificent slain animals. She felt, as she always did, that she had truly entered the domain of an authentic male chauvinist, a genuine museum piece, a kind of living fossil of an old-fashioned male. He was so extreme he seemed almost a parody — though in Los Angeles practically everything was a parody of something or someone; you were nervous only until you worked out what or who the original was. Could a man parody maleness in the same way that a male drag artist parodied women?

It was this element of self-consciousness that caused Cynthia to exercise caution in her final assessment of Emhard. Parody was very close to humour, if not exactly the same thing, and humour itself was the indication of intelligence, maybe even of humanity — a dangerous thing for a feminist to ascribe to a male, of any species. It was as if Emhard too knew he were playing a role, a role constructed for him out of tradition, a tradition of being reared by an aristocratic father and a mother who played bridge and went to parties and left him in the hands of a series of nurses, a tradition of the lonely single child who is given into the hands of others because his parents have too many concerns of their own to bother with the secondary one of raising their offspring. He had emerged out of private school, then Yale, and the first part of a career in a law firm before journalism finally took hold of him and compelled him into the arcane world of newspapers.

But his humour (if you could call it that) was a two-edged sword. He had constructed a role for her too — the image of an extreme feminist that was the inverse of the role she had constructed for him. Curiously, in his presence she found herself playing up to this role, as though to balance his own. They approached each other like stage personalities, each trying to live up to the monstrous image created by the other. In its outer aspects at least, it was just another case of Los Angeles gothic.

31

There was another press release from Dr Holocenter on her desk a few days later, printed on LAPD notepaper and signed by the chief psychiatric adviser.

To the members of the press and public:

It is our duty to inform you that there has been yet another vicious attack by the so-called "City Hall" rapist. The victim, whose identity has been concealed for her own safety, is a young woman who has been subjected to the now familiar pattern of an assault by a dangerous obsessive. The victim reported that during her ordeal the attacker repeated over and over again that he would like to meet F-woman.

We can only emphasise the most obvious deductions, drawn from the closest possible analysis of this case, that the motivation of the offender is clearly to meet the vigilante. He perceives the rapes as simply means to that end.

Accordingly, we appeal to F-woman to give herself up. It is our considered opinion, based on the most careful psychiatric analysis, that by so doing she will remove the temptation to the City Hall rapist to meet her at large. By placing herself in custody, F-woman will remove all possibility of the meeting which he desires. This in turn will encourage him to desist in his attacks on innocent victims.

We believe that if F-woman is true to her supposed calling, of attempting to reduce the number of rapes on women, she will have little choice other than to do as we suggest.

As chief psychiatric adviser of LAPD, I would like to add my personal appeal to F-woman to cease her attacks on suspected rapists and to give herself up to the due processes of justice.

Dr James Holocenter, Chief Psychiatric Adviser, LAPD.

"What do you think of that?" Emhard said.

Cynthia swallowed. "It seems to me he's exploiting this particular case to get at Fuckwoman. He hasn't been able to capture her, so he's using this thing to gain leverage."

"Goddamn, Cynthia. We're talking about rape here. We're talking about real harm to women, not some abstract theory of motivation about the chief psychiatric adviser. Isn't that what we should keep in mind?"

"There's no guarantee that if she gave herself up, the City Hall rapist would stop his attacks. For all we know he rapes women because that's the way he is, and he uses his obsession with Fuckwoman as a *post facto* rationalisation."

"It seems to me there are some mighty cold calculations

going on here. Don't you think that even on the off-chance that it might stop, Fuckwoman should hand herself in? If she's so concerned about women's safety against rapists... Isn't this exactly how she should put her money where her mouth is?"

"Is that what you'd like me to write, Gore?" Cynthia said. "A piece which sets out to encourage Fuck-woman to give herself up? You want to me act as a mouthpiece for Holocenter?"

"If I were doing it," Emhard said, "that's the line I'd take."

"Do I have any independence here?"

"Well, of course you do."

"How long do I have?"

"We have missed this evening's edition. So I want it ready for tomorrow."

"OK, I'm going to take you at your word." She picked up her bag and nodded to Emhard out of brisk courtesy, then moved out.

There was something else that annoyed her about the press release, that caused her to lie awake in her small apartment, staring at the ceiling, with the evening flights from LAX rising upwards through the sky beyond the window sill. What was Holocenter's motivation? He'd surely know that his exploitation of the City Hall rapist case to encourage her to give herself up was useless. He'd know that she'd have enough sense to reason the rapist was using her as vindication — no sane man would rape women to obtain a meeting, not unless he was inclined to rape women anyway. So what were Holocenter's motives in constantly pressing that line? Was he just trying to provoke her, to keep her off balance, hoping she'd make a slip? Possibly. If so, it seemed a lot of effort on a fairly slender and hypothetical outcome.

She could not entirely disband the uneasiness that he was compelling her to behave in a certain manner. If she would not give herself up in response to a blatant piece of exploitation, what were the alternatives? To avoid the matter entirely? Even though she knew Holocenter's reasoning was suspect, the constant taunting still bugged her. The best solution of all was to capture the rapist herself — assuming that was possible, given the complete absence of any information on him. At the very least that would eliminate Holocenter's opportunity to continue to exploit the case, and it would reinforce the impression that the LAPD weren't capable of bringing major serial rapists to book. In the meantime, she'd counter Holocenter's propaganda with some counter-statements of her own.

Perhaps in the event she concentrated too closely on the contents of her article to predict Emhard's reaction. Or perhaps she knew, at least subconsciously, what his response might be. Whatever the precise cause, the effect was the same — the following morning Emhard hit the roof.

32

"God in hell, Cynthia, you expect me to print this?"

"Why not?" Cynthia asked. "It's true."

Emhard said, "Quote: *Police psychiatrist Dr James Holocenter is clearly in love with his own authority. His use of psychiatric language to establish an* a priori *case against F-woman amounts to an abuse of professional ethics. In his persistent attacks on F-woman's motives, Dr Holocenter has substituted speculation for fact, and dressed up his fanciful theories in the recondite language of professional psychiatric diagnosis.*"

Emhard looked up at her, shook his head, and returned to the text. "Quote: *Dr Holocenter seems to regard F-woman's mere presence as a personal affront. Rather than give further publicity to his persistent and obsessive attacks upon the self-styled vigilante, perhaps it is time we gave our attention to Dr Holocenter's own motives in this matter. Does Dr Holocenter's hostility towards F-woman have anything to do with the fact that LAPD were outwitted for three years by the serial rapist Pablo Cipasso? Does the fact that Larry Delamous was able to rape women over a number of years until apprehended by F-woman constitute a more coherent explanation of LAPD's current manoeuvres? In short, does F-woman represent such a challenge to the authority of the LAPD — and thus to Dr Holocenter's own authority — that he is forced to display his frustration in continuing criticism of her? And finally, is Dr Holocenter perhaps projecting his own frustration with LAPD's performance onto F-woman herself? These questions, though speculative, have no less validity than Dr Holocenter's own tendentious theories about the suspect."*

Emhard looked up and said, "What in God's name is the matter with you? This isn't journalism. This is the pursuit of some kind of personal vendetta. Rewrite the whole thing."

"No," Cynthia said.

Emhard's eyes narrowed.

"What?"

"No. You're asking me to go against what I believe in."

It was the first time she'd really heard Emhard roar. Actually, he reminded her of the MGM lion. His voice appeared to rise from somewhere close to the pit of his stomach and to expand through his ribcage. His head and chest seemed to fill with rage. He shouted, "I'm asking you to write a proper article."

Cynthia waited for the final echoes of his outrage to wash over her. Then she stood up and put on her coat. "Is this what you mean by giving me latitude to write my own work?"

"It means behaving reasonably."

"I see."

Emhard lowered his voice. "Come back here, lady."

Cynthia picked up her bag and walked away.

"You go out that door now," Emhard said, "you don't ever come back."

Cynthia paused at the glass door. At her approach the heavy pane slid back on soundless hinges. For a moment she seemed to be considering her situation. But she knew what she had to do. There were things out there that she had to pursue personally. Without looking back, she stepped forward and through the doorway.

Emhard watched the door slide back and observed her figure striding away, merging with the dark. He heard the final hiss of the door motor. For a while he stood there, watching the empty corridor. He didn't look around at the other journalists. Instead he walked back into his own office and — in an almost monumental calm — he closed the door and ignored both the stunned silence and then the furtive outbreak of whispers in the main newsroom, whispers which appeared out of the atmosphere like the first morning dew.

33

At the Aztec Health Club, Cynthia walked by the kiosk beneath the porticoed entrance. The building behind hovered, huge and hushed.

"Evening, Miss Lelague."

"Evening, Matthew."

The attendant pressed a button and the side-door opened. Cynthia walked through into the cool, damp atmosphere.

The interior of the Health Club was as sepulchral as ever. The night lights burned low in the tiled, empty building.

In the dark spaces of the main hall the swimming pool steamed. She walked down the side of the pool and towards the great sapele wooden doors of the gym.

At the doorway Cynthia halted and looked around.

She could see no sign of Juan in the shadows, no telltale breath. It was silent, in that living resinous calm that seems almost solid. She called out softly, "Juan?" and waited for her echo to return.

There was no answering sound. Behind her she could hear the wavelets of the swimming pool touching the sides. Ahead of her the silence seemed as heavy as water.

Carefully, Cynthia advanced into the room. She took up her position in the centre of the wrestling mat. Before turning, she glanced once more around the obscure peripheries, searching for the trace of feet or toes protruding beneath the weights and other apparatus, the faint husk of warm breath. There was no sign of Juan.

She looked up at the moonlight through the high windows with their alloy frames and glass panes. Pale oblongs of light fell on the boarded pinewood floors. The gym was built in that type of California secular style which hinted at older traditions. To her eye the interior resembled nothing so much as the nave of a church — perhaps an apt metaphor given that an obsession with physical health was the average Angeleno's deepest spiritual concern.

She heard a faint sound, as of a coin being dropped. It seemed to come from the darkest part of the room, where she could see nothing. Maybe Juan had thrown it there to distract her from where he was really hiding. She imagined the coin sailing softly through the air, spinning in its own dream.

Cynthia tensed slightly. If he wanted her to think that was where he was, she would call his bluff. Slowly, she turned away from the direction of the sound. With her back to the main body of the room, she waited for perhaps a full minute.

The running footsteps, when they came, had a precise configuration. Their very regularity seemed part of a dream. She listened to their staccato patter, trying to gauge from sound alone the direction and predisposition of her attacker. If he had run at her from the darkest part of the hall, he would have taken several seconds to reach her. But she realised, too late, that he was attacking from another direction, from behind and to her right. He must have been hiding amongst the closer wall equipment, amongst the knees of the presses and the strange spinal columns of the lifting weights. It was too late to prepare herself. Instead, before she could take counteraction, she was hit with terrible force from the side. With wolfish strength, a figure grappled her onto the mat.

They fought furiously in the obscurity, rolling over and over as first one and then the other gained a temporary hold.

Her attacker gained the ascendancy. His hands closed over her throat. She struggled to break free. Her head was being forced back and she could feel her neck was on the point of dislocation. There seemed no mercy in his hold on her. A deep and primal fear overcame her — of being in the power of someone outside her.

Suddenly she shifted, disconcerted his grip, punched back a fierce blow into her assailant's kidneys.

She heard the expulsion of his breath. She rolled and followed up with three devastating punches to his head and neck. He collapsed on the wrestling mat.

Panting, Cynthia rose into the moonlight falling from the high windows. She stared down at the lifeless figure on the mat. He lay on his front. The thick dark hair lay next to the skin, as sleek as an otter's pelt.

"Oh God," she whispered.

She knelt down and rolled Juan onto his back. He appeared

dead. His eyes were closed, his mouth open. His body had an unnatural limpness. She could not hear his breathing.

Cynthia lay beside him, parallel, staring at the profile of his face. For several moments she studied him.

Juan's eyes opened.

Cynthia said, "You bastard."

Juan did not move, staring at the ceiling contemplatively. He smiled. "You soft on me, Cyncy?"

"Bullshit."

"You can't help it."

"You goddamn creep."

Cynthia stood up and looked down at him, her hands on her hips. He moved his shoulders and flinched, then smiled up at her. "Give me a little while. Those were hard blows."

"Serves you right," Cynthia said.

She turned and walked back through the gym doors and stood on the edge of the pool. The warm, heavy air coiled and rose towards her. She removed her leotard like a faint outer skin and left it at the side of the pool. She looked down at her feet, hooked her toes over the edge, and leaned over the water. For a moment she glanced down at the reflection, at the milky limbs, the triangle of fur.

Juan's feet appeared beside hers at the edge of the pool. He looked at their two reflections briefly but didn't smile. Instead he stared down the length of the pool, gauging the distance to the end. There was something that she had always noticed about him — that he hated to look into another person's eyes. He was like a fox, both furtive and self-contained.

"Ready?" he said.

She nodded.

Their splashes were like twins. Then they were moving in ghostly parallels across the surface. She was a fast and decisive swimmer, but whenever she glanced to the side, his own slim limbs seemed to flicker alongside hers. As she came up to breathe, she could hear the gasp of his own breath, and sense the punch of his arms as he fought to stay with her.

The end wall approached, undulating in the underwater light. She was about to do a racing turn, but instead, as they reached the shallows, she reached out, put her arm around his waist, and lifted him clear of the water onto the side. He rolled several times like a fish over the tiles, then lay on his back, laughing at her anger.

She said, "What were you trying to do back there? Hurt me?"

"No," he said. "Proving a point, maybe."

"What point?"

"Those were people I knew."

"Which people?"

"The ones you attacked out there."

"You knew them personally?"

"We all have relations and cousins."

"So?"

"Those were the people I came from."

The only sound was the steady dripping of condensation on the tiles. She said, "And what's between us now?"

"Nothing bad," Juan said.

He stood up and came back to the side. He reached down, she held his wrists and he lifted her out of the water in one clean movement.

It was the first time for a long time that she had felt naked. He was already excited. In the darkness he rose upwards into her embrace.

Afterwards, they lay on their backs, staring up at the ceiling.

Cynthia said, "I gave up my job this evening."

"You can't go back?"

"No."

"Why not?" Juan asked.

"There are certain things I have to do."

She was aware, almost instinctively, that he would not enquire further. He had a kind of reticence when it came to other people's emotions. She knew he was not the sort of person who would press her for an answer.

After a while he rose and walked through the shadows to the place where he had left his knapsack against the furthest wall. She watched him kneel in profile and undo the buckles and take something out.

He brought back two apples and handed one to her. "Why don't we stay the night?" he said, looking over into the darkness. "No one else here."

"I have to go out."

"You seeing someone?" Juan asked casually.

He turned towards her. It was the first time she had seen that direct, categorical stare. He seemed unafraid and open, and for a moment she had the impression of looking into him. She knew that of all the memories that evening it was what she would take away with her, that this was what she would remember with longing when she thought of him.

Cynthia said, "It's nothing like that."

She glanced over at his face. He seemed locked into himself, poised and quiet. He turned away from her again, and shrugged his shoulders.

They ate their apples in silence, staring out across the surface of the water.

34

She went out into the night. Lights lay on the city precincts like pollen. Planes tilted in the western sky, faint geometric shapes with port or starboard navigation lights rising out of LAX. Above her the Harbour Freeway poured its east-west stream of glowing traffic. She walked under the freeway and past the Sheraton Grand. Almost alone on the sidewalk, she watched the red tail-lights of the passing traffic. At Spring Street she swung left and walked towards the Civic Center.

If you turned away from the bright lights into side-streets you began to move through the familiar territory of hoardings and urban degradation. There were hookers and drunks, but no gangs that she could see. They were present but usually invisible. She turned a corner and the Civic Center buildings rose up monolithic and luminous. She walked parallel with them, then turned a corner onto a path through the park on the south side of City Hall.

She was crossing the park when something caught her eye. A figure of a man moved in the furthest shadows, drifting like a cat. He seemed to disappear into some shrubs and trees. At the end of the path there was no sign of the elusive figure. She looked down another path, then another.

At the furthest point a figure moved across a patch of light into shadow.

Cynthia stood for several seconds, perplexed. Then she heard a woman's scream. It was high-pitched and far off. Before it had ended she was moving forward into the night. It seemed to come from the south-east corner of the park. She ran through a group of laurel bushes and emerged into a small space bounded by low walls. Panting from her efforts, she halted to catch her breath. She looked around. It was an area of mown lawn and trees, with tall palms planted evenly along the street. Moonlight turned the palm leaves silver.

The second scream was nearer than the first, shrill and light. It seemed to come from beyond a set of thick hedges. She had to run parallel for a good seventy or eighty yards before she found a gap and broke through into another area of lawn and small shrubs.

The street lamps were widely spaced. She hunted the darkness between them with her eyes. The silence rolled towards her.

She called out, "Who's there?" and heard her echo shimmer off the sides of the buildings at the edge of the park like light on the edges of a swimming pool.

There was another scream, so near the night itself seemed alive. Perhaps fifty yards away was an area of darkness fringed by trees, in which the light from the streetlamps could not penetrate. She ran towards the deepest shadows.

The scream came again, this time choked and thick and curtailed, from the other side of a high white stone wall. At the bottom of the wall she backed off several steps, then took a sprinting run, vaulted and grabbed one of the coping stones. She hauled herself up and slid her body over the top and fell silently on the other side.

Looking around, she saw she was in an empty quadrangle. Grass floated close. A set of concrete steps moved down to a second lawn, set below the first.

The screaming seemed to have stopped. Concentrating with all her senses, she heard something that sounded like a faint thudding or drubbing sound. She turned into the sound, directly into its hollow reverberations. She could hear the silence now, as heavy as breathing.

Until then she had seen nothing, as though her hearing and her sight had been separated. But now a faint commotion caught her eye. Two figures were struggling in the shadows against a wall.

She broke into a charge. She could hear the bursting of her lungs as the distance narrowed, the rhythm of her feet, the pounding of blood in her head. As she closed with the struggling figures they both split and moved apart casually, like lovers separating.

Cynthia hit the roughcast wall between them, almost winding herself. She turned, leaning against the wall, sucking in air and expelling breath as though she had risen from under water.

The woman on her right was in the uniform of a policewoman. She was fully clothed and seemed totally unharmed. Cynthia stood facing her, motionless. As she watched, the woman reached down towards her waist and carefully and deliberately snapped out a pair of cuffs from her belt. Cynthia turned to look at the man.

He was smartly dressed, straightening his tie. She did not need to see the distinguished mane of white hair, the mandarin face.

"Miss Lelague," Dr Holocenter said. "I hoped we'd meet again." He paused. "You're under arrest."

Between breaths, Cynthia said, "How did you know where to find me?"

"Come now, Miss Lelague," Holocenter said. "I issued a challenge to you about the City Hall rapist. That was, so to speak, my final throw. I knew that you wouldn't be able to resist that temptation."

She could see his lips smile in the low light, and it seemed to her that he smiled like a man giving a tutorial, an academic smile of lofty disdain. "It was a matter of staking out the area, of sending out the appropriate signals, and waiting for you to find us. We set out scouts to watch for your approach. And we drew you into our trap."

She said to herself, *Make him feel superior. Let him believe he caught me against my will.*

Cynthia said, "Who was your soprano? I have to congratulate her."

She turned towards the policewoman, who was edging towards her crabwise now, using the wall to block Cynthia's escape. She could see she was a burly woman, her close-cropped blonde hair showing beneath her cap.

There was a sound from the shadows where the quadrangle wall made a right angle. She could see the shapes of dozens of policemen were advancing out the shadows towards her.

Her own body was preparing itself to fight, crouching back into herself. Her intention must have communicated itself, because Dr Holocenter said, "Like to take issue, Miss Lelague? Want to fight the whole police force?"

She knew he was trying to tempt her, that if she were to show violence at this stage it would increase his hold over her. But she knew too that this was the final stage in the drama, that in some indefinable sense she had willed this outcome as much as he did. She understood too that, for purposes of record, she must not go down without a fight.

When she charged him, she crossed the distance between them so fast that even he was taken by surprise. She hit him carefully and hard with the heel of her right hand, between his left cheekbone and the bridge of his left eye. It wasn't profound enough to do damage, but she felt the discharge of it into her shoulder. The force of the blow knocked him backwards. In the same movement, she managed to hook her right leg behind him, push hard against his chest with both hands, and send him backwards over her leg and down. Because of his height, he fell heavily and in slow motion. She fell with him, intending to wind him with her weight. They hit the ground together and she felt the breath go out of him. She managed to get her hands to his throat and her thumbs on his windpipe before a police baton descended on the back of her head.

35

In the foyer of City Hall the main doors flew open and a trolley carrying the figure of Cynthia Lelague came driving into view, with a heavy guard of four policemen. She was in a straitjacket, strapped down to the trolley. It was a classic moment of official power designed, at some subconscious level, to intimidate and impress. The four troopers who pushed the trolley stared ahead in their dark glasses. They had blue jackets with epaulettes and peaked caps. In their dark leather belts were mace canisters, handcuffs, fighting sticks. They looked like four Sylvester Stallones. Their boots hit the polished marble floor like a perfectly drilled squad. The sound ate up the air.

That was the image that struck the press waiting in the foyer of City Hall. A hundred shutters were pressed. Photographic flashes reflected off the polished surfaces of the marble. That image remained part of the iconography of Cynthia Lelague's capture, another instance of pure Los Angeles gothic.

At the head of the convoy a fifth police trooper shouted, "Make way! Make way there!" at the ranks of photographers and journalists who crowded the passageways. The photographers swung back and the convoy entered the main hall, pushed aside a further crowd of reporters, veered right in co-ordinated precision and went through another set of swing doors. Two officers of unusual girth swung into the wake of the departing convoy and prevented the press from following the trolley into the interior of City Hall.

Moving toward the LAPD subsection offices that were installed there on the ground floor of the building, the convoy turned down a corridor in sudden silence. Only the faint squeal of the wheels and the slightest creak of the leather belts and holsters of the troopers could be heard over the regular striking of boots on the polished floors. Immured in her confinement, the patient seemed to be trying to shout or say something behind her gag. Her limbs flexed and struggled. But these spasms of a muted life merely served to emphasise the pace and implacable momentum of the central event. She, who had taunted the LAPD and the city authorities, was now their prisoner, and this was simply the formal expression of that inalienable fact.

The LAPD facilities in the City Hall were largely administration and liaison, but they also kept several single cells there for overnight stays. The trolley and its entourage entered the police subsection and pushed through open prison bar doors into the waiting cell. Two officers were detailed to stand guard over the patient. Then the cell doors were pulled shut.

Cynthia looked up and saw Dr Holocenter above her.

He wore a white lab coat and white rubber gloves. In his

right hand he held a syringe with a long needle from whose end he was squeezing a few drops to eliminate air bubbles. The procedure seemed to engross him. Now that he held control over her, he appeared both deliberate and detached. She noticed a discoloration on his left cheekbone where she had struck him, but his attitude towards her seemed to be unruffled and calm. While she was regaining consciousness after her arrest, she had been put in a green surgical gown and strapped down to the stretcher. She could not use her arms or legs. She could move her head slightly and she looked down at the restraints holding her body to the stretcher.

Dr Holocenter approached. He bared her shoulder for the needle and rubbed the skin with a little pad of disinfectant. He put the pad of disinfectant in the dish. The needle was all that she was aware of in the room. She felt the buzz of its hot tip. They were trying to penetrate her mind, and she knew she had to bear it.

"This won't hurt, Miss Lelague," Dr Holocenter said. "It's for your own benefit."

Cynthia screamed behind her gag. At some level she knew that what he intended was not for her benefit, but perhaps more broadly and philosophically in pursuit of his view of the public benefit, or perhaps even some hidden agenda of which he himself was not aware. Perhaps, in that moment of instinct and fear, she saw that universal figure who is there to enforce the particular conformism of society upon the lawless and outcast, even perhaps the isolated and crazy figure of the independent artist. Whatever may have passed through her mind at that heated moment as the needle went in, a rich darkness filled in and surrounded it. She started to float away.

36

In the offices of the *Angel Times*, Gore Emhard knocked on the outer door of the locked main office. A faint shape resembling the night editor appeared on the other side of the reinforced frosted glass. The locks were turned and the door opened with a faint flush of cold air.

"It's three in the morning," Emhard said. "Jesus, Hal, what's the meaning of this?"

Hal Barton said, "You always told me to call you if something big occurred."

They walked through to the main office. A single television monitor was switched on.

"So what's happened, Hal?" Emhard asked. "President's been shot, the Middle East has blown up? What the hell has made you call me out?"

In patient and subdued silence, Barton turned up the volume of the nearest screen. The announcer said, *"In a special sting operation carried out this evening, LAPD have trapped and captured* the famous, or perhaps infamous, vigilante known as F-woman."

"Serves the bitch right," Emhard said. "There are too many crazies running around."

"*We can reveal that F-woman has been identified as Cynthia Lelague, a reporter for the* Angel Times.*"*

Gore Emhard's face froze. He swallowed. Hal Barton, standing beside him, observed the long, convulsive movement of his Adam's apple. At that moment Barton thought maybe Emhard was going to quote something from Apuleus or Catullus, something a little lofty and hard-bitten, about the follies of the world. But after a while Emhard breathed out, "Fuck me."

"That's just what I said," Barton replied. "Exactly the words I used, in fact, when I heard the earlier broadcast."

Emhard sank slowly into his chair. It seemed to take some time while his long form took up the chair's declensions and declivities.

Hal Barton said tenderly, "Want me to get you anything, Gore? I keep a little whisky somewhere."

Emhard didn't seem to hear the question. He whispered to himself, "Goddamn."

"Like you say, Gore," Hal Barton said. "We have to keep a sense of perspective here. I didn't know Cynthia like you did — she kinda kept to herself — but I guess it always has to be someone."

Emhard looked up at the ceiling. He said, "Sweet Jesus."

Barton was keeping an eye on the screen. "Something's happening."

The announcer began, "*An emergency press conference has been called at police headquarters. Our chief reporter, Myron Overbear, is there now. Myron, what's going on?"*

Myron Overbear said. "*Thanks, Jill. I'm here in the auditorium of the police headquarters building, where Dr James Holocenter, chief psychiatric adviser to LAPD, is set to give a briefing. The word is that Dr Holocenter masterminded the operation to catch F-woman, who we now know has been identified as Cynthia Lelague, a reporter with the* Angel Times. *I understand the capture of F-woman is important enough even to have got Mayor Dally out of bed. Here come the Mayor and Dr Holocenter now.*"

There was a flurry of movement as a side-door opened and the short, burly figure of Mayor Dally moved towards the stage, followed by the almost absurdly taller Dr Holocenter. Mayor Dally stepped up and took the rostrum.

"*Ladies and gentleman of the press. I'm glad that you have been able to gather here so quickly. Having been the subject of so much criticism at LAPD, it is something of a pleasure to be able to announce that after a carefully organised sting operation, our officers have captured the notorious and dangerously violent vigilante known as F-woman, who can now be brought to trial for her various assaults upon members of the male population in our city.*" He paused. "*I want to quote a great and venerated lawyer of the past, Judge Boyle, on the subject of the relation of the law to the individual citizen. 'Be ye ever so high, the law is above you.'*

"*This is an important time, not only for us but for the state of the law in general. The woman who styled herself as F-woman thought she could get away with numerous assaults upon suspected rapists who themselves were fully entitled to be tried by the due process of law. She believed she was above the law. She thought she could act as God, and ignore those rights which are fundamental to free citizens in our great republic. And so she not only mounted an* attack on men who were not yet proven guilty by due process, but by so doing she assaulted those very processes and institutions which we Americans hold dear."

"Hell," Emhard said. "I hate it when politicians start to get pompous."

Mayor Dally paused again. *"The fact is, two wrongs do not make a right. Now, I'm going to hand over to senior LAPD psychiatric adviser Dr James Holocenter, who has masterminded the trapping of F-woman."*

Mayor Dally sat down as Dr Holocenter stood up and took the rostrum.

Dr Holocenter said, *"I'd like to thank Mayor Dally for introducing me so that I can give some account of the complex and well-organised police operation which resulted in the final entrapment of F-woman."* He glanced around him at the assembled reporters. The flashlights picked up his angular features. *"After a detailed analysis of F-woman's psychotic personality, we set out to entice her by appealing to her vanity. We actually constructed the entire notion of the City Hall rapist, who would act as a decoy for her illegal activities."*

At that stage there was the first sign of a murmur among the pressmen present. Myron Overbear, who seemed to be some kind of unofficial spokesman for the fourth estate, called out, *"Are you saying, Dr Holocenter, that the City Hall rapist was a complete fiction created by the LAPD?"*

Dr Holocenter would not be hurried or harried. He waited until the hubbub had died down again before speaking:

"That is wholly correct. To enable us to proceed with our plan, we required a decoy that we effectively controlled. So we created

the fiction of the City Hall rapist in order to attract F-woman to the scene. As you now know, I am able to confirm that the operation has proved entirely successful."

There was a hush in the auditorium, a sound like dry leaves rustling as the details were set down simultaneously on dozens of notepads. Out of the silence, Myron Overbear said, *"Hold on a minute, Dr Holocenter. Are you saying you were prepared to frighten to death half the women in the Civic Center area with this fictional being called the City Hall rapist — just so you could bring F-woman to book?"*

"Yes, sir. We decided to take that risk. I believe strong measures were called for. We arranged to give out a set of press announcements which were carefully calibrated to attract F-woman to the area, where we could set our trap. As I say, the operation was entirely successful in achieving its end. We naturally apologise for any fear or distress caused, but on balance we thought it even more important to bring this major criminal to justice."

Over the hubbub, Myron Overbear said, *"Just one more question, Dr Holocenter. Aren't you pre-judging F-woman before she gets a trial?"*

"No, I don't believe so. I will accept the verdict of that trial unequivocally. The important point is, we have taken every necessary step to catch the suspect and bring her to trial so that she can be subject to the due processes of justice."

Myron Overbear maybe got a little hot under the collar at this point. Certainly he seemed to be sweating slightly in the spotlights that had been hastily assembled for the press conference. He looked a little flushed, just like a big-time reporter on the track of a salient truth. *"Dr Holocenter, wasn't F-woman's greatest crime that she showed up the inadequacy of the police department in catching rapists at large?"*

"Sir," Dr Holocenter said, *"that is a piece of rhetoric which is unworthy of such a distinguished commentator as yourself. The suspect is a psychotic who was a danger to the citizens of this country. After an intensive police effort, we have captured her so that justice may now take place. You have been kind enough to criticise my own role in this matter. Perhaps I could take a leaf out of your own book and suggest to you that I believe you should be grateful for what we have achieved on behalf of those citizens you purport to represent."*

Uproar erupted amongst the press gallery.

Gore Emhard looked over towards Hal Barton. "I know Cynthia was a trifle eccentric," he said. "I mean, no woman of normal character could fail to be charmed by my bison's penis pencil-holder. But a dangerous psychotic? Does that strike you as an accurate depiction of her character?"

Hal Barton said, "That bison's penis pencil-holder excepted, I am not so sure that it does."

On the monitor, Dr Holocenter stood down and Mayor Dally stepped up again.

"Ladies and gentlemen. Many of us have been summoned here out of our warm beds and, given the importance of the occasion, perhaps some of us are a little excitable. Speaking on behalf of LAPD and the City Authorities, I am very proud indeed we have brought to book a dangerous vigilante. I believe, when we all have time to reflect on these matters in the sober light of day, the basic principles will become clear. In a law-abiding society, there is no room for people who think they are above the law. I

want to thank you all for gathering here to hear this important announcement."

At that point Mayor Dally stepped down from the rostrum. He and Dr Holocenter walked back and out of the side-door.

The announcer said, *"Well, Myron, what do you make of that?"*

"Well, Jill, you heard me attempt to articulate what I think is a legitimate doubt amongst many members of the press. A suspicion remains that the Mayor and LAPD have been less interested in catching rapists than in silencing F-woman, because she has shown them up."

"Thank you, Myron. That is the end of our early morning emergency broadcast. We now return to the normal programme schedule."

Hal Barton switched off the set.

With the television switched off, the empty newsroom had taken on a vertiginous calm. It was like the deck of a submarine when the crew is sleeping.

Emhard turned towards Barton and said softly, "Hal, who would have thought our quiet, introverted, infinitely patient Celia Lelague, who could tolerate even you and me, was Fuck-woman?"

"This has really got to you, hasn't it, Gore?"

"You think you know other people just like you think you know yourself," Emhard said. "Except you find you didn't know them at all. And then, maybe you start to doubt whether you even know your own mind."

Hal Barton let that one rest for a few moments. "It's one hell of a strange world, Gore. It surely is."

37

Cynthia lay motionless on her stretcher. She woke up and looked around the cell.

Dr Holocenter's face was above her. He was preparing her for the now familiar syringe.

The needle went into her arm. Not long afterwards Cynthia was being helped along the corridors by two large female warders. She felt groggy and tired. Her hands were tied by handcuffs and her legs seemed like water.

She was manoeuvred down several flights of stairs, into the depths of the building's basement. The green-painted corridor appeared to move away in front of her. She entered a further cell in which there were various items of instrumentation and equipment. The two female warders handcuffed her to a metal chair that was in turn anchored to the floor by heavy bolts.

Dr Holocenter must have entered the room shortly afterwards. She felt his presence like a shaft of cold air. She sensed the deference of the warders too, the odd, sliding recognition of animals moving round the edges of the room when their master has appeared.

Dr Holocenter pulled up one of the metal chairs and sat down opposite her. He considered her with the same concentrated calm of her first interview. After a while he nodded slightly. The two warders left the room as though in acknowledgement of intimacy.

Perhaps it was then she knew that he was hunting something in her, he was looking for some part of herself that would reveal itself to him. She did not know what this was, just as an actress might not know precisely what her director wants from her in her performance.

He reached forward and, for the first time since her capture, her gag was taken off.

Cynthia said, "I have a statutory right to speak to my lawyer."

He nodded, not in agreement, but to himself, in recognition of her state. Then he began, almost patiently, to explain her position.

"When we first met, and you challenged me to arrest you, you were a free citizen with certain rights under our Constitution. We went to a great deal of trouble to set up our trap for you. It had a specific purpose — to bring you under our jurisdiction. Perhaps you assisted us, unwittingly, in acting with extreme violence while resisting arrest. You see, as a result of your efforts, your status has undergone a transformation. I don't think you quite realise the extent of that transformation."

She could see more closely the damage she had done when she had hit him. There was a substantial bruise around his left eye, a discoloration beneath the skin to the bridge of his nose which flowed from his nose across his cheek and over his left cheekbone. There were two marks on his throat, two parallel bruises, set close together, where her thumbs had dug into his windpipe. She examined each of the marks carefully, attempting to assess whether they had made any impression upon him, whether he had been subject to the notion of what it was to be a victim of violence, rather than its perpetrator. But when she looked into his cold eyes she could see nothing there, no spark of communication between them.

Dr Holocenter was in no hurry, and proceeded at his own speed. "When we last met, you were a reporter from the *Angel Times*. Since then you have, so to speak, taken another identity. You are now a dangerous psychotic with extreme violent tendencies. You attacked and attempted to strangle a police psychiatrist in the process of his lawful duty. We may only speculate what might have happened if matters had been allowed to continue." He smiled a little regretfully. "I hope you will forgive me for being long-winded."

"Everyone has rights," Cynthia said. "Even psychotics have the vote."

"Apart from a rabble who support you, Miss Lelague, because they are predisposed against legitimate authority, I do not think you have a friend in the world." He didn't smile this time. "Even your family have made no effort to contact us. As things stand, I believe we are able to do whatever we believe is necessary."

Cynthia sensed the drugs had drained her. She felt dry, as empty as a husk.

"As your psychiatrist and guardian," Dr Holocenter continued. "I have permitted you one visit. Your former editor, Mr Gore Emhard, phoned me this morning to congratulate me on capturing you. He was obviously shaken by the fact that you could so easily assume two identities. I was able to reassure him that dangerous psychotics are often able to assume a sane appearance for a long time. But in due course the inner character will show itself."

She didn't say anything, but she wondered at the strange transfiguration of language. She was exactly the same person he had addressed at the first interview. She was the same person whom he had described as admirable, focused, sane, even ironic. Now the terms were different — "insane", "dangerous", "psychotic". It was as if he believed language itself could transform identity. She wondered which of them was actually engaged in creating fictional identities — he or she.

Dr Holocenter said, "Mr Emhard is coming over here in a short while to identify you directly as Miss Cynthia Lelague, former reporter of the *Angel Times*. Once he has identified you, we will transfer you to the special psychiatric award for the criminally insane at Hopkins Penitentiary. I have obtained Federal authority to conduct a series of tests to determine the full nature of your psychosis. When that is completed I have further authority, once our conclusions have been drawn, to apply if necessary a full abreaction therapy and chemical programme to cure you of your dysfunction."

One of the warders knocked on the cell door, entered and whispered in Dr Holocenter's ear. He nodded and said, "Please replace her gag, Miss Otisbeam. We don't want her to create some kind of a scene in front of our visitor."

Cynthia struggled, but the warder was insistent. It occurred to her while she moved her head backwards and forwards to avoid the gag, that authority exacted a self-fulfilling prophecy. It imposed restrictive conditions upon you, and if you resisted them, you were clearly dangerous and in need of further restriction. She knew that if authority chose, there was no end to the cycle of resistance and restriction. It was clear that the amiable female warder took her resistance as evidence of her psychosis. When the gag was installed, Dr Holocenter said, "All right. Let him in."

She had never really seen Gore Emhard out of his office or his home before — off his own habitual territory, so to speak. Now that he appeared in front of her in such unusual circumstances, he seemed a different man. He had donned with his light suit a slightly wary and supercilious elegance. His spare frame imposed clean lines upon the cloth. He could have been a museum curator. He glanced at Cynthia, trussed-up like a chicken, with a certain worldly objectivity.

"My goodness," he said in his southern drawl.

"Glad you could join us, Mr Emhard," Dr Holocenter said. "I appreciate your making the journey."

It seemed to Cynthia, immobilised behind her gag, that Holocenter and Emhard might have been brothers. They were of similar height, both somewhat spare. Each of them was possessed of an air of authority which appeared simultaneously to focus on her and exclude her.

"Would you care to sit down?" Emhard asked

"Thank you."

Emhard sat down in front of the trolley on which Cynthia lay.

Dr Holocenter said, "Now, Mr Emhard, if you would take a close look at the subject in order to identify her, I would be grateful. Please take your time."

Emhard appeared to examine Cynthia closely.

"To the best of your knowledge," Dr Holocenter said, "is the person you see before you Cynthia Alouette Assumpta Lelague, former reporter of the *Angel Times*?"

Emhard said softly, *"Alouette Assumpta.* Wow, Cynthia. You never told me that."

Cynthia would have liked to say something in reply, preferably something brisk and rude. But it occurred to her that Emhard might be joking for Holocenter's sake, rather than her own, and that beneath this show of levity he had his own interests and concerns. He was watching her carefully now, looking directly into her eyes. Those eyes were hunting, searching out something. She knew that he was trying to assess someone who had worked closely with him all this time.

While he examined her, she considered what lay behind that look. Was Emhard wondering how she had managed to fool him? Or perhaps he was considering how he could have trusted someone who went out at night and supposedly assaulted people for obscure, feminist motives he could not begin to understand. She wondered whether this was how Patty Hearst's relations must have regarded her when she was finally apprehended — as someone they knew, but at the same time did not know.

Dr Holocenter said, a little more sternly, "Mr Emhard?"

"Yes indeed," Emhard said. "This is Cynthia Lelague, Dr Holocenter. Am I glad to see her so…confined. You see I didn't know that living right next to me, sharing my office day after day, hiding her full nature from me, was such a dangerous criminal."

"No one knows his neighbour entirely, Mr Emhard."

"I am not my brother's keeper," Emhard said softly, almost to himself. "Is that what you're saying, Dr Holocenter?"

"I don't believe I fully catch your meaning."

"What happens to her now, Doctor?" Emhard asked. "I mean, she looks mighty dangerous."

"We will be taking her to Hopkins Penitentiary, to the special department for the criminally insane. After careful analysis, the likelihood is that she will be placed on a full course of chemical and abreaction therapy."

"This is, ah, before she's been tried?"

You would have thought Emhard was commenting on the weather. He continued all the time to look directly into Cynthia's eyes. She had never seen that calm, searching stare before. It reminded her a little of that open stare of Juan a few nights before. It occurred to her that only in extreme circumstances could people look one another directly in the eye without embarrassment.

"Are you surprised at that, Mr Emhard?"

Emhard seemed to make and effort to remove himself from his own thoughts, though he still didn't take his eyes off Cynthia. "Well, now that you come to mention it, I am a little surprised. I thought that the purpose of the trial was to establish her guilt. If I understand you rightly, you seem to be assuming her guilt and are already proceeding on that basis to punish her."

"You're mistaken about that, Mr Emhard. Whether someone is insane or otherwise is not established by a court, but by a senior psychiatrist following specific agreed procedures of diagnosis. Miss Lelague demonstrated a manic frenzy in attacking me, which was directly witnessed by more than thirty detectives and police officers. Accordingly, I have the authority to confine her and apply appropriate treatment. That is an entirely separate matter from the legal process, which will be followed meticulously."

"I see," Emhard said. "And what course of therapy are you intending to apply?"

"The likelihood is that Miss Lelague will be treated with what we call the IS2 programme."

"Independently of any trial?"

"Independently of any trial."

"Well, Dr Holocenter. It is been something of a pleasure to meet you at last. I shall return to my newspaper to write up a report of what I have witnessed."

"I trust you will, Mr Emhard."

Emhard seemed to disengage his concentration only with an effort of will. He stood up and shook hands carefully with Dr. Holocenter.

Cynthia watched Emhard as he turned away towards the door. She was hoping he would turn and glance back at her, as relatives or friends did — that final gesture of parting which meant something more than mere words, a sign that she was not alone, that whatever he might think of her, she was at least in his thoughts.

Dr Holocenter said, "Miss Otisbeam, would you be so kind as to accompany Mr Emhard to the main door of the building?"

Emhard walked through the cell doors out into the corridor. When he was out of sight of Dr Holocenter, Emhard stopped, patted his pockets, as though he had lost his glasses. He found them and put them on. And then, unexpectedly, he casually turned towards Cynthia and looked at her through the open door for perhaps several full seconds, as though fixing her image directly in his mind. She thought — though she could not be certain — that he gave a single nod, hardly more than the faintest inflection of his head, before he turned away and followed Miss Otisbeam's substantial frame down the long corridor.

38

In the offices of the *Angel Times*, Emhard sat at his desk, tapping away at his computer.

Hal Barton knocked on the door and entered, closing the door behind him.

"How you doing, Gore?"

"Just finishing my editorial. What you got for me, Hal?"

"Something that might interest you. You asked an old reporter to dig away. I've been going through records, finding what I can on the net."

Barton put down on the desk several pages of close typescript.

"I went through every reference I could on Dr James Holocenter, senior police psychiatrist. He's been at LAPD for sixteen years. Before that the trail went cold. Couldn't find any records. Until I got this."

"Read it to me, Hal."

"Item in the *Utah Enquirer*. A programme was carried out on the chemical treatment of prisoners judged to be criminally insane in the special hospital department of the penitentiary. Programme was run by a Dr James Holocenter."

Emhard stopped typing. "What else does it say?"

"Programme was discontinued after three years."

"Say why?"

"Says here, 'Effects on prisoners of the intensive chemical treatment included a pattern of long-term docility, but there were some doubts about permanent effects after long-term treatment. Programme discontinued pending further investigation of said chemicals.'"

"Anything else?"

"No. But I assume Dr James Holocenter was out of a job."

"Any sign of subsequent investigation?"

"No. Approximately three months later Dr Holocenter applied for the job of police psychiatrist with LAPD, no doubt with excellent references."

"Any name given to the programme?"

"What programme?"

"The programme of chemical application to criminally insane prisoners."

"Let me see now," Barton said. He moved through the three pages of text, running his figure down the margins. "Wait a moment. Here it is. Says here it was designated the "Lockdown" chemical programme. Programme was designed to render certain dangerous individuals permanently docile and tractable. Programme has been discontinued pending further evidence."

Emhard turned to face Barton. His face had gone white, and

his voice took on a certain coldness. He said, "We have to find a way of getting Cynthia out."

"Gore, you OK?"

"Sure I'm OK. Far as I can see, he's intending to put the same programme into effect against her shortly. May have started already. Tell me one more thing, Hal. They mention the chemicals used in that programme?"

"Only one they mention is codenamed Y372. Made a note of it. It rang a bell so I put it in a search engine and found that was the chemical used by the former Soviet psychiatrists when they wanted to destroy the resistance of dissidents and other people who were proving uncomfortable to the state."

Emhard was about to question Barton further when there was a knock on the door. Emhard shouted, "Who is it?"

"Come to collect a parcel, sir."

"OK, come in."

The door opened. Emhard looked at the young man standing in the frame. He had black leather motorcycle boots, faded jeans, a kind of short-sleeved denim overshirt which displayed his bare tattooed arms, a Mohican haircut and a brass ring through his nose. The haircut in particular seemed to attract Emhard's attention. Technical virtuosity of any kind absorbed him. He looked with fascination at the way the roots of the hair turned from a deep aquamarine blue into a violent violet, and then climaxed in a shimmering chemical yellow, like the last explosion of fireworks on a dark night.

"Jesus," Emhard said.

The young man was perhaps not wholly unused to contemplation of his coiffure.

"You wanted me to deliver a parcel, sir?" he reminded Emhard.

Emhard emerged from his consideration.

"Sure," Emhard said, though he allowed himself to consider the finery of the hair a little longer. There were a number of signs recently that contrived to persuade Emhard he belonged to an older, different world, and the young man's hair was just one of them.

Emhard picked up a wrapped parcel from his desk and handed it over.

"That'll be twenty dollars fifty."

Emhard reached into his pocket for some notes and change.

"You sending something to a girlfriend, Gore?" Hal Barton asked.

"Sending something to a friend, Hal, that might just give her some heart."

The courier took the money, nodded, and left. As he turned down the corridor his hair gave off an electric shimmer that seemed to hang in the afternoon light.

39

Two female warders were standing guard outside the doors of the prison cell when a courier approached down the corridor.

"Parcel for Miss Cynthia Lelague. Will you sign for it?"

One of the warders applied her signature. The other took up her mobile telephone and spoke into it.

"Dr Holocenter. We are in receipt of a parcel for the prisoner. I guess you might want to vet it yourself." She paused. "Yes, sir, we'll hold it over for you."

Dr Holocenter arrived not long afterwards. The door was opened and he walked through and, taking no notice of the warders, looked at his patient directly. She was still gagged and she could only stare back.

The warder handed the parcel to him. Dr Holocenter examined the outer wrappings, then held it up to Cynthia's face.

"You expecting a parcel, Miss Lelague?"

Cynthia shook her head.

"Well, in that case, it's probably from a crank. Accordingly, for your own safety, I'm going to open it right here under the witness of the warder."

He proceeded to open the parcel, and studied the object carefully.

"It's a pencil-holder, covered in — let me see, now, if I'm not mistaken — the penile sheath of a large American ruminant."

Dr Holocenter's mobile phone bleeped. He pulled the phone out of his pocket.

"Holocenter. Yes, hello, Mayor. They printed what? I'll come over right away."

Dr Holocenter handed the pencil-holder to one of the prison warders.

"It seems relatively harmless, though somewhat bizarre. I have to go. Would you kindly deal with this, Miss Otisbeam?"

When Dr Holocenter had left the room, Miss Otisbeam regarded the object with evident distaste. She seemed, however, a benign figure, and she leaned down with it towards the patient, holding it in both hands at a little distance from her body.

"You want us to keep this thing for you? You have the right to some personal possessions. Otherwise we can get rid of it."

Cynthia considered the object carefully, but she made no sign.

"Looks like some kind of sick or weird person must have sent it. You want to keep it, or for us to get rid of it?"

Slowly, Cynthia began to nod her head.

The warder was surprised. "You want to keep it?"

Cynthia nodded her head again.

"Well, bless my soul. Guess I'll put it down here on this side-table. You sure, now?"

Cynthia nodded her head again.

40

Mayor Dally sat at his desk, watching a television monitor. He was concentrating so hard that at first he ignored the knock at the door. Then he called out, "Come in, come in."

Dr Holocenter entered.

"Sit down," Dally said. "Take a look at this. I'm due to go on the air in a few minutes."

Dr Holocenter sat down in front of the screen.

The announcer said, *"In a truly astonishing editorial this morning, Gore Emhard, the editor of the* Angel Times, *has accused the LAPD's senior psychiatric adviser, Dr James Holocenter, of authoritarian behaviour in his mistreatment of Cynthia Lelague, the suspect who police believe is the self-styled vigilante otherwise known as F-woman. Mr Emhard is known as a conservative, and even prides himself on being something of a chauvinist. Nevertheless, he has written a moving account of Cynthia Lelague's seven-year stint as journalist at the* Angel Times, *praising her for her patience, her balance, and her commitment to finding the truth. On the basis of his own long-term knowledge of her as a working colleague, he has said Dr Holocenter's characterisation of her as a dangerous psychotic is an example of character assassination which ranks with the abuse of psychiatry in the former Soviet Union."*

In the offices of the *Angel Times* Gore Emhard and Hal Barton were watching the screen.

"Odd what that television does," Barton said. "Seems to flatten everything. Puts it through some kind of universal mincer."

"Our chief reporter, Myron Overbear, has been covering the F-woman case. Myron, how do you see things developing?"

"Well, Jill, this is starting to look like a mighty interesting confrontation. I understand a meeting took place yesterday between Gore Emhard and Dr Holocenter, ostensibly to ensure that the suspect arrested as F-woman was independently identified as Cynthia Lelague. During the course of this interview, Mr Emhard became increasingly concerned that Dr Holocenter himself was showing signs of obsessive behaviour. Mr Emhard points out that in his attempts to capture and treat Miss Lelague, the police psychiatrist has broken a number of the usual rules or guidelines of law-keeping. In particular, his elaborate strategy of 'inventing' the City Hall rapist, and using fake briefings which caused terror to many women in the Civic Center area, is itself cited as evidence of what the Angel Times *calls Dr Holocenter's dangerous over-reaction. According to Emhard, the police psychiatrist clearly placed a higher priority on capturing Cynthia Lelague than on the mental anguish caused to thousands of women by his subterfuge."*

"Is that where we are at present? A stand-off between both parties?"

"Not quite, Jill. In a further development, Mr Emhard claims that Dr Holocenter was employed some years ago as the supervisor of a programme to treat 'criminally insane' prisoners in a Utah penitentiary. The programme was a bona fide government project, but it was abandoned when severe doubts were raised that the medications used were causing long-term effects on the nervous systems of the patients under treatment. When the programme was refused further funding, Dr Holocenter found himself out of a job. He subsequently travelled to Los Angeles, and used his otherwise impeccable qualifications to apply for the position of senior psychiatric adviser to the LAPD."

"Is there any suggestion that he has in any way misled LAPD?"

"No. The research in question was a carefully structured programme which was apparently carried out to the letter. It was decided at the time not to proceed further because of possible risks to the nervous systems of those treated."

"But the programme has been finished and is now closed?"

"No, not exactly. That is another interesting facet of this affair. We learned since then that efforts have been made to reduce the danger of toxic side-effects. Permission has been granted to reopen the experiment using the new chemical combinations on human subjects."

"Do we know whether Dr Holocenter intends to apply this?"

"I'm afraid we don't. There is very little information on the specific nature of the treatment currently being applied to the suspect."

"Thank you, Myron. In a short while we will go to the Mayor's office for an interview with Frank Dally about the latest twists in the saga."

Mayor Dally was sitting at his large desk in the Mayoral office. He said, *"I believe the attack on Dr Holocenter is one of the worst cases of abuses of freedom of the press I have ever seen. Dr Holocenter is a practising psychiatrist of high reputation who has served the LAPD well. I believe it ill behoves a senior journalist of Mr Emhard's distinction and experience to mount a personal attack upon such an eminent practitioner."*

"Isn't that the point the Angel Times *is making, Mayor? Dr Holocenter seems to place serving the LAPD above the due processes of the law."*

"Frankly, Jill," Mayor Dally said. *"I don't know where this interview is leading. If serving the LAPD isn't serving the law, I don't know what is."*

"Goddamn, Hal," Gore Emhard said. "He doesn't know the difference."

"Where does that leave Dr Holocenter?" the announcer asked. *"Are you supporting his behaviour?"*

"Dr Holocenter has my total and unequivocal support."

"What about the claims in the Angel Times *that he is intending to practice a form of therapy that bears a resemblance to that practised by former Soviet psychiatrists on dissidents?"*

"Psychiatry is a complex process," Mayor Dally said. *"I believe it should be left in the hands of the experts. All the evidence is that Dr Holocenter has practised conscientiously within the official guidelines pertaining at the time. Perhaps you would permit me to ask a question here. Since when is Mr Gore Emhard an authority on psychiatric practice?"*

"Doesn't it say something about those guidelines that an earlier programme, apparently using the same chemicals as the Soviet

psychiatrists, had to be abandoned because of possible damage to the nervous systems of the patients involved?"

"What point are you making?" Mayor Dally asked.

"I am making the point that the official guidelines are not always perfect."

"The official guidelines are the very best that can be set out at the time and in the prevailing state of knowledge. If I may make a point, the crucial difference between our system and the former Soviet system is that when there are clear signs the guidelines are not working, we have the freedom to adjust them."

"And what response do you have to the rumours that Cynthia Lelague is shortly to be transported to a hospital for the criminally insane and treated there before she has been bought to trial?"

"There is a vigilante element in the community who appear only too keen to take the law into their own hands," Mayor Dally said. "For her own protection, I shall be giving my full support and personal authorisation for Cynthia Lelague's removal to an institution where she has greater protection."

"To a hospital for the criminally insane?"

"To wherever we feel is necessary to protect her."

"Hal," Emhard said. "I'm getting just a little tired of all this pontificating. How about you?"

"I am too, Gore."

A telephonist appeared at the door. "I know you didn't want to be disturbed, Mr Emhard, but there's an urgent call for you."

"Who from?"

"The call is from LAPD. He wouldn't give his name. Said it was important."

"OK, put him through."

The telephonist returned to her desk. The phone trilled.

"Who is that?" Emhard said.

At the other end of the line, Ed Stevens said, "Mr Emhard, I just wanted to say that I thought your editorial was telling the truth about Cynthia Lelague. I know her a little bit and your character assessment is something I happen to agree with."

"And who the hell are you?" Emhard said.

"You don't know me, but I think maybe I can help you."

"What do you mean?"

"I'm from LAPD, seconded to the City Hall building to help with guarding the patient. I'm using a payphone at the moment so I can't be identified."

"Why are you phoning me?"

"If you want to gain access to this building, I mean without specific authority, I can leave side-door 6 open for you."

"Is that so?"

"I can pull back the main bolts, but you'll have to break the lock yourself. To get the key I'd have to sign the register, so they'd know who opened it. But I reckon I can ease the bolts without anyone noticing. Once the bolts are eased, the lock will give way if you hit it hard enough."

"You're encouraging me to behave like a common criminal and break into the building? This is a new role for LAPD."

"I'm not encouraging you to do anything, Mr Emhard. I'm supplying you with certain information. What you do with it is your own business, and any action you may take is at your own risk."

"I'll ask you again. Why are you doing this?"

"Let's just say I'm a friend of Miss Lelague."

The phone went dead.

Emhard seemed locked in thought. After a while he said, "Looks like we got a friend inside LAPD."

Hal Barton nodded.

Emhard said, "I've been hearing a lot about juvenile crime recently, Hal. What are your views on senile crime? Doesn't seem so much of it about."

"I'm in favour of a balanced society, Gore."

"Well, I think it's time we got a little balance on the situation here."

"Are you suggesting we do something irrational and irresponsible, that we are likely to regret maybe for the rest of our lives?"

Emhard considered the question, then nodded carefully. "I believe that's exactly what I'm suggesting."

"Are you saying we should take the law into our own hands?"

"Now that you mention it, that's getting pretty damn close to the kind of thing I had in mind."

"Well, answer me this," Hal Barton said. "Do you have in mind that we should do something right now?"

"Not right now, maybe. But the way I see it, we may have to take our opportunity when it comes."

"Taking account of all the factors, I have to say I'm against that kind of thing in principle."

"So what do you feel about it in practice?" Emhard asked.

"I have to say I'm with you."

"I was hoping you were going to dissuade me, Hal. Put some kind of a case for my better judgement. If we all behaved like that, the very fabric of society would collapse. That kind of thing. Frankly, that's what I'd expect from a deputy editor of your standing."

"I think this is a case where rescuing someone in genuine need takes precedence over other things."

"That's what I feared," Emhard said. "That's just exactly what I feared."

41

One morning in an interlude between treatments, the heavy metallic doors of the cell opened. Cynthia heard the prison warder say, "Yes sir, she's just woken up."

Dr Holocenter appeared at her bedside. He removed the gag and put it on the table and sat down in a chair opposite her. He nodded to the prison warder. She left the room, closed the door and waited outside.

Holocenter leaned forward and said, "Have you ever read Gore Vidal's *Myra Breckenridge*?"

Cynthia nodded, wary of her questioner's apparent earnestness.

"What do you think of the philosophy embodied in that book?"

She tried to turn her head so that she could see him more clearly, but tied down as she was, it was difficult to get him directly in view. She felt oddly and unnaturally calm under the effect of the drugs. After a while, she said, "That seems to me a rather strange question, even after our earlier literary discussions."

"You're familiar with the book, though?" Holocenter persisted.

"Yes, I've read the book. What point are you making?"

"The heroine is a man who becomes a woman and then takes his revenge on men."

He paused, waiting for her reply.

"Why is that relevant to me?" Cynthia asked.

"The notion of taking revenge on men is perhaps relevant to your case, is it not? At one stage, for example, Vidal's heroine penetrates a somewhat unwilling male victim with a dildo."

"Have I ever done that?"

"You used to exercise control over your...victims."

"Anal penetration with a dildo is not one of them, I assure you. That would simply be following a male pattern. I wouldn't do that."

"But, nevertheless, your practice is to humiliate those who you believe have offended."

"The only thing that is necessary to humiliate a man is to take away his control over a woman."

"Then you regard the fictional precedent of *Myra Breckenridge* to be irrelevant?"

"What are you saying? That Gore Vidal should be held up as some kind of model for feminists?"

"What about the philosophy", Holocenter said calmly, "of a woman taking revenge against men?"

"I don't take revenge, Dr Holocenter."

"Do you not, Miss Lelague? You see, I rather think you do."

In the oddly stilted atmosphere between them, Cynthia said, "Perhaps you would permit me ask you a question. Have you ever seen a film called *Barbarella*?"

"Miss Lelague, I am sorry to disappoint you, but I have no interest in discussing film history."

"If you will be patient with me, I would be interested in your answer. You see, I think it will enable me to answer your question."

Holocenter's smile seemed to float briefly across his features. It occurred to her that he believed he had all the time in the world, that he would simply use his drugs and his questioning to wear her down at his own leisure.

"What point are you making, Miss Lelague? I am prepared to be entertained."

She said, "In *Barbarella* the heroine, played by Jane Fonda, attempts to force her sexual attentions upon an angel. The angel says, 'An angel cannot make love, an angel *is* love.'"

"And what conclusion do you draw from that?" Holocenter asked.

"The point I'm making is this. You don't seem to understand that being a female in this society is tantamount to being a permanent victim. If I may paraphrase the angel, I am not taking revenge. I am revenge."

Dr Holocenter smiled again. "These...er...somewhat literary points are all very well, Miss Lelague. But if I may say so, in the context of this situation," he indicated with his eyes the small cell, the heavy bars, the stainless steel-framed bed to which she was securely strapped by her wrists and ankles, and the frame which in turn was bolted to the floor by heavy steel screws, "you are hardly in a position to make such...absolute pronouncements."

"I believe," Cynthia said, "you will find out the meaning of the phrase in due course."

"Which phrase is that?"

"I am revenge," Cynthia said.

Dr Holocenter smiled again.

"Miss Lelague, you have entertained me a great deal. I came here to ascertain whether the medication we have administered has had any beneficial effect on your state of mind. Clearly it has not. You show no sign of contrition or even of understanding your situation. I must now pronounce you truly beyond the reach of any normal means of communication and, as such, a suitable case for further treatment."

There was a moment's silence. It seemed to Cynthia important to preserve the formality between them. She said, "In response to your own diagnosis, I have also been studying your own behaviour. I feel obliged to inform you that I believe that you are incapable of contrition or even of understanding your own situation. I agree with you that there is not a single word of reasonable communication that can now pass between us."

Dr Holocenter nodded, a precise inclination of the head that was almost as formal as their conversation. "Then I believe we have reached agreement. I came here this morning intending to inform you that once we reach the John Hopkins penitentiary, you will be subject to the full course of IS2 drug therapy. I am going to adjust that schedule. As you know, a collection of troublemakers is demonstrating outside this building, and it is therefore impossible to remove you from here without undue disturbance. I see no point in delaying that course until we are able to transport you to the penitentiary hospital. Accordingly, we will begin the final treatment now."

42

In the days before her incarceration, when she looked out over the city, Cynthia thought of the earliest inhabitants, from the Gabrieleno to the Chumash Indians. She considered the Spanish mission settlements and their attempts to make the natives conform to the tenets of Catholicism. She thought about this as the breakers came in on the Redondo and Venice beaches. It seemed to her the whole earth was liquid, the waves no less than the molten lava and magma on which they floated. The waves and tremblers and earthquakes and the smog that came in over the city, even the hot and humid Santa Ana winds that blew down the valleys, were all manifestations of the liquid beneath everything, that feminine core of immutable emotion that sometimes lay silent and then, after years, erupted in its own display of anger. The earth seemed to her to be a hard masculine layer or crust upon the surface of the female core of the world. That same male crust seemed solid, immovable, but in fact it was thin and brittle, and ultimately fragile. When she lay in her hospital bed, trying to regain consciousness between treatments, she hung on to that belief.

She did not know how long she floated in and out of consciousness, and she lost track of the days.

43

Gore Emhard was talking to one of the features editors in the main newsroom when his assistant appeared beside him and stood anxiously waiting.

"What is it?" Emhard said.

"Phone, Mr Emhard."

"Male, female, or animal? I'll only answer if it's female or animal."

"Male."

Emhard said, "Tell him to call me back in a little while."

"He says it won't wait."

"Tell him to phone back in ten minutes."

"It's from a payphone. He says it's important."

"If it's important, he'll phone back."

"He says it's from LAPD."

"Why didn't you say so in the first place?" Emhard said.

He moved back into his office, closed the door behind him and picked up the phone.

"Who is this?" Emhard asked.

"Your friend," the voice said.

Emhard was an expert at extracting information. It was one of the skills of a newspaperman's job. He knew it was best to sound a little gruff, as though suspicious of the quality of the information. He also knew that all informants are nervous, and that the slightest hesitation or trace of insincerity could terminate a conversation. With this particular caller he sensed a serious man who was willing to take risks for what he believed. Emhard moved as if by instinct into the appropriate register, somewhere between suspicion and respect. He said, "What exactly have you got for me?"

"I've been out gathering evidence with a couple of colleagues on a homicide case. We've been working six hours solid since early this morning. Right now, they're parked in a side-road, having a cup of coffee, so I don't have too much time. I'm calling again from a standard payphone at the side of a road because I don't want this call traced."

Emhard knew that what was needed at this point was reassurance. He said, "I understand."

He waited for the brief pause while he imagined his informant glanced down the road to see if the coast was clear and he could talk without interruption.

"I know one of the female warders who looks after Cynthia Lelague. She happens to be my sister-in-law."

Suddenly Emhard found that his concentration excluded everything else — the faint buzz of tapping from the main newsroom, the phones trilling in a neighbouring office, the sound of someone arguing with someone else on a telephone. He said, "I'm listening."

"My sister-in-law and her husband came over for supper at my place last night. She and I are both in law enforcement work, and I guess we talked shop a little."

"Sure," Emhard said. "We all like to talk shop."

"Well, she just informed me straight out that Dr Holocenter has already started his planned drug treatment on Miss Lelague."

Emhard recovered from his own silence. He said, "How does your sister-in-law know this?"

"Dr Holocenter told her so himself. Said they were using chemicals in a controlled experiment and that she was to keep an eye on the patient at all times. Told her particularly to call him immediately if there were any changes in her behaviour."

"What changes?"

"They got her strapped down on that steel-framed bed in there, and they got monitoring equipment all over her. They're looking for reactions to the chemicals — heart pulse rate, blood pressure, temperature, all those things."

Emhard said, "What made Holocenter start now? I thought the programme was going to begin after she'd been taken to the penitentiary?"

"The crowd outside's preventing her leaving. That's why he decided to start."

"In the City Hall building?"

"They have an emergency hospital suite in the basement. Dr Holocenter's taken over that facility. That's where they're keeping her."

"Why couldn't they sneak her out at night?" Emhard asked. He was trying to get a handle on the situation, trying to run down the alternatives.

"The word in the building is that the Mayor is supervising the matter personally. He says to sneak her out would inflame the crowds. Their instructions are to move her when the atmosphere has calmed down."

"If Holocenter's doing this inside the City Hall premises, he must have had the Mayor's permission to start in on the chemical programme."

"I guess so."

"You guess so?"

"That's my feeling."

"Do you know what kind of drugs Dr Holocenter is using?"

There was some interference at the other end, as if a heavy truck had gone by the payphone. Emhard could sense the nervousness of his informant under the mask of the detective's calm accounting.

"Can you repeat that?" the voice said.

"What kind of drugs is he using?"

Emhard thought he had lost his informant again, but then he came back strongly. "Matter of fact, I asked my sister-in-law just that question."

Emhard approved. Detectives were like journalists; they hunted for information naturally, almost by instinct, even in their sleep. This man had been working his sister-in-law for additional knowledge, maybe not even consciously. The point was, how much did he recall?

"What did she say about the drugs?" Emhard said.

"She specialises in dealing with mental patients. Works quite a lot with psychiatrists like Dr Holocenter. She's also a trained nurse, so sometimes she is called on to give pills or medication. She told me one or two things about the chemicals they're using."

"Oh?" Emhard expressed something like polite interest. He didn't want to pump too hard.

"She said the main drug they're using is something that was used in a controlled prison experiment some time ago. The experiment was discontinued."

Emhard waited a little, until the pounding in his temples had stopped. He said, "I heard of something called IS2. I don't know what it stands for."

"She says it stands for Isomer 2."

"What's that mean, exactly?"

There was another pause. Emhard had the impression his informant had put his hand over the receiver and was looking around again. Maybe someone had walked by the payphone. Maybe he was just checking his colleagues in the car. Then suddenly he was speaking fast and relatively distinctly, as if he had just been making sure everything was clear and he could start in on things. "Look, this is kind of complicated, and I don't have too much time. My sister-in-law says there are some chemicals which have a certain number of atoms, but those atoms are set up on the molecule in different ways, as if they're left-handed or right-handed. Those different forms of the same molecule are called isomers."

"Left-handed? Right-handed?" Emhard asked. "What the hell does that mean?"

"Your hands both have four fingers and one thumb, but you'd agree that your left hand and your right hand are not alike. Same with these molecules, my sister-in law says."

"OK," Emhard said. "I'll have to take what you say on trust."

"The point is, these different isomers have different effects on the body. Now it happens that the chemical that was used in the original experiments has more than one isomer."

Emhard's mind started to move ahead a little. He said, "Keep going."

"My sister-in-law says they want to test this new isomer, Isomer 2. They tried it out on rats firsts. It's supposed to be less toxic than the original isomer."

"I think I'm beginning to catch your meaning."

"Well, the thing is, in the light of those experiments with rats, the Federal Drug Administration have given Dr Holocenter permission to run the tests again on humans, this time using Isomer 2."

"Jesus," Emhard said. "Sometimes I wonder about these authorities." He checked himself. "So that's what he's using on Cynthia now — this Isomer 2?"

"That's what my sister-in-law told me."

Emhard said, "How come the FDA assumes the effects on rats will be the same as on humans?"

"That's just their assumption."

"What does that mean — their assumption?" Emhard said. "Take an example. You might assume my ass is blue. But I wouldn't bet on it."

"It's the standard assumption, I'm told. I mean rats and

humans are usually affected by chemicals in pretty much the same way. I guess that's the whole basis of experiments with animals."

"You guess," Emhard said. "So they're using Cynthia as a guinea pig?"

"That's about it."

"Thank you for your information," Emhard said. "I'm truly grateful."

"That's OK. I have to go now. The other detectives are giving me these looks from the patrol car. They think I'm speaking to a girlfriend or something."

"Wish I could call you by your name."

"That don't matter."

"Listen," Emhard said, "Maybe you'll tell me one day who you are and I can return a favour."

"I'm not after favours. Just remember what I said about side-door 6 at City Hall."

"Just one more question."

"Make it quick."

"If you're LAPD, what are you doing at City Hall?"

"LAPD has a suite of offices at City Hall. There's a liaison section and a security section. They each have representation in one another's buildings. OK?"

"OK. I guess if I made a determined search, I could find out who you are."

"You could try. But what good would it do you? I've given you the information you need."

"That's right, you have," Emhard said.

"Now I guess it's over to you.

Then the line went dead.

Emhard had an intuition the detective was a big man, from the way he breathed and spoke in the confined space of the phone booth. He could imagine him opening the booth door and walking back to his companions in the patrol car. They would open the car door for him. He'd get in and pull the door closed, looking as nonchalant as he could. Emhard imagined the patrol car moving out of the side-road and easing into the suburban traffic.

44

When he was not applying his therapy to his patient, Dr Holocenter had taken to explaining his role on television. As the captor of Celia Lelague, he had become something of a media celebrity.

It seemed to Gore Emhard that the eminent psychiatrist was behaving like a circus owner who had caught a fabulous or dangerous animal. There was an element of P. T. Barnum in the way that he conducted himself, the way that he was positively free with his time. He was asked questions by interviewers, and he seemed entirely at home on the screen. Now he would answer inquiries on almost anything in his authoritative, avuncular manner. Emhard imagined him returning after the interviews to the place which his LAPD informant had described — to a cell in the basement of City Hall where his patient was confined against her will. It seemed to Emhard that Holocenter had taken over the role of publicly defending LAPD too. But somehow he had also contrived to represent himself as a defender of the liberal order.

Emhard watched him performing with a mixture of fascination, repugnance, and surprise. On one programme Dr Holocenter was responding to the question, *"How should our society deal with dissidents?"*

"California is a libertarian state," Holocenter said. *"It is in the nature of libertarian societies to criticise their institutions. Frankly, it doesn't matter how well LAPD performs its duty, every institution is capable of criticism, and in a free society that's what we have to expect."*

"You don't think that the criticisms of LAPD are justified?"

"You'd be wrong to assume that's what I think. I do believe the criticisms are justified. But that's just part of the healthy operation of the system. People have every right to criticise us, and we should respond to that criticism."

"But some people think the situation is so bad that they feel inclined to do something directly. You feel that they should never do that, whatever the circumstances?"

"I think that type of behaviour, where someone says, 'I am taking the law into my own hands,' is dangerous."

"Let's take an extreme instance. Isn't it historically justified under some circumstances — for example, with Hitler?"

"That's an extreme case where the democratic institutions have broken down. I think if you have workable institutions, controlled or supervised by democratically elected representatives, you ought to function within that system."

"But if we take the case of Cynthia Lelague — if she sees women being raped, and she knows in certain cases she can stop that

happening, don't you think she's honour bound to do what she can? If she knows she has the means to prevent even one woman being subjected to a horrific violation, don't you think it's up to her to do what she thinks is necessary?"

"That's one of the prices we pay," Dr Holocenter said, *"for living in a lawful society. She's violating a central principle of our liberal state. The criminal has the right to the full protection of the law until he is proved guilty. If you removed those processes and burdens of proof from the authorities, we could probably catch and punish more criminals earlier. But in the course of time we'd be abolishing those very processes which protect the individual from the tyranny of the authorities."*

"You're saying the key difference between the authorities and Cynthia Lelague isn't that she got to the criminal first, but that she ignored all the due processes — such as the burden of proof and trial by jury in a legally constituted court?"

"That's precisely what I'm saying. One of the things Mussolini was credited with, maybe correctly, was that before the Second World War he virtually destroyed the Mafia in Italy. The thing was he didn't feel constrained to operate inside the law. As a Fascist dictator, he thought he was above the law. Everyone pretty much knew who the Mafia were, but getting legal proof of their activities that would stand up in a court was another thing entirely. Mussolini just went ahead and arrested them on suspicion, shot them or put them in prison. Now, the point is, which society would you prefer to live in — one where you can be arrested on suspicion and shot or imprisoned without trial, or one where you are innocent until proven guilty?"

The interviewer said, *"Are you identifying Cynthia Lelague with Mussolini?"*

"I think Cynthia Lelague is the equivalent of some kind of po-litical fascist. I think she's arrogant and authoritarian. She refuses to acknowledge that all democratic institutions are imperfect. She refuses to accept the arduous processes of proper proof and trial by jury. She wants to impose her own solution unilaterally, by force. I think in a free society we all have a duty to resist people like that."

Emhard and Barton were watching the television screen in Emhard's office like a pair of old desert hawks sitting on a cac-tus. Their mouths were set in that kind of expression where maybe one or both of them had a thorn up his ass. Emhard was leaning slightly to the right, Barton slightly to the left, as though they were trying different strategies to ease the discom-fort of their predicament. Neither of them was looking happy.

"I have a problem with that guy," Emhard said. "What he says is all very good — in fact I agree with every word he says. I've been writing editorials like that for the last thirty-eight years. But I worked with Cynthia and I know she's no dangerous psychopath. He can talk all day about representing liberal, democratic institutions and about all us good liberal people in a lawful society. But the fact is he's got her strapped down and he's applying chemicals to her that could wreck her nervous system and change her character. His way of dealing with someone that challenges the system is to try to obliterate her. And as far as I can see he's doing it outside the proper scrutiny of the law."

"So what are we going to do?"

Emhard said, "That is some slick operator out there and I don't like it. He accuses Cynthia of being a fascist, and he hides behind the due process of law. But actually he's the one who's acting more like the fascist. By the time she comes to trial, she risks having her character changed by those chemicals. She could be an entirely different person."

"You haven't answered my question."

"Just look at that rabble," Emhard said, glancing down through the window at the crowd of people that were gathered around the City Hall entrance. "I am the goddamn editor of one of the great newspapers of this land. Temperamentally I'm a conservative. I like this country and I'm proud of its institutions. What do I have in common with Dykes on Bikes and Queens with Spleen and every goddamn crank in this city?"

"You asking me or telling me?"

"I'm asking you and I'm telling you."

"Just so I'm clear," Hal Barton said.

"So why in goddamn hell should I put everything I hold dear at risk and go in and try to get out someone who has only herself to blame?"

"No reason at all," Hal Barton said. "The way I see it."

"No reason at all. So why am I itching to get my old bones out on the street and raise Cain with all those sons-of-bitches at City Hall and kick the ass of that smooth-talking psychiatrist?"

"Senile deterioration of judgement?" suggested Hal Barton. "Old-life crisis? Hormonal imbalance?"

"And what I want to know," Emhard said, "is why the fuck are you egging me on? What evil elf in you is trying to annoy me to that point where I just might finally lose my rag and go in there and cause some mayhem?"

"Beats me," Hal Barton said. "Seems to me you got a real problem."

"What I want to know is, why are you shifting your weight from one leg to the other like a goddamn schoolboy just because you want to get on down there and raise some mischief?"

"You tell me," Barton said. "I don't know why."

45

The unruly crowd that had gathered at the entrance of City Hall had been there nearly three weeks now, partitioned off by police. Emhard, observing them as he walked down the approach road with Barton, didn't quite know how they sustained themselves. They seemed to be operating some kind of rota system. For the first couple of weeks it had been a matter of a few hundred people. But there had been increasing numbers for the last few days, and the crowd seemed to be swelling slowly but inexorably. The tribes of the earth appeared to have been summoned: there were pony-tailed hippies and yuppies from Venice, Latinos from El Segundo and La Habra, blond surfers from Seal Beach, a detachment from Dykes on Bikes, a full regiment of Queens with Spleen from Silver Lake. Mixed in were the unemployed, the vagrant, the alcoholics who slept rough in Griffiths and MacArthur and Exposition Park. They seemed to represent the fullest congregations and denominations of the earth. All the more remarkable, then, was the cheerful collective spirit that seemed to animate them.

The crowd raised fists high and chanted: *"Fuck! Fuck! Fuck! Fuckwoman!"*

Emhard moved towards the front, pushed this way and that by the press of people. Sometimes the crowd rolled forward like a sea, and you had to move with them.

Between times the crowd sang, "What do we want? *Fuck!* What do we want? *Fuck!* What do we want? *Fuckwoman!"*

Then they surged forward like a wave against rocks, and the police enthusiastically beat them back. Undaunted, the crowd re-gathered.

Mayor Dally appeared at an upper window above the colonnaded entrance, looking down at the mêlée. The crowd saw him and responded with sudden and unaffected spontaneity, as though greeting an old friend, *"Fuck Dally! Fuck Dally! Fuck Dally!"*

Mayor Dally observed them though his dark glasses. He was wearing a blue double-breasted suit, a cream shirt and white tie. His face was tanned and every hair was in place. He seemed to be engaged upon some internal debate, some profound meditation upon the nature of politics and society. Amongst other things, his consideration ranged over such matters as democratic voting methods and working majorities. He was wondering, more precisely, how many of those gathered below had ever voted Republican. His calculation was that of the four or five thousand people assembled there, you could count the number of Republican voters on the fingers of one hand, or possibly even upon one finger of one hand. This calculation had important moral and social implications. It seemed, in short, a heaven-sent opportunity to chastise a substantial group of hostile voters without in any way jeopardising his own constituency of supporters.

On the contrary, building upon the knowledge of many years' experience as a working politician, he had good reason to believe that a great many of his constituency would like to see the crowd gathered there subjected to some degree of official disapproval, if not outright chastisement. He believed that this disapproval should take the form of some type of direct action against them, partly because of the provocation of their somewhat varied and unorthodox lifestyles, but also their means of assembling there in the form of a large and unruly crowd, not to mention their particular comments and stated intentions in regard to his own person.

"Those people are animals," Mayor Dally said to Miss Tarzanna, as if he had identified a particular species. "I can smell them from here. A great many of them have little use for personal hygiene. Tell Gonzaga to order in the water cannons."

Miss Tarzanna relayed his orders on the mobile phone to Captain Emile Gonzaga, in charge of the squadron of vehicles arranged beneath them. The heavy diesel engines of the water cannon trucks, gathered at the side of the small square, coughed and started into low, grinding life. The crowd heard the sound and seemed to pause.

Then the machines rolled forward like tanks. At first no one believed they would open fire. They moved around the periphery of the crowd, nearly a dozen of them, painted black as mourning and with the silver police livery on their sides. They halted and turned towards the assembled people, and then they waited.

The crowd watched them. There seemed to be some kind of stand-off for a while. Then a youth with a bright blue Mohican haircut started to run along the adjacent sidewalk, waving his arms and shouting. At first his attempt at provocation seemed to be ignored. Then a single arc of water spurted out towards him. The crowd watched the youth with the blue Mohican haircut being rolled over and over until he lit up against the wall in a heap. Using the wall for support, the youth rose up, pulled off his shirt and downed his trousers. The crowd roared their approval. Dancing naked in the blasting jet, he was doing a rendition of "Singing in the Rain", tap dancing along the wall, when another jet caught him and he disappeared beneath their combined blast like a spider being flushed down a lavatory pan.

After a short while the hoses were turned off and in the ensuing silence the crowd was given a chance to consider its options.

"That'll teach those sons-of-bitches," Mayor Dally said.

The assembled people watched the two lines of water-cannon trucks. They were being invited to disperse. They were sullen and quiet but at the same time they weren't going to move. Slowly, the water-cannon trucks gunned their engines. The crowd remained silent but unmoving.

Miss Tarzanna's hand-held radio crackled. She snatched the headpiece up to her ear and listened intently for a few seconds. Then she said, "Captain Gonzaga reports the demonstrators are not dispersing, and he is requesting your further orders, sir."

Mayor Dally had treasured this moment. There is a time in the life of all men when the good must come to the fore. He said, "As the demonstrators refuse all reasonable requests to obey lawful dispersal orders, I believe I have no option other than to order the officers of the law to take appropriate action."

Miss Tarzanna listened and then carefully abbreviated the order to, "Give 'em hell, Emile."

Two concentrated white jets curved out casually towards the crowds. People were being knocked over, and women were screaming and an elderly tramp was being pushed along the sidewalk as though on a water-chute, still holding onto his bobble-hat with his small dog under his arm. The dog was looking dignified and restrained. After that, half a dozen other hoses began to spray the crowd mercilessly. Those operating the water-cannons could vary at will the type and frequency of the chastisement they rained upon the crowd. By raising the jets high they could soak several thousand people as thoroughly as in a tropical storm. By lowering their aim they could pick off individual demonstrators or malcontents like the youth in a Mohican haircut. They engaged in this sport for several minutes. Mayor Dally watched approvingly from the balcony while the crowd was doused collectively from above and at the same time unappetising elements were individually selected and chastened with water-jets directly upon their persons. The water-jets were not sufficiently strong to cause permanent damage, but any person on whom they were directed for any appreciable length of time would be well advised to collect loose objects about his person, such as his hat, toupee or dentures, from the Lost and Found department in neighbouring Orange County.

Apart from the satisfying work of chastising sinners, there were aesthetic sights to be enjoyed too. The volume of liquid created a rainbow arc which had a pleasing effect in the sunshine, dispersing its translucent and multicoloured lights upon the scene. Mayor Dally considered himself a happy man as he watched the sights below, and perhaps even allowed himself to take solace from the thought that the Almighty, surely a conservative figure if not a devout Republican, seemed to smile upon the work that was being done there.

In the middle of the crowd, Emhard was trying to make himself heard above the shouting.

"Pass the word. We know a side-entrance."

"A what?"

"A place where we can get into the building."

Around them the crowd continued to chant, "What do we want? *Fuck!* What do we want? *Fuck!* What do we want? *Fuck-woman!*"

The word moved through the crowd. They were beating their hands and alternately shouting. Clap clap clap. *"Fuck!"* Clap clap clap. *"Fuck!"* Clap clap clap. *"Fuck!"*

Emhard was tapped on the shoulder. He turned round. A long-haired young man with a thin face said, "Lead the way, brother."

Emhard and Barton moved off down a side-alley, with a substantial portion of the crowd following.

Mayor Dally, looking down, said to Miss Tarzanna, "Where in God's name are those riffraff going?"

Miss Tarzanna wore Electra shades. She looked down and tried to make out the two men leading the way. "I believe, Mr

Mayor, sir, that the man out front is Mr Gore Emhard, the editor of the *Angel Times*."

Mayor Dally looked over and saw Emhard making signs to some large and particularly hairy-looking people. There were certain things that Mayor Dally knew. He knew about divide and rule. And he knew that when the forces of reaction and the forces of disorder are to be found in flagrant proximity gesturing and communicating in inescapable sign language, then the peaceful order is under the most severe threat.

Mayor Dally said, "Who is that person Mr Emhard is addressing now?"

Miss Tarzanna stared out across the square through her shades. Her eyes were as sharp as pins.

"I believe that is Mr Crispin Grace, editor of *Queens with Spleen*."

A cold shiver went through Mayor Dally. Inadvertently he clenched his buttocks.

"Miss Tarzanna, I believe we are witnessing a seditious dialogue between two dangerous intelligences. Tell the Captain I want those people stopped at all costs."

Miss Tarzanna barked into the mobile radiophone. Almost before the order had been issued, an entire detachment of water-cannons, backed up by policemen on foot, was detailed off to block the path of the breakaway group and prevent them from whatever sedition they intended.

But a crowd filled with reactionary and revolutionary elements united in profane community of purpose is a dangerous thing. Because that was precisely the moment when a diversionary tactic took place akin to the use of cavalry in warfare.

From another part of the crowd an entire squadron of Dykes on Bikes and Queens with Spleen took off in the opposite direction, travelling in a motley crowd, whooping to their friends and looking as if they owned the place. You could no more expect any red-blooded police officer to pass up a provocation like that than you could flush up a partridge under the nose of a bird-dog and expect that bird-dog to show no emotion. The fact was a whole troop of screaming dykes and queens peddling on their bicycles past a line of police-operated water-cannons with pressure hoses at full strength and with their operators' trigger fingers cocked is just too much temptation to offer on this mortal earth. The detachment stopped in their tracks, took aim with their water cannons and let fly.

It was a graphic demonstration of the power of water and the military efficacy of concentrated fire. A lot of queens and dykes went head over elbow at the first salvo. But even as they went down, behind them and seemingly beside them a whole bunch of other queens and dykes starting cycling even faster and whooping it up, causing a severe continuation of the provocation. It required a redirection of effort and real concentration before every single dyke and queen had been knocked off his or her bicycle and laid low. But by the time the water cannons had finished demolishing the cavalry regiment, and those aiming the water cannons had got over their satisfaction with the general turn of events, a substantial portion of the crowd had followed two elderly reprobates into the lane on the side of the City Hall building.

Emhard and Barton moved round several huge pails of refuse and arrived at side-door 6. It was bright orange with an aluminium handle. Beneath that was a lock for something like a Benson key.

Emhard tried the handle, but it didn't give. He commanded imperiously, "Bust down this door!"

Crowbars and pickaxe handles came out of nowhere, and without further preparation or formal address the crowd started laying into the door. Each time the metal was hit, the door sprang and quivered, but it seemed to hold. They seemed to be there for quite a few seconds, and were losing the vital element of surprise, when Emhard shouted, "Hit the lock area, for Chrissake. The bolts are already open." From the sudden surfeit of force he could hear the lock squealing, then the crack of breaking steel. As the double doors swung open, Emhard saw that, just as his informant had promised, the heavy additional bolts had been pulled from the inside.

The crowd streamed through the open doorway in a blind, soft rush that became entangled there for a few moments, then it was through and into the inside of the building. For a few seconds, after the bright sunlight, Emhard stumbled in the cool dark of the interior.

He looked behind him and saw some heavyweight individuals of both sexes with "Pink Panthers" and "Gay Hussars" and "Hairy Fairies" on their tee-shirts. Emhard was a man used to thinking in terms of headlines, and the title that went up in his mind suddenly was:

ELDERLY EDITORS LEAD FURIOUS GAY ASSAULT ON CITY HALL

He wondered whether he'd ever live that one down. He saw another tighter, more abbreviated version:

EMHARD AND BARTON IN PINK RAMPAGE

It was going to be difficult as guest speaker at the local chapter of the National Rifle Association with a reputation like that. As it happened, there were other things demanding his attention. A thin line of police officers, hastily thrown together, blocked their way across the corridor. More reinforcements were arriving every moment, shuffling into place. Many had riot helmets and clear plastic shields.

A sergeant, attempting to rally his men, shouted, "I warn you, you are breaking the law!"

Two rows back from the front line, Gore Emhard called out, "Let's kick their asses, people!"

They surged forward. The thin line of blue shuddered briefly. Emhard could smell sweat and fear and rage in the air as they pressed the chain. Then the line gave at its weakest point. He saw looks of horror and surprise on the faces of the police officers as they swept past and through them.

The crowd moved like a tide down the corridor, chanting its war-cry: *"Fuck! Fuck! Fuck!"*

46

Inside Cynthia's cell, Dr Holocenter was about to inject his patient with a full capsule of IS2 when he paused. He had filled the syringe and had taken up the antiseptic swab, but stood arrested for several moments, entirely motionless, listening. The noise he heard was like the far-off howling of wolves.

"What in God's name is that?"

It was difficult to make out at first. Now it sounded more like the yelping of dogs or the baying of hounds.

One of the prison warders said, "I'll check it out."

She walked out of the cell, then he heard her voice outside in the corridor rise to a shrill protesting tenor.

The crowd burst in, led by Emhard and Barton.

Holocenter looked at the distinguished editor of the *Angel Times* and his deputy as the crowd swarmed in with him and gathered behind the two ringleaders in the confines of the cell. To Emhard's left was the lanky figure of Crispin Grace, editor of *Queens with Spleen*. Behind Grace was a phalanx of Gay Hussars.

They all seemed to have eyes only for Holocenter. He chose his words carefully and said, softly and silently, "Good God almighty."

Holding the large syringe like a weapon, Holocenter started to back slowly away towards the protective angles of the corner of the cell.

In the ensuing stand-off, Emhard reached toward Cynthia and untied the gag. Released, Cynthia breathed out a great sigh of relief.

Emhard set about untying her, unclasping the ties from legs and arms. Freed, at first she sat there for a moment unmoving, and it occurred to Emhard they might have arrived too late, that she was beyond revival. She had bruises under her eyes and her face was puffy. Her head hung a little to one side, she was breathing heavily and she seemed groggy. But Emhard looked past the frame and peered into her face, and saw something flicker behind her eyes.

Emhard went over to the wall basin and filled one of the metal jugs with water. He came back and carefully and ceremoniously threw a jug-shaped column of water over her face and shoulders.

Cynthia spat out water and shook her head. A little more light came into her eyes, as if a curtain had been opened in that dark room. Slowly she rose from her chair and stood up with care and with difficulty. Her legs were stiff and she had pins and needles. Emhard wanted to help her, but she put up her hands to keep him off. She shook her head again to gather herself and the water fell in fine droplets from her mane of curled brown hair. Standing, she appeared like a beast that had roused itself from a long sleep. Her green patient's pyjamas seemed to the observers watching her to be some kind of emblem or insignia. She was truly Amazonian.

She turned and looked around the room and her gaze fell upon Dr Holocenter, backed into a corner by the crowd. She said in a low voice that was more like a hiss, "Leave him to me!"

The crowd heard the tone in her voice and stood back.

Cynthia advanced down the long axis of the cell.

Holocenter brandished the syringe. "Keep back, I'm warning you. One step nearer, and I'll give you the full dose."

"You can't do that to a post-feminist icon," Cynthia said.

Dr Holocenter moved backwards carefully using the corner to keep her from getting round the side of him. "Back off now. I'm warning you."

A thought seemed to occur to Cynthia, a recurrence of memory. There was something missing in her life and, instinctively, she knew what it was. Her glance moved around the room as though she was hunting for something. Then her eye alighted on the bison's penis pencil-holder, standing upright on the sideboard.

It was like the Mark of Zorro, or when Arthur took hold of Excalibur, or Charlemagne seized his sword *Joyeuse*. It was iconic. The weapon had found the man — in this case, the woman. You could see in Holocenter's eyes that he was witnessing some truly mythic conjunction of forces, some arcane amalgamation of the magical and physical that transcended mere formal narrative.

Gripping the base of the bison's penis pencil-holder in both hands, holding the object like a two-handed samurai sword, Cynthia advanced down the diagonal towards the bisection of walls against which Dr Holocenter stood, the syringe held in front of him as though fending off blind fate.

Cynthia said, "What happens when a post-feminist meets a postmodernist vampire?"

"Is this a riddle?" Holocenter asked. His eyes moved towards the door, attempting to judge a possible avenue of escape.

"More in the nature of a demonstration."

"I sincerely hope," Holocenter said, "you're not going to attempt something too...ah...*gothic*."

In the brief duel which followed, the syringe was no match for the massively tumescent pencil-holder. With a clatter the syringe fell to the floor.

Cynthia closed in. Dr Holocenter said, "Sweet God alive!"

"Open your mouth wide now," Cynthia said. "Time for your medicine."

Horror entered the expressions on Gore Emhard's and Hal Barton's faces. It was mythical, it was symbolic, but was pretty disturbing and disgusting too.

Dr Holocenter said something that sounded like, "AAAAARGH!"

You could see in the faces of the crowd the horrible thing that was being enacted. Some turned away. One man threw up over the adjacent wall.

"Jesus!" Emhard said.

Then Emhard and Barton were tugging at Cynthia's shoulders.

"That's enough now, Cynthia."

The crowd that entered the door caught a brief glimpse of Dr Holocenter lying prostrate on the floor, his eyes swollen with fear, the bison's penis pencil-holder rammed down his throat.

They could hear other noises, other rhythms, the pounding of boots, the heavy beat of police reinforcements arriving. With Cynthia at their head, the crowd surged out, chanting, *"Fuck! Fuck! Fuck!"*

47

Outside, the battle was still raging.

The power of the media is a strange thing. In the half-hour or so of direct engagement between the forces of law and order and the forces of anarchy, the television cameras had been relaying the battle live to the homes and offices of the populace. As the conflict gathered pace, commentators gave their views on the state of the conflict and experts were consulted on the mechanisms of civil disobedience and the movement of forces. There were military strategists whose opinion was sought on the state of the pitched action between the entrenched police and the waves of Dykes without Bikes and Queens with Spleen that had regrouped and were even now throwing themselves in infantry waves against the police barricades.

In that half hour between ten and ten-thirty, a huge proportion of the workforce of the local offices abandoned their coffee-break and walked the few hundred yards from the city area to the Civic Center to observe directly the rolling battle that was taking place there. Though they were not in the forefront of the crowd, sharing in the death-or-glory massed charges of dykes and queens, they were nevertheless interested spectators to the events that were unfolding directly beneath their view.

The day was bright and there was a clear sky, deep blue interspersed with small cirrus clouds and a single thunderhead over Van Nuys, overseen by a beautiful rainbow from the heavy artificial rain which fell from the upturned firehoses upon the centre of the battle — rain which did not seem to dampen the spirits of the combatants but rather, as at Agincourt when the English faced the might of the French cavalry, appeared to inflame the spirits of both sides.

Mayor Dally watched as the periphery of the crowd grew and swelled with male and female executives from the surrounding offices. After some little while he calculated that perhaps there were a hundred thousand or more in total out there, most of them representatives of the business community of Los Angeles. It seemed to him that there were events taking place that were not only quantitatively but qualitatively different from those pertaining when the battle had commenced. The young executives and secretaries and business people, who had taken a temporary respite from their work to witness an historic battle, by no means could be described as inherently disorderly or radical, and it seemed to him that very few would have been sufficiently depraved to be tempted by a Democratic ticket, even in the deepest and darkest recesses of a polling both. It did not take a mathematician of Einsteinian proportions to perceive that when approximately ninety-five thousand Republicans are added to five thousand Democrats, the broad configuration of political allegiance within that crowd has undergone a subtle change.

Mayor Frank Dally was not insensible to these subtle changes. He was a man of highly developed moral conscience, with a capacity to be stirred by humanity, particularly those aspects of humanity which yielded some workable, operating idea of voter intentions. There was another factor which caused him deep concern. The larger outer circle of the crowd seemed to be blending with the smaller hard-core into one homogeneous entity, business suits combining with tattooed torsos and brightly coloured punk hair. What was more, the shouts of the hard-core, *"We Want Fuckwoman!"* were being taken up and magnified by the larger crowd, so that it seemed to Dally he was witnessing again, on a larger scale this time, the unwelcome and eerie unification of the forces of reaction with those of disorder.

A political crisis of unimaginable proportions was forming. Parents who had tuned in on their television sets, respectable parents in Culver City and Pacific Palisades, would soon be witnessing their children, their Martins and Cecilias, hurling themselves against police barricades shouting *"Fuck, fuck, fuck!"* and trying to rip the asses off large policemen whose only sin was that they had signed municipal contracts and had a sense of civic responsibility, which in practice meant doing what the Mayor ordered.

The Mayor knew that these are precisely the moments that test politicians and separate the men from the boys, the women from the girls and the sheep from the goats; or maybe the men from the sheep, the women from the boys, and the girls from the goats, depending upon your orientation. These are the moments when there has to be a new and building democratic consensus, when out of a sense of overwhelming moral certitude, based on the deepest and most abiding convictions of the public good, those who lead must not back down or bow out. At such times it is necessary for upstanding men of virtue in all fields, not excluding politicians, to come forward — that is to say, not to hang back but to come from behind and lead from the front.

It happened that Mayor Dally was such a man.

48

Inside the building, the crowd led by Cynthia and Emhard rounded a corner and came face to face with a phalanx of police. In front of them, standing on a box behind a hastily mounted lectern, was Mayor Dally.

It seemed as if Dally had not only called up the LAPD divisional reserves, but had also hauled every old trooper out of his hospital bath-chair and personally guided him back to the station. They had never seen so many police officers in one place. The hall was so full there were officers backed into the side-lobbies, into the window recesses and every available space. Down one of the corridors there could be seen other officers with long hoses that seemed to be connected up to the building's main water supply.

The two groups confronted each other. Mayor Dally stood in front of the crowd with a megaphone. Directly behind him were maybe a dozen officers in full riot gear who were ready to close around him and provide an avenue of escape. He looked as cocky as a sparrow and as cute as a bandicoot.

It occurred to Emhard, leading the crowd, that Dally was going to give them a speech about freedom and civil justice and the due process of law, then back out and allow the heavily armed forces of the law to beat them all to a pulp for daring to challenge his authority. Instead, Dally cleared his throat and seemed about to speak. While the stragglers came up from the back and joined them in the confrontation, the crowd was sufficiently awed by this unexpected array of police power to pause for a moment or two.

"I have an apology to make to you," Dally said into the microphone. He smiled a smile Emhard would not easily forget, a smile of confidence and wiliness, as if he had been summoned for precisely this moment in life and he was ready and in his element.

Emhard and Barton listened with expressions of acute scepticism.

"I believe, in the circumstances, and taking account of all the evidence, that we in the Administration and the LAPD may have acted overzealously in our prosecution of Cynthia Lelague, otherwise known as, er…Fuckwoman."

In the silence that followed, Emhard said, "What do you mean, you old buzzard?"

"Well, to be sure, er, Mr Emhard, it would appear that there were indeed…irregularities in the course of action taken by Dr James Holocenter, our chief psychiatric adviser. There were errors committed as a result of some over-enthusiasm…"

"Spit it out, Dally," Emhard called out.

"In the process of her arrest and arraignment, I believe that Miss Cynthia Lelague's rights as a citizen may have been jeopardised. It stands to reason that Miss Lelague must be subject to the due processes of law. But meanwhile, to allow feelings to calm down, with the agreement of the Chief Prosecutor, I'm granting Miss Lelague a temporary amnesty of one month — during which time, among other things, she will have an opportunity to recover from the treatment she has received and prepare her defence…"

At this point Mayor Dally smiled again, as if he had personally invented amnesty, and perhaps charity and several other virtues associated with amnesty as well. "In addition, given the nature of the provocations offered to the defendant, we, the City authorities, will overlook this break-in, and those who have been involved will not be prosecuted." He paused. "That is all I wanted to say."

There was a strange atmosphere that followed. The police were maybe hoping that they would have an opportunity to deal directly with some of those who had been taunting them for nearly three weeks. They watched Dally step down from the temporary rostrum and retire behind the cordon of his personal police protection perhaps with a certain disappointment. In the ensuing silence, Gore Emhard could be heard saying to Hal Barton, "My God, it's amazing what some people will do for votes."

For a few moments the forces of the law and the forces of civil unrest examined each other. They would have loved to get stuck into one another, and put aside former differences and become physical and emotional, may the best man (or woman) win, but it was not to be.

Instead instructions were called out and the police stood by to let the crowd pass. It was like the parting of the sea — a blue sea that seemed to stretch interminably. Lieutenants and sergeants were barking out orders. The police shifted back and a clear corridor opened out towards the entrance of the building that seemed about as long as the Panama canal, though not as pretty.

On the outside an even larger crowd was gathering. The word had gone out. The siege had been covered on TV. People had been collecting from all over the place, streaming out of offices in their coffee-breaks.

When they saw the crowd outside, a voice went up from the people inside the building, small at first, like the far-off yelping of dogs. And the crowd outside, separated by a long run, started to call out to them like relations in airway lounges that have seen their loved ones on the other side of the customs barrier. It was a thin sound, an outbreak of thin cheering like the ululation of Berber women when they mourn their dead.

Cynthia, Emhard and Barton had stood silent while the array of forces rearranged themselves. Now there was a movement behind them amongst the crowd to lift them, however much they might object, and then there were more cries of appreciation as Cynthia, Emhard and Barton were finally raised on the shoulders of the crowd inside.

They started to advance down the long tunnel of policemen, and they were perhaps halfway down that distance when another sound started that they had never heard before and would never hear again. It was like something waking in its sleep, a deep cold roar that starts in a cavern, and for a moment the crowd was disconcerted by it before they knew what it was or even guessed what it might be.

But it grew steadily, and before they fully knew it or could properly identify it, maybe a thousand or fifteen hundred officers of the LAPD, much abused by local media and local interest groups, were starting to give voice, starting to cheer, starting to roar out their approval. There was no sign of any breaking of ranks or of any external show of enthusiasm. The sound came from deep inside the body armour, from inside the human being in the uniform.

Emhard couldn't tell what they were singing. Maybe it was the LAPD choir singing its divisional anthem. Maybe the words came from 'The Star-Spangled Banner'. At one stage he thought he heard a refrain from 'She'll Be Coming Round The Mountain When She Comes'.

The crowd heard it too and went silent. That was the thing that they would all remember afterwards, the strange, thunderous power of the LAPD's disciplined salute, an odd moment of unity between the forces of law and the forces of anarchy and civil disobedience.

It put the fear of God into those that witnessed it, but the person it frightened the most was the Mayor, climbing up the stairs to his office. He stopped dead when he heard it. It seemed like the howling of all the hounds in hell, the mythical conjunction of revolutionary and reactionary forces. He shivered involuntarily on the stairway, and then he went on.

When they got to the end of line of police, into bright sunlight, the crowd outside finally broke out into full voice and began to shout, *"We want Fuckwoman! We want Fuckwoman!"*

Emhard and Barton had not before seen a crowd like it, at least not in the city of Los Angeles. They couldn't easily put figures on it but it seemed half the population was there. They filled the spaces and surrounding streets so tightly that all traffic in the area had been halted. In the sky above them there were helicopters hovering like dragonflies, police planes for aerial control and other aircraft with cameras and television link-ups.

Maybe the only time Emhard and Barton had seen or participated in a crowd as large as that was at Woodstock when they were younger and had long hair and smoked a lot of marijuana and banged eighteen-year-old and sometimes sixteen-year-old chicks — though you would not be able to get either Emhard or Barton to admit it now, because neither would be prepared to concede that the most fervently radical people in their youth tend to become the most deeply entrenched conservatives in their old age. They had seen crowds like this, but the very fact of admitting it recalled layers in their own psyche which they had done everything they could to repress, so it was an uncomfortable experience and one they wouldn't want to repeat.

There was a kind of sigh behind them and a meshing of shields as the police shifted back across the steps of the main entrance, sealing their retreat and closing off the City Hall buildings against further intrusions.

High above them the Mayor was on his balcony, waving to the crowd and taking the credit for the massive demonstration, as though it were his own popularity entirely that had caused it to gather and as though he had invented not only popularity but the very notion of popularity itself.

Emhard and Barton, those old reprobates, managed to dismount from their unaccustomed position as heroes of civil disorder and mass action. They got down and joined the others and watched the tongue of people carrying Cynthia Lelague move into the heart of the general body of the crowd.

They saw the crowd receive her and roar. The sound rose upwards until it was reflected off the high buildings and the twenty-eight story City Hall. They heard the crowd roar again and then move like a surface impacted with fierce rain as they raised their bunched fists. The sound reached up the dizzying heights of the buildings to the air amongst the helicopters, and then went higher still.

POSTSCRIPT

CYNTHIA ALOUETTE ASSUMPTA LELAGUE was tried for the crimes of the notorious vigilante known as "Fuckwoman". She was given a two-year suspended sentence.

GORE EMHARD retired three years later as editor of the *Angel Times*. He was succeeded in the post of editor by Cynthia Lelague.

MAYOR FRANK DALLY was re-elected with an enlarged majority.

DR JAMES HOLOCENTER was admitted to emergency hospital with an enlarged pharynx and other, more minor, traumas. He was disqualified from psychiatric practice and became the proprietor of an old people's home in Miami.